The
WIDOW *of*
SAUNDERS
CREEK

Center Point
Large Print

Also by Tracey Bateman and available from Center Point Large Print:

Thirsty

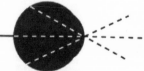

This Large Print Book carries the Seal of Approval of N.A.V.H.

The
WIDOW *of*
SAUNDERS
CREEK

TRACEY BATEMAN

CENTER POINT LARGE PRINT
THORNDIKE, MAINE

This Center Point Large Print edition is published
in the year 2013 by arrangement with WaterBrook Press,
an imprint of The Crown Publishing Group,
a division of Random House, Inc.

The text of this Large Print edition is unabridged.
In other aspects, this book may
vary from the original edition.
Printed in the United States of America
on permanent paper.
Set in 16-point Times New Roman type.

ISBN: 978-1-61173-705-9

Library of Congress Cataloging-in-Publication Data

Bateman, Tracey Victoria.
The widow of Saunders Creek / Tracey Bateman.
pages ; cm.
ISBN 978-1-61173-705-9 (library binding : alk. paper)
1. War widows—Fiction. 2. Bereavement—Fiction.
   3. Large type books. I. Title.
PS3602.A854W53 2013
813′.6—dc23

2012050817

To Pastor Rick Morrow.
Your compassion for those who are trapped
in Satan's grip inspires me.

The
WIDOW *of*
SAUNDERS
CREEK

PART ONE

The LORD is my shepherd,
I shall not want.
He makes me lie down in green pastures;
He leads me beside quiet waters.
He restores my soul.

Prologue

Corrie

An easy spring wind blew through my open Jeep, lifting my hair and ruffling the cloth seat covers as I turned off the interstate and traveled east toward Saunders Creek. It was the last leg of my nine-hour drive from Dallas to the tiny, unassuming Ozarks town that bore my husband's family name.

Towering oaks, full maples, and evergreens hugged the narrow, winding road in a way that even a few months ago might have felt intrusive. But today the trees seemed to embrace me, welcoming me.

Déjà vu came over me, as though the scene before me came out of my own childhood memories instead of recollections of stories my husband told about growing up here.

I wanted him beside me, flashing his *Top Gun* Maverick grin.

Jarrod had died the way he lived—reckless, but heroic. Saving at least fifty lives in a little Iraqi settlement on the east bank of the Tigris River. Leaving me to pine after him, sick with love for a man who would never hold me again. I couldn't breathe. *God, just take me too.* But every day my eyes opened, air filled my lungs, and I forced myself to go on.

Six months ago, I buried him according to his wishes, in the Saunders family graveyard. After the funeral, my mother demanded that I return home to Dallas to grieve—as though I could just put the last seven years behind me and move on. Forget the consuming, crazy, once-in-a-lifetime love who had rescued me from her in the first place. Every night since then I had dreamed of my husband's childhood home. A force compelled me to come here, and I couldn't ignore it any longer.

Jarrod was gone, but as I drove my Jeep up the path that led to the two-story farmhouse, I finally understood why I had been so drawn to this place.

I had come here to find the man I loved.

One

The memory of my husband's funeral returned with an uncomfortable clarity as I navigated the winding road to Saunders Creek.

I barely made it through the service with all my pieces intact. My skin crawled from the unfamiliar embraces. Everyone wanted to hold me. Fat, clammy arms threatened to suffocate me. Muscular arms would have gladly relinquished their strength for my weakness, because that's the way Jarrod's vast, extended family was. Motherly arms, fatherly arms, arms of women who could only imagine how they would feel if it had been their husbands and were thanking God it was mine instead. So many people clawing at me I wanted to tuck in my elbows, jerk my arms upward, and watch everyone scatter. Instead, I soldiered on—a good army widow.

But that had all happened what seemed a lifetime ago, and after spending the winter with my mother in Dallas, I hoped Saunders Creek would still want to embrace me. Still want to gather me in and allow me to live among them like one of their own.

I pulled up to my tumble-down house, relishing the solitude. I'd been smothered in Dallas, forced to mingle with Mother's kind of people, when all I wanted was to stop and catch my breath, to remember how to breathe again.

I owned my pain. Hid it deep inside. I couldn't let anyone see me fall apart. Mother taught me that. I hadn't dared show weakness during those months in Dallas. I'd kept my tears close and silent. My grief was my own, every tear sacred.

Quiet surrounded me as I slid the Jeep into park and stared at my new home. An old white farmhouse built at an angle to the road. Windows everywhere. The waning sun shone on the front porch, and I pictured how well lit the east side of the house would be in the morning.

On either side of the house, vibrant lilacs bloomed. The wind carried the sweet rose-and-vanilla fragrance from their purple flowers through the open windows of the Jeep. I smiled. Jarrod knew how I loved the smell of lilacs. Perhaps he'd had them planted for me.

I climbed the rickety wooden steps to my rickety wooden door and turned the wobbly knob. Apparently the contractor hadn't bothered to lock it. I didn't blame him. If anyone wanted in, they'd get in about as easy with a lock as without.

Fresh grief splashed over me like ice-cold water as I stepped inside. I looked around my new home, which had once belonged to Jarrod's grandparents, and my stomach tightened until it hurt. Did I actually believe Jarrod would be here? No. I wasn't crazy. But in coming back to this place he had loved so much, the home where he came on weekends and spent most of his summers, I hoped to feel something that my heart recognized.

But there was nothing, unless you counted dust motes and stale air. And a deep sense of disappointment.

My furniture had arrived and had been placed in some sort of order, rather than thrown into the house for me to deal with. Boxes stretched along the hallway, politely moved to the side. Jarrod's cousin Eli had unlocked for the movers, and this was his way of welcoming me, I assumed. I appreciated the order more than I could say.

The scarred wooden floor groaned beneath my weight as I walked slowly into the kitchen and dropped my purse onto the kitchen table. My gaze fell on the trifolded flag the officer had handed me during Jarrod's military funeral. I stopped short and stared. I hadn't wanted it that day. I was so grief-stricken, so angry, that I left it on the chair at the cemetery. My mother and I had left directly after the funeral. We hadn't come back to this house, and I couldn't imagine how it had turned up on my kitchen table.

I stared at the red, white, and blue symbol of death and felt nothing but cold rage. What did I care about the American flag anymore? My pride at the sound of the national anthem or the president's voice beseeching, "God bless you, and may God bless the United States of America" died six months ago with my husband. I would never again lay my palm reverently across my heart and recite the pledge. That day, I hated the "purple mountain majesties" and "sea to shining sea" as much as I had once loved my country. I would have crawled on top of Jarrod's coffin and let the dirt tumble over me as willingly as he had tackled a twelve-year-old zealot and carried him to an abandoned building before they both exploded into a million pieces.

The images haunted me.

I yanked my thoughts back before they could spiral into a dark place I might not be able to escape. There were suitcases and a couple of boxes to bring in anyway. I went back to the Jeep and started unloading, glad that the furniture had all been sent ahead so I didn't have to deal with getting it here.

If he had not died, he would have been home by now, out of the military, and ready to put down roots here.

In my grief, I'd almost abandoned our plan to live out our days in the heart of the Ozarks, and his family, but night after night, dream after dream, Jarrod seemed to be drawing me. How could I stay away?

Besides, mid-May seemed like a good time to move. Perhaps the beauty of nature's rebirth would somehow speak to my soul and help me make sense of the pain I couldn't escape.

After my last trip from the Jeep, I dropped, exhausted, into a kitchen chair and kicked off my flip-flops. The flag stared back at me, and I made a mental note to stuff it in a closet the next day. My phone trilled. I fished it from my purse and smiled at a text message from my sister, Lola. "Did you find your birthday present yet? Look in your pink duffel bag."

My birthday wasn't actually for a couple of weeks, but that wouldn't stop me from taking an early present. Curiosity overcame fatigue, and I padded barefoot into the living room, where I'd dropped most of my things.

I didn't have to dig around. A box sat on top of my clothes, along with a card. I unwrapped a huge bottle of brandy. I couldn't resist a smile. My city-girl sister had been joking for a month that I'd have to be drunk to actually live in "the boonies."

"Got it," I texted back. "Thanks."

"No problem. Try not to drink it all in one night. You're going to be there a long time. You'll need it."

I wouldn't, of course. I'd never been a drinker. The gift was an expensive joke. And it made me laugh the way only Lola could manage now that Jarrod was gone.

As the sun shifted, preparing its descent, the house began giving up light. The loneliness set in, and I blamed Jarrod for that. He should be here. My emotions ran the gamut these days, vacillating between grief, love, numbness, and finally, though not as often lately, anger. I didn't want to be angry. I wanted to idealize him the way everyone else did, but he'd gone off to save the world and left me to die of grief.

Tears blinded me as I pulled the bottle from the box. I'd always felt a little superior to people who used alcohol to numb their pain, but now I decided to join their ranks. What did it matter? There was no one to care what I did.

After rummaging through the boxes, I found

17

my dishes and pulled out a glass. I rinsed it out and poured a drink for myself. I downed it without taking a breath. My throat burned, but I barely noticed as I poured another and downed it too. I wandered out to the porch and settled down on the rickety porch swing. I had no idea how long it would take the alcohol to affect my brain, but I was ready for it.

I wanted to be numb and dizzy. Anything to stop the images of Jarrod's last few minutes on this earth. I turned sideways and stretched out on the porch swing, crossed my ankles along the wobbly armrest, and looked up at the rusted chains. I decided it was a good thing I wasn't very big because from the looks of the chain, a good hard yank would pull the whole swing down.

I poured another glass, then set the bottle on the porch. Staring out across the tree-laden hills, I raised the tumbler to my lips. I sipped the contents, despising every sweet, fiery drop that landed on my tongue. But as the warmth spread from my throat and moved through my body, I began to relax.

I could smell the creek beyond the tree line, and I breathed in deeply. The brandy slid straight from my empty stomach into my bloodstream, and my head started to spin a little. I liked catching a buzz. It made the trees greener. The birds sang a little louder, and the tree frogs chirped in better rhythm. And the more I drank, the better the brandy tasted.

I had to laugh a little at my circumstances. I, a debutante raised in Highland Park—the Beverly Hills of Dallas—was living in a dilapidated one-hundred-fifty-year-old home. My greatest joy in the past six months had been the look on Mother's face when she saw the house before the funeral. "Oh my dear Lord," she'd said, over and over. Her dismay was like Mozart to my ears.

As much as Mom hated it, I loved my new home. The house had sat empty since Jarrod's grandma passed on years earlier. Jarrod inherited fifty acres and the house two years ago when his father decided he'd like to go ahead and pass it on rather than wait until his death for Jarrod to move back home. Apparently, his grandmother had made it clear in her will that Jarrod should eventually end up with the home place—that's what the family called the part of the land with the house. From the moment I caught sight of the old two-story, I felt a kinship with the broken structure. It reminded me of *The Waltons*, and we had hoped to fix it up and fill the rooms with children. Mine and Jarrod's. I started the renovations while he was overseas. He suggested I contact his cousin Eli to do the work but that I make my own choices about how to fix it up. I wanted to surprise Jarrod with the changes. I fantasized about picking him up at the airport and bringing him home to a beautiful renovated house he would love.

What a cosmic joke.

But despite the insinuations I'd heard, I had no intentions of signing it back over to the family now that Jarrod was dead. The house sat empty, getting more and more run-down, for years before we started renovations, so I saw no reason to give it up if I had the means and desire to restore the place.

"Stupid Jarrod," I said to the sky, hoping he was up there somewhere listening. "You should have run away when you saw the kid had a bomb strapped on him." I raised the glass in the air, not as a salute, but so I could show him I was getting loaded for the first time in my life and it was his fault. "You think you're such a hero, sitting up there"—I leaned over the side of the swing and looked down at the porch—"or down there while everyone cries over you and talks about that stupid baby fox you saved when you were ten." My words were beginning to slur a bit, and the tears were stinging my nose. "Well, congratulations, my darling. You saved the world and left me alone. And don't you dare tell me to stop throwing myself a pity party, because I have one coming!" I downed the rest of the glass. It was burning less now with each tumbler.

I tried to negotiate the bottle, but it slipped from my hands, spilling half its contents onto the porch. The liquid made a winding trail through the cracks on the wooden porch. "Now look what you made me do," I sobbed. I sat up, my head spinning and swaying, feeling as crazy as I sounded. I lay back down and curled into the fetal position, using my arms as a pillow. I shut my eyes against the dizziness. The tears kept coming, bursting through my closed lids like water through cracks in Table Rock Dam.

I would never see him again. Jarrod, the hero of my heart, was gone, and he was never coming back.

"You jerk," I whispered through tears. "They gave you a medal."

The chain groaned above me as the swing moved forward, then back, as though someone were pushing from behind. My eyes popped open, and I glanced, half-fearfully, around. There was no wind. Not even the slightest breeze. And drunk as I was, I knew I hadn't moved the swing.

"Jarrod?" I whispered. Had he somehow found a way to come back to me? If he wanted to be with me as a whisper of wind, a shiver up my spine, I'd take him any way I could get him. I sat up, my heart racing with fear, anticipation, excitement. The remnants of twilight were gone, and nothing was left except the stars and moon. It was so dark I could barely see the white railing in front of the swing. I hadn't even bothered to turn on a light earlier, so there was no glow through the windows. Only the sounds of the tree frogs and crickets broke up the quiet of the hill on which the farmhouse sat.

"Jarrod?" My voice shook and echoed so loudly in my ears it sounded like I was speaking through a bullhorn. "It would be just like you to break all the rules and come back to me. I'm freaking out a little bit, and to be honest, the brandy has me really drunk. If it's you, make the swing move again."

I held my breath, waiting for . . . something. "Jarrod?"

Still nothing. I had never felt so utterly alone in my entire life. "Aw, Jarrod," I whispered, my throat choking with tears again. "For a minute there, I thought you were really back."

The rusty chains began to creak, and slowly, the swing moved back and forth. My heart lurched and I smiled—the first real smile to touch my lips in weeks. The songs of the night insects became a lullaby. I didn't open my eyes, but I knew if I did, Jarrod would be sitting at the end of the swing, cradling my feet in his lap and swinging me to sleep.

Eli

I thought for a second she might be dead. Curled up in the swing, a strand of honey-blond hair stuck to her face, her skin so white it was almost pasty.

She moaned and moved. I set down my coffee thermos, released the breath I'd been holding, and leaned against the porch rail, trying to decide whether to rouse her or let her wake on her own.

The gentleman in me wanted to lift her and carry her inside. She was shivering and shouldn't be lying there in the dewy, cool spring morning. She wore a pair of black exercise pants and a thin, long-sleeved shirt that might have been plenty warm for her to wear inside the house but didn't cut it out here. What was she thinking?

She moaned again and moved.

I knew there was an afghan on the rocking chair in the living room, so I went inside and got it. When I stepped back onto the porch, she was sitting up. She didn't act embarrassed when she saw me.

"So, you're the one I heard walking around," she said, her voice strained. "I thought it might be Jarrod."

My heart went out to her. "You'll be looking for him for a while. My mom said after Dad died she heard him in every room and saw him 'round every corner for months."

Corrie's eyes widened. "Does she still see him?"

I shook my head. "No. She never really did. She just wasn't ready to let him go, so her mind played little tricks on her."

"Oh."

She shivered and reached for the afghan. "For me, right?"

I handed it over. "You looked cold."

"I am. Thanks." She settled it around her shoulders as I leaned back against the railing again.

Corrie pressed slender fingertips to her temple. I could only imagine the way her head must be pounding. Her gaze found my coffee thermos next to me, and blue eyes flickered with interest. I lifted the container, unscrewed the top, and poured her some. She blushed, which I admit I found appealing, though I had no business thinking any such thing of my cousin's widow. She took the steamy mug I offered. "Was I that obvious?"

"It's okay. You need it more than I do." She smelled sour. The bottle of brandy sitting on the porch next to her feet was half-empty. And unless I missed my guess, this girl wasn't a regular drinker.

She took a sip and made a face. Then sipped again.

"You don't like it?"

Corrie's cheeks dimpled. "I don't usually drink coffee without sugar."

"I'll try to remember that."

Corrie took another sip and stared down the hill at the fog above the tree line. I couldn't imagine what she was thinking, and I wouldn't intrude to ask, so I kept my mouth shut and left her alone with her thoughts.

I searched for small-talk topics and was just about to ask her about her trip the day before when she spoke up first.

"Do you believe in ghosts, Eli?"

The question took me aback. I didn't like talking about spirits. The house held memories I'd just as soon forget. Too much family folklore that whispered of visitations and dreams and slamming doors. But she had asked an honest question. And she didn't seem spooked, which encouraged me. "You mean like if someone dies they don't leave until they get their unfinished business wrapped up?"

She nodded and took another sip.

"No. I don't." I had no evidence from the Bible or from reality that supported the existence of the dearly departed.

"Then how do you explain haunted houses? And ghost hunters on TV?"

I had my own theory about ghost hunters but kept that to myself. "I don't claim to have all the answers," I said slowly, gathering my thoughts. "But I imagine if there is an entity in a house and it's not an angel, it's probably a demon."

Corrie's expression dropped.

I frowned. "Is everything okay?" I asked. "The house isn't—"

She shook her head. "No. Just thinking about Jarrod. Wondering if he's thinking about me."

"He'd be an idiot not to."

She gave a short laugh. "He could be idiotic at times. Like blowing himself to kingdom come."

Her words startled me. "Most people think he's a hero for that."

A shrug lifted her shoulder, and the blanket slid down over the thin shirt. Absently, she pulled it back up, keeping her gaze fixed on the horizon. "I guess a lot of Iraqi families are glad he was so brave."

"But you don't see it that way?"

"It was heroic. I see that. But when a man has a wife waiting for him, I think he should consider the cost to her before he makes a choice like that." She pursed her lips, then spoke again. "If he'd been shot instead of sacrificing himself, I might feel a little differently."

I knew she spoke from a place of deep grief and not from a rational mind. She had to go through the process. Clearly she was in the angry stage of grief, and I didn't begrudge her feelings. I stood. "I best get busy."

"What were you planning to start on today?"

"The upstairs bathroom." That one had flooded several times, and the whole thing needed to be gutted. The floor had to be pulled up and replaced. It would take awhile to finish. "Unless you would prefer I take off a few days to give you some space and quiet time?"

She shook her head. "No matter how long we wait, I'll never be ready to let him go, so there's no reason for you to delay your work on my account. Let's just get on with it."

Once more, my heart went out to her. She was working through anger, grief, and acceptance. "All right. I'll plan to work on the upstairs bathroom, then."

"Before you get started on that, can I ask a favor?"

I stared into her pixie face and nodded. "What do you need?"

"Could you secure the swing better? I think you'll need new chains. It's just that I don't want to press my luck on this thing, and I'd like to enjoy the spring weather on the porch."

"Not a problem. I'll have to run into town and pick up some supplies at the hardware store. But that shouldn't take too long."

Her face lit up and she smiled at me, flashing those dimples and blue eyes. My heart responded to the sweetness of her face, and I smiled back.

The thermos at my feet slammed over, jerking my attention away from Corrie's pretty face. I picked it up and handed it to Corrie. "You need this more than I do," I said. "I'll grab a cup at McDonald's."

"You sure?"

"Yep."

"It's strange that it fell over like that."

I smiled at the way her furrowed brow wrinkled her nose. "The porch is slanted," I said, although the tilt wasn't pronounced enough to make the thermos fall without a nudge or a gust of wind.

But given our ghost discussion, I didn't want to spook her. "I'll be rebuilding the porch soon."

"Sounds good, Eli." She stood up, wrapped in the afghan like an Indian princess, then wobbled. Even with my gimpy leg, I got to her before she tilted backward. I grabbed on to her, feeling her tiny bones. "Steady," I said. "You might want to take it slowly until you get your sea legs."

She let out a soft sigh and pulled back, pushing her palm against my chest. "Thank you, Eli. I should never have touched that brandy. I'm paying for it now."

I chuckled, keeping my hands on her forearms to make sure she stayed steady before I let her go. "I'm sure you are."

She gave me a wobbly attempt at a smile. "Thanks, Eli. And thanks for going into town for the chains. I know it will derail your plans."

I grinned. "You're the boss."

As I drove slowly around the sharp curves and steep declines down the road toward town, my mind drifted back to Corrie's question: *Do you believe in ghosts?*

I heaved a sigh. *Are we doing this again, God?*

Two

Corrie

My head felt like I'd been sentenced to death by squeezing. I slumped against the side of the shower, and I'm sure I didn't get the soap rinsed out of my tangled hair. But at the moment, I didn't even want to live, so what did I care about soap? I stepped out of the shower, but I didn't feel any better after rinsing off yesterday's pain. I guessed I was experiencing my first ever, and I hoped last ever, hangover.

I couldn't bear the thought of the blow-dryer screaming in my ear, so I wrapped a towel around my hair and slipped on another pair of workout pants and one of Jarrod's old flannel shirts. The soft black pants were the most comfortable I owned. And comfort was what I needed most today.

Eli hadn't returned from town by the time I got to the kitchen. I knew I should try to get something down besides coffee. Maybe some dry toast. Wasn't there some kind of hangover concoction made with tomato juice and raw eggs? Was there something about Tabasco sauce? Where had I heard that? Some movie probably. Surely no one would actually drink that. I shook my head. How could that possibly help when just the thought . . . ugh. My stomach roiled. Of course, the more I tried not to think about nauseating dishes—runny fried eggs and globby oatmeal—the more those images stayed in my brain. I ran for the first-floor bathroom.

Thirty minutes later, I still couldn't bring myself to get off the bathroom floor, even though there was absolutely nothing more that my stomach could try to eject. My entire torso was clenched in the kind of muscle cramp we used to call a charley horse back in my track-star days. Maybe I'd be getting my wish after all and was about to be reunited with Jarrod. I could see our double tombstone now. "Jarrod. Beloved husband. Died a hero. Corrine (because Mother would insist upon my full name even though I hated it). Drunken wife and disgraceful daughter. May she rest in peace."

"I'm comin' to join you, Jarrod," I said out loud, in my best imitation of Fred Sanford of *Sanford and Son*. We used to watch the old seventies sitcom and laugh our heads off. I figured he'd appreciate the gesture.

I heard the front screen door swing open and then slam shut, and relief floated over me. Eli was back. I waited for him to call out for me. Listened carefully for the sounds of chains being dropped on the kitchen counter, but nothing happened. I frowned. Come to think of it, I hadn't even heard his footsteps. I'd only heard the door open and shut.

"Eli?"

No answer.

I shrugged, figuring I must not have heard the door after all. Did hangovers cause hallucinations? I made a mental note to ask Eli when he really did get back from town. I also made a mental note to dump the rest of that brandy down the drain the second I could stand to smell it. Just the memory of the smell . . .

I fought my churning stomach, still too weak and shaky to even care that I was sitting on the floor inches from the toilet.

Tucking my legs into my chest, I wrapped my arms around my shins. The position helped my stomach cramps, and for the first time since I woke up on the porch swing, I felt optimistic that I might actually live to see tomorrow. I pressed my forehead against my knees, closed my eyes, and wished like anything I'd used a little more self-control the night before.

I must have dozed off, because I woke to the sound of someone knocking on the front door. Then the telltale sound of the rusty hinges, followed by Eli's voice. "Corrie? I'm back."

"In here," I called, not at all sure he'd hear my thin reply. How could I possibly feel any worse now than I had earlier? My legs trembled and my head hurt so badly I wanted to cry, but I knew it would only make the pain worse. It seemed like every nerve ending in my body shook just below the surface of my skin, like a hyperactive version of restless leg syndrome. The good news was that my stomach had settled down, and despite the cramping, everything else was letting up. "Eli?"

"Coming," he replied, and I was never so glad for parchment-thin walls. My spinning head stopped me from standing. If Eli hadn't been there, I'd have had to crawl all the way to the living room.

The sound of his heavy boots echoed in the hallway of the nearly empty home. Our small apartment on base didn't have enough furniture to fill this place, so all I had was my kitchen table, a couch, a couple of rocking chairs, my bedroom furniture, and the futon that I noticed someone— Eli, probably—had set up in one of the spare rooms. I'd finish furnishing when we were done renovating.

He tapped on the bathroom door. "Corrie? Do you need help?"

For the first time today, I had the presence of mind to be embarrassed. He was about to open the door and see me sitting on the bathroom floor. I tried to at least stand up, using the wall as support, but my head and legs were having no part of my attempt at movement.

"I can't stand up."

He hesitated. "Are you . . . decent?"

"I'm sitting on the floor in front of the toilet wishing I were dead, but yes, I'm fully clothed."

The door opened and he wrinkled his nose. "Gross."

"That's the way you talk to a sick person?" I tried to be irritated but couldn't drum up the energy.

"If you were really sick, no, I wouldn't talk like that." He bent down and slid one arm under my knees, the other at my lower back, and lifted me effortlessly into his big, contractor-strong arms. "And I'm sorry. I shouldn't give you a hard time anyway. You've had a tough year."

"Can you carry me with that leg?"

He smiled. "I'm not carrying you with my leg."

I would have laughed, but it seemed too much effort. "Don't make jokes. I'm sick."

"It's just a limp, Corrie. I'm not crippled."

I nodded, hoping I hadn't offended him but sensing he'd rather drop it.

My head protested my attempt at holding it up, and the pain became unbearable in seconds. "Can I put my head on your shoulder?" It felt intimate, and I didn't want him feeling awkward when he was doing me such a kindness.

"Sure, honey," he said. His tone was so kind that I felt safer than I had in a very long time. He carried me out of the bathroom. "Your bed or the couch?" he asked softly.

"Bedroom, please," I mumbled, already

almost asleep again. "If it won't bother your leg."

I felt myself being lowered to the bed and then a soft, warm chenille throw floating over me. Eli's boots thumped as he left the room and descended the steps. I rolled to my side and pulled my legs up into the fetal position, hoping to stop the stomach cramps as I had earlier.

As I drifted to sleep, I felt the mattress move, as though someone had stretched out next to me. Breathing in deeply, I shook it off, chalking up the feeling to my spinning head and an active imagination. There! I felt it again. Movement on the other side of the bed. I jolted awake. That definitely hadn't been my imagination. I sat up quickly—too quickly. Blood rushed to my head, and nausea hit me full on. I closed my eyes and lay back down. I knew there was no one there, but I also knew what I felt. My mind returned to the night before, when I felt the swing move. A shiver ran up my spine, and my jitters got the better of me. I had to get out of that room. Jarrod or no Jarrod, I couldn't lie next to a ghost.

Eli

I didn't know how on earth I got the new chains hung on the swing without waking Corrie. Most people would have woken up a hundred times from the drilling and hammering, even from her bedroom upstairs, but she slept soundly, although for some reason she had come downstairs and passed out on the couch.

My heart hurt for Corrie. I, of all people, knew what it felt like to be under the spell of Jarrod Saunders. And his death had done nothing to stop the admiration people had for him, especially since his death had been so heroic. Jarrod would forever be the favorite son of Saunders Creek, Missouri.

I sat on the swing and shoved back, then let loose, looking up at the new chain and hooks. They would hold.

Jarrod should have been here helping with this kind of stuff. He hadn't even really wanted to join the army, but September 11 brought out the patriot in him, and he dropped out of his second year of college to enlist.

I had known better than to try again. Even with a war on, they didn't want guys like me. I stared at my twisted leg. With the naked eye, you couldn't see anything wrong. The problem was under the skin and muscles, in the bone, where my horse had fallen on me during a race with Jarrod. We were only eighteen years old at the time, a week and a half away from graduation. I was only two weeks away from boot camp. I'd signed up and was just waiting for graduation. I already had my orders and was headed for Fort Sill, Oklahoma. And then the accident changed everything.

According to the doctor, I should thank my lucky stars and Jarrod's quick thinking that I'd even kept my leg. I'd landed hard, and my thigh slammed into a stray log. As I tried to clear my head enough to figure out what had just happened, I watched, horrified, as my horse slid down onto his side. I couldn't react. I heard the snap as my leg broke, and I went into some kind of shock. I barely felt the pain until later. I'd have a limp for the rest of my life. Jarrod had coaxed the lame horse off me, helped me up the ravine, draped me over the bare back of his horse, and hopped up behind me. He rode like a twister all the way to town.

I had Jarrod to thank, all right. For whipping his horse around me on that narrow, muddy path, knowing the horses could easily miss a step. I had Jarrod to thank for my horse losing his footing and sending us both sliding down the steep hill to the bottom of the holler, where I lay pinned while Jarrod carefully made his way down the hill.

He had indeed shoved and coaxed the wounded horse until I was able to wriggle free. But then he had paced and panicked, trying to figure out how to get me back up the steep incline. I would have punched him if I could, but in the end I was forced to yell at him to shut up and get the rope from my horse.

He helped tie the rope around me—thanks to our Boy Scouts training, we both knew how to create knots that wouldn't come loose. He crawled back up the embankment and started to pull, while I used all the upper-body strength I possessed and dug my elbows into the ground. If the path had been wider, we could have had Jarrod's horse pull, but we both knew that with the mud, it was likely his horse would plummet as well, so I crawled my way to the top while Jarrod tugged on the rope.

I can only imagine the spectacle we made entering Saunders Creek. By the time we rode the thirty minutes to town, I'd passed out from the pain. Jarrod was declared a hero. After several surgeries and a medical release from the army, I watched as Jarrod deployed with his unit from Fort Leonard Wood, Missouri.

I never really knew how much I resented my cousin all these years until his funeral six months ago. A hero's funeral; a hero's life. Sure, he was a hero, but Jarrod had always been reckless and impulsive. His last impulsive action had cost his life.

I stopped the swing and sat without moving for a while, taking in the sunny, breezy spring day. There was no place I'd rather be than sitting right here on Granny and Pop's front porch as I had during my childhood. Pop smoked a pipe, but Granny didn't allow it inside, so every time he got a hankering for a smoke, we'd come here. I could almost smell it now as I remembered our talks on summer nights.

I spent most of my vacation nights here with Pop. Granny was always partial to Jarrod, with his love of old movies and TV shows, but I wanted to be outside experiencing things for myself, just like Pop. It's amazing that I grew up to be the one to go to seminary while Jarrod did the macho thing.

I reached forward and rubbed my aching thigh. The pain told me we'd be in for another afternoon or evening storm. Nothing new for springtime in the Ozarks, but boy did it ever keep me popping the Advil.

The door opened, and I turned to find Corrie, pale as a ghost and still shaky. She had wrapped her blanket around her, and she seemed so small and alone. If there had been a way to transfer my strength to her and take some of that pain away, I would have gladly done so. I scooted over so she could sit on the swing next to me.

A wan smile came to her pretty lips as she glanced up at the new chains. "You fixed it. Thank you." She sat abruptly, as if she was about to fall.

"How you feeling?"

A shrug lifted her tiny shoulders. "Better than earlier, but still not so good. I don't see how social drinkers can function."

I couldn't help but laugh a little at that. "What you did last night was a little less 'social' and a little more 'binging.' "

"That stuff sneaks up on you." She closed

her eyes. "Can we stop swinging before I barf?"

I planted my foot and the swing halted. "What made you decide to sleep on the couch?"

She shrugged. "The bedroom doesn't feel right to me."

"Do you want me to wait to start on the upstairs bathroom? I was going to take out the floor and replace the rotted boards this afternoon, but it'll be noisy because I'll be nailing."

"Do you mind waiting until tomorrow?" she asked. "But I can tough it out if it'll throw off your schedule."

"My schedule is your schedule, boss."

We had spoken on the phone a couple of weeks ago and mapped out a plan for how the renovation would proceed—what needed to be done, what had to be taken care of first. The plumbing, for instance, had been finished over six months ago, before Jarrod died. Now there were brand-new pipes fitted throughout the house. The electrician would have to come and rewire the entire house, but the soonest we could get him in was a month away, and that was iffy. It would be okay for a little while, as long as Corrie didn't run too many appliances at once.

"Where do you live, Eli?" she asked. "I'm ashamed that I never bothered to ask you before. Close by, I assume, since most of the family lives on land your grandparents owned. Right?"

The question caused a bittersweet response in

me. I'd honestly always believed Granny and Pop would leave me this house and the land above the river. I loved it best and spent a lot more of my time here before and after college than Jarrod ever did. But Pop went first, and Granny made the decision to give it to Jarrod once his dad passed. Uncle Fred decided to go ahead and pass it on. There was a lot of grumbling right now among members of my vast family that Jarrod had passed the land and house to Corrie rather than his parents, who would have for sure kept it in the family.

Sitting next to Corrie now was the first time I didn't begrudge him the inheritance, though I knew there were some in the family who were livid over her decision to come back to Saunders Creek and move into the house. What right did she have to live on Saunders land without Jarrod, or at the very least a Saunders child? I understood their fear. What if Corrie married an outsider and raised a bunch of non-Saunders in the house? I didn't like the way that looked either, but I certainly couldn't begrudge her the home Jarrod had given to her.

I smiled at her. Poor thing looked so miserable. "I live down the hill and a jog to the right. Go a couple of miles, and I'm the two-story brick. If you keep going a few miles, you'll run into Aunt Trudy's place. Her grandson, Ray, lives with her. If you turn left instead of right at the end of the hill, you'll come to my mom's, and past that is Jarrod's parents."

She nodded. "I remember where Liz and Fred live. We came a few times over the years. Just not enough for me to keep my directions straight with all these back roads. Let's see, though. If I go straight, that road takes me into Saunders Creek, right?"

"Yep." I pointed in the other direction, away from the road, and her head turned so her eyes could follow my finger. "If you're ever out walking, you can get to my place by crossing the covered bridge down yonder. Take the trail beyond it, and it curves around so you come up on the backside of my property. That's where the cabins are."

"Hmm, okay." Corrie squinted, trying to see where I was pointing, and I knew from my own teenage experiences with too much beer at our riverside parties that she was having a hard time with the sun. I reached into my shirt pocket and pulled out my sunglasses, a ten-year-old pair of Ray-Bans.

"Here. They won't win you any fashion awards, but they'll keep the sun from stabbing your eyeballs."

"God bless you and your descendants," she said, and I smiled, unbelievably charmed by her. How could Jarrod have signed back up after his first tour? If Corrie were my wife, I'd have gotten her pregnant as soon as she was willing, kept her that way for as long as she would have it, and

41

filled a home with beautiful kids that looked like her. I'd have happily spent my life doing everything in my power to keep her happy.

Not that I was in love with my late cousin's wife. But I liked her. A lot. And it wasn't hard, even for a knucklehead like me, to see how lucky a guy would be if she surrendered her heart to him.

"Did you say something about cabins?" she said, resting her head against the new chain.

My mind worked for a second to catch up, then I remembered. "I run a summer camp for military kids."

"Really?" She lifted her head and observed me. Or I guess she did. The glasses were pretty dark. "That is so cool. How'd you get into that?"

"I went to seminary with an army chaplain. He was telling me how at loose ends a lot of the kids are. They move every couple of years when Mom or Dad gets reassigned, and there are so many with at least one parent, sometimes both parents, deployed. Summer camp is a place for them to come and feel special."

To be honest, I was a little surprised she didn't know about the camp. I had spoken to Jarrod about it when he was stationed at Fort Leonard Wood the last two years. I asked him and Corrie to come and be part of it. I guessed he never said anything to her. But I wasn't going to tattle on a dead guy.

"Jarrod told me you went to seminary," she said. "I'd forgotten about that. He called you parson, like an old-time preacher."

"Yeah, no respect for the cloth."

She grinned. "Seriously, though. If you went through all the years of seminary, then why did you go into contracting?"

The truth was, I'd been given the opportunity to preach in large churches, in small churches, and as part of missionary programs, but my heart was here, in the Ozarks. I'd never be happy anywhere else, and unless I felt strongly that God was leading me, I'd never leave these hills. "I can't leave my mom alone, for one thing," I said, which, of course, was the short answer. "I do preach, though. I pastor a very small rural church just down the road."

Her eyebrows went up above the rim of the glasses. "I didn't know that. I'll have to come and hear you. I guess I especially need to after last night's drunken pity party." She laughed. "But I guess God understands, huh?"

I gave her a wry sort of smile and shrugged. "I personally think God's grace is all over situations like the one you are in. But given the choice, He would much rather you turn to Him for comfort than anything else."

Her face grew a little red, and I felt bad. I hadn't meant to shame her.

Corrie nudged me and looked toward the

direction I'd indicated for the camp. "So, this camp of yours," she said. "How long does it run?"

Relieved to change the subject, I dove into the new topic. "Six weeks. Different age groups, one week at a time. It'll take most of my spare time between now and mid-June to get things ready."

The wind picked up a little again, and a cool pocket of air floated up from the creek. She grew quiet. I respected the silence and kept quiet too.

She nudged me. "Hey, Eli?"

"Hmm?"

"Is there a store close by that sells porch swing cushions?"

Okay, so we were going to completely change topics. That was okay. I respected that too. "Lowe's down in Springfield, I imagine."

"Well, I need to get some. This wood swing might look pretty, but it's too hard. My behind is protesting."

I chuckled because, now that I thought about it, I reckoned she was right.

"Can you drive me in?" she asked.

"You mean now?"

"I'd have to stick my hair up in a clip and put on some mascara, but yeah, since we're not working on the bathroom anyway." She paused. "Unless you have someplace else you need to be?"

"Nope. I'm just surprised you feel like making a trip to anywhere but bed."

"I'm feeling a little better, and I'm afraid if I go to bed now I'll be up all night. I'd rather not get my days and nights mixed up. With remodeling going on in my house, I'll never get any sleep." She shrugged and looked up at me. "But I could probably drive myself if you don't want to go."

I waved aside her comment. "It's okay. I could use a couple of things from there anyway. So it'll kill two birds with one stone."

"Okay, thanks." She stood, clutching the light blanket around her. "Be back in a sec." She slid the sunglasses from her face and handed them to me. "Thanks for these. I have some inside."

Her eyes were starting to lose that dull, pain-filled look, and I could see a little of the spark I admired.

The door slammed hard behind her, and I heard her gasp.

I stood and got to her as fast as my limp allowed. "You okay?" I asked. I decided not to remind her that the frame on the screen was fragile.

"Yeah, the slam just surprised me. I didn't realize it was so windy."

I knew then that the door hadn't slammed itself, and she hadn't slammed it either.

A frown crossed her features, and she looked out at the tree line, presumably looking to see branches swaying—but they were still. "It's really not windy, is it? Sheesh. I best be more careful." She shrugged. "Be right back."

I hated to acknowledge what had slammed the door and turned over my thermos earlier today. Half the family believed in ghosts and thought the strange things that had happened around this place for as far back as I could remember could be attributed to an ancestor—or more than one. I sensed something was here too, but as I told Corrie earlier, I didn't believe people were allowed to come back as ghosts.

Prayer whispered from my lips. *Lord, keep her safe.*

Three

Corrie

The four-hour nap had done me more good than I'd originally believed. When I woke up earlier with the sun slashing my eyes, I thought I would be sick for a week. It had taken sleeping most of the morning to make me feel that maybe I wouldn't die after all.

Still, I regretted my impulsive decision to go buy cushions the second I entered my house to get ready. But Eli had already been so nice, I hated to back out on him. Besides, I needed a few grocery items too. I probably should have driven myself, instead of imposing on poor Eli, but I felt pretty shaky still. I wasn't sure how long the effects of alcohol stay in a person's system and had no intention of tempting fate.

Eli opened the car door for me. He drove a nice Ford 4 x 4 with a backseat and a heavy-duty body. "Wow, you boys don't play around with your trucks, do you?"

"Sort of like the guys in Texas?"

I smiled. I'm sure he was right, but I wasn't really raised with the country side of Texas life. Mother had dinner parties and invited politicians and TV preachers. They drove luxury cars and got massages. She most definitely didn't hang out with good ol' boys who drove half-ton trucks.

As we started down the hill, he pointed toward the double cup holder in front of the radio. A stainless-steel travel mug occupied one, a bottle of water the other. "I made coffee while you were getting ready," he said. "Figured you could use some. And after last night, you're probably pretty dehydrated. So the water seemed like a good idea."

I couldn't help but be touched by Eli's thoughtfulness, although today he'd been nothing but thoughtful and kind. I found myself wondering why he was single. As a matter of fact, thinking back, I couldn't recall one instance during any of our visits that I'd seen him with a woman. Over the past eight years, Eli and I had met a few times during family holidays, and of course my wedding, but we never really had too many conversations before we started talking about renovating the place.

Within a few minutes of calling Eli about the work, I knew he was the best choice for the job. I had no firsthand experience to tell me what a gem Eli was, but I could see why Jarrod had always said Eli was more than a cousin. He was like a brother and the best friend Jarrod would ever have. I knew that was why Jarrod felt comfortable having me work on the renovations. He knew Eli would look after me. Of course, it hadn't worked out the way we'd planned, but here I was, and Eli was steady as a rock beside me.

Staring at the cup holders, I thanked Eli and made a grab for the water first. I drank down all twenty ounces in seconds. I set the empty bottle back in the holder, a little breathless. "I didn't know how thirsty I was until I started drinking," I said a bit sheepishly, then eyed the coffee and decided the caffeine might help the dull ache in my temples.

By the time we reached the town of Saunders Creek, I had downed half the coffee, and I needed to make a pit stop before we went any farther.

"Um, hey Eli. Has Jarrod ever mentioned to you that he didn't let me have liquids while we were driving?"

He turned to me and shook his head, a frown piercing the space between his eyes. "No. Why?"

"Small bladder."

I couldn't see behind the dark sunglasses he'd loaned me earlier—which I was sure looked way better on his tanned, solid face—but I was pretty sure his eyes were smiling. At any rate, his mouth curved upward. He didn't say anything but pulled immediately into a small shopping center —Saunders Creek's version of a strip mall, I supposed. Five stores shared the L-shaped center. Eli parked the car in front of a quaint little shop with a window sign that read, The Nature of Things.

"This is my mom's health-food store," he said, opening his door. "You can go in there. Hey, she might have something natural for you to take for that hangover too."

I gasped, and my jaw stayed dropped as he walked around and opened my door for me. "Eli, if you say one word to your mom about me getting drunk last night, I'll punch your lights out."

He laughed. "Don't worry. I was just teasing."

"Well, good Lord. Don't give me a heart attack." That's all I'd need, starting a life in a town like this where everyone knows your name. I'd never live down being the town drunk.

He laughed again. "Honey, you're in corn liquor country—not to mention that the meth capital of the world is just down the road. A night of overindulgence due to grief is nothing to most of the people around here."

Eli opened the door for me. One thing about these boys—Jarrod and Eli—they were gentlemen to the core. I hadn't opened my own door in eight years as long as Jarrod was around.

When we stepped inside, the conflicting aromas of jasmine, sage, rosemary, thyme, and basil almost made me gag, given my still-precarious state. A sign across the back wall advertised organic meats, including buffalo roast and locally raised chickens.

Eli's mom handed a customer a small cloth bag and smiled. Her eyes landed on Eli, and her already beautiful face glowed even more. "Have a good day," she said to her customer, then slipped out from behind the register and headed toward us. I'd met Mrs. Murdock only once, but I knew she was the youngest sister on Jarrod's dad's side. Her eyes smiled the way Eli's did, and he'd gotten her height. She towered over me, standing at least five foot ten, which to my five foot three seemed Amazonian.

"Eli, baby," she said. "You didn't tell me you were stopping by." She turned her gaze to me and without asking reached out and pulled me close for a quick hug. "It's good to see you again, Corrie. How you holding up, honey?"

My throat clogged at the kindness. "I'm making it," I said. "Thank you for asking."

"Well, I'm surprised to see you out and about after such a long drive yesterday. Of course just a trip to St. Louis tuckers me out these days. That's the price of getting old."

"Sure, Ma," Eli said with an exaggerated drawl. "You're real old."

"Oh, what does he know?" she said, addressing me. "Now, honey, don't you dare bury yourself out there at that old farm or I'll come looking for you."

"Yes ma'am," I said, reverting to my southern belle upbringing. I already regretted leaving the farm today, but I didn't tell her that. Once I got some food for the house and some cushions for my swing, I probably wouldn't force myself off the property again until I had no choice. For instance, if I ran out of shampoo or toilet paper or, even more tragically, coffee.

Eli nudged me and pointed to the sign in the back that said Restroom.

"Oh, that's why you stopped in," his mom said. "And here I thought you missed your mother."

He rolled his eyes. "How could I? You don't give me a chance to miss you."

"Fine," she said with mock hurt. "I'll stop calling."

"Sure you will. Anyway, we're on our way to Springfield," Eli explained as I made a beeline to the back. "Corrie has some things to pick up, and so do I."

I closed the door behind me, and I heard the muffled conversation. I trusted Eli. He wouldn't blab my business. But gee whiz, doesn't a girl have a right to drink herself dizzy on her first night in the house she was supposed to share with her husband? Just the thought of Jarrod's burial brought burning tears to my eyes. I tried to fight them back, knowing that Mother would be mortified to know her daughter was bawling in a tiny bathroom in a tiny hillbilly town.

The thought made me smile and helped me control the sudden rush of grief.

I finished my business and washed my hands in the tiny sink. Then I shoved my sunglasses back on my face before I went out. I knew it would look a little funny—sunglasses inside—but better that than Eli's mom noticing the tears and going all motherly on me. I'd be a blubbering pile of mush in the middle of the store, and we'd never make it to Springfield if I let that happen.

Thankfully, she was helping a customer anyway. I spotted Eli over by the shelves all the way across the store. You couldn't really miss him. Tall as a basketball player, broad contractor shoulders, and a gorgeous tan already. If it had been Jarrod, I'd have accused him of popping into the tanning bed a few times after the gym, but I was pretty sure Eli wouldn't even fit into a tanning bed.

He looked up from the supplements he was eyeing and smiled when he saw me. I moved toward him, and his expression changed from happy to dread. For a split second, I felt the weight of rejection land on my shoulders, then in my peripheral vision I saw I had company. I turned and my eyes widened. At first glance, the woman could have been Mrs. Murdock's twin, with her blond hair and height and slender build. On second glance, however, her face definitely looked older, by at least twenty years. She stared wordlessly at me, and her eyes were the wildest shade of blue I'd ever seen. Something between sapphire and aqua. "Jarrod's widow." She said the words, not as a question, but as a statement of fact. "He misses you."

An eerie sort of cold moved through my back and over my scalp. The feeling reminded me of the way I'd felt earlier in my bed. I shivered. Then Eli was at my side, and I felt the warmth return. "I-I miss him too."

"Aunt Trudy," Eli said, slipping an arm lightly around me until his palm touched the small of my back. I felt strength in that action, and my mind began to run through the extended family members I had met the few times Jarrod brought me to his hometown. Then I remembered one Thanksgiving get-together five years ago, and Aunt Trudy's face came to mind.

With a rush of relief, I reached out to shake her hand. "Of course, Aunt Trudy. I remember you."

She smiled, and all I saw were gums. My stomach started to protest. "I remember you too. Jarrod's pretty, delicate wife."

Delicate?

Her gaze shifted to Eli, and something akin to hostility hardened her expression. "She's not for you," she said. "I love you, but don't let your competition with Jarrod lead your heart down the wrong path."

Eli's face darkened a shade. "Aunt Trudy . . ."

For a second I didn't know what she meant, then in an awful moment of clarity, I realized she meant me. Of course I wasn't for him. What did she mean?

Dismissing Eli with an upraised hand, she turned her attention back to me. A slow smile lifted one side of her mouth. "Jarrod isn't lost to you. Death's not the end." She peered closer. "But you already know that, don't you, honey? Where else would he have gone but back to the home place?"

My eyes went wide, and the hair on my neck stood up. I wanted to ask her about the swing moving and if that might have been Jarrod comforting me, and how did she know Jarrod was here with me, and how could she hear him speak? But I could tell Eli wasn't happy with the encounter, though I wasn't sure why. His mom finished with her customer and walked back to us. She slipped her arm around the old woman. "Aunt Trudy, I see you've met Corrie. She and Eli were just headed into Springfield. We'd better let them go." She gave Eli and me a conspiratorial wink behind Aunt Trudy's head. "I need to close up anyway. Auntie, will you help me cover the bins? Then I'll drive you home."

Aunt Trudy nodded. "Of course I'll help, but there's no need to patronize me, Samantha," she said in that blunt way that only old people can get away with. She looked at me again. "All you have to do is whisper, and he'll present to you."

"Okay," Eli said. I sensed he was trying to protect me, but I wanted to shake him off and ask this woman the questions rushing through my mind.

She ignored him anyway and studied me, her eyes narrowed. "Do you know magic?"

The unexpected change in topic threw me. I shook my head. Beside me, Eli's tension was palpable. Aunt Trudy's eyes narrowed to mere slits.

I shivered at her words, but I had to admit that somehow she seemed to know I was wondering about my experiences in the house last night and today.

Growing up in the Bullock home, we had never discussed the possibility of ghosts. In fact, there was a cut-and-dried explanation that went something like this: mediums and witches are an abomination to God. Conjuring spirits is forbidden. It opens doors that almost always result in demons wreaking havoc on your life.

I knew what my mother believed, but I didn't

really have an opinion one way or another. And I had to admit the occurrences—or whatever they'd been—frightened me. I wasn't much of a brave soul anyway. But if there was a chance Jarrod wasn't finished with me, if he wanted to help me through the transition of moving to his family home, I welcomed the chance to be in his presence again, however God allowed it. But given the tension I felt radiating from Eli, I instinctively knew this wasn't the time to discuss the issue. "It was a pleasure to meet you, Aunt Trudy," I said. "I'll see you again soon."

She gave me a slow nod and turned her back.

Eli's mom smiled warmly. "If you need anything, honey, you just give me a call. Eli, give her my number so she has more contacts around here, okay?"

"Will do, Ma." He kissed her cheek and kissed Aunt Trudy too. The old lady brightened and patted his face.

"Drive carefully," she said, and the gesture made her seem almost normal and a little less spooky.

I was shaking when we walked outside. The sun stabbed as it slowly descended. I was glad we'd be driving west. "Wow, I had no idea it was so late."

"Lowe's is open for a few more hours." Eli opened the door to his truck and waited for me to buckle up before he shut the door. I looked out the window toward the shop, hoping to catch a glimpse of Aunt Trudy. I wasn't disappointed. She had come to the store window and stood staring out at me as though she knew.

I almost felt guilty as Eli slid into the driver's seat and cranked the engine. I knew he'd want to avoid the subject, but my curiosity refused to let it go.

"So, she's an interesting character," I said, giving her a little wave and a smile as we pulled away.

"To say the least."

"How exactly are we related to her?"

"She's Pop's youngest sister." He cut a glance toward me and missed his opportunity to pull out of the parking lot into traffic. "The youngest of thirteen kids. She's only seventy-five but looks about ninety."

"That's only because she doesn't have teeth."

He laughed. "She does that on purpose, I think. Her way of seeming more witchy."

His tone and lack of respect for an elder surprised me, and I stayed quiet. He must have understood my silent condemnation, because he elaborated.

"I don't mean that in a disrespectful way. I mean she honest-to-goodness wants the mystique of being a witch. She practices the old magic from around here. Everywhere else in the world, the witches want to get rid of the stereotype of warts and wrinkles and pointy hats, but she likes it."

"Is that why she asked me if I knew magic? Did she think I might be a witch?"

He got an opening and maneuvered the truck into traffic. Then he turned toward the main street that would lead to the outer road, which would lead to the interstate. We had a good forty-five-minute drive ahead of us. And I was getting hungry, but no way did I want to walk into a restaurant today. The thought of being in a room full of people sent a wave of panic through me.

Eli glanced at me again. "Aunt Trudy seems to have taken a personal interest in you."

"I liked her. I thought she had character. When the house is finished, I'll have her over for lunch one day."

"Just be careful, Corrie. As much as I love her, Aunt Trudy isn't playing games. She honestly believes the things she said to you."

"So she's a witch for real?" I grinned and put on my Glinda the Good Witch high-pitched voice. "But is she a good witch or a bad witch?" He gave me a blank stare, then frowned. I gave a mock gasp. "From *The Wizard of Oz*? Don't tell me you've never seen it. That's un-American."

"Oh yeah, I saw that." He watched for traffic and pulled onto the outer road. "And to answer the question, she's a good woman. I love my aunt. But we have fundamental differences in what we believe." He hesitated. "My faith tells me she's deceived."

"Deceived how?" I felt bad for teasing about *The Wizard of Oz* when the topic of his aunt clearly troubled him.

He expelled a heavy breath. "The old-timers around here still hold to the superstitions the ancestors brought with them from Appalachia in the early nineteen hundreds. Our family has been filled with healers and naturalists as far back as anyone has bothered to trace."

I shivered a little in spite of myself. "Your mom running a natural-food store, for instance."

"Yes, that's bringing the tradition into the twenty-first century. Aunt Trudy and Pop's mother sold charms and love potions and served as midwives to most of the women around here for a couple of generations."

The thought made me smile. "No harm in that." I felt like I'd been charmed from the moment I laid eyes on Jarrod, and even death hadn't eased the effects of his spell on my heart.

"She was said to be a medium."

"Conjure-up-the-dead medium?"

"It's called spirit communication, but yes. And the Bible says to stay away from it."

"She said she heard Jarrod say he misses me."

Eli's jaw tightened. "She might have heard something speaking to her, but it wasn't Jarrod."

"Just like that?" Irritation hit me. "You can't even consider the possibility he spoke to her?"

"I believe the Bible." He shrugged. "Anyway,

it's part of our heritage. You're living in the house where she grew up. I just thought it might interest you."

Actually, since he put it that way, I had to admit that I was more than a little intrigued. I reached over and put my hand on his upper arm. "It does interest me. To be honest, Aunt Trudy did get me a little spooked."

He shook his head. "She's a good person, basically. Mainly she's into nature and trying to set things in balance. You have nothing to worry about from her unless . . ."

Okay, when someone leaves a sentence open-ended like that, I can't help but worry. Especially when it has to do with worrying about a witch—good or otherwise.

"Unless what? Is she going to cast a spell on me or curse me?"

His lips twitched, and I was glad to see him lighten up a little. "Of course not. Unless you make her mad—just kidding."

"Jerk." I punched his arm, and he laughed. But he still hadn't answered the question. "I don't need to worry unless what?"

"Aunt Trudy is kind and a good woman . . ."

"But she dabbles in the black arts so I should be careful?" I thought I was starting to catch his drift a little.

He shook his head.

Or maybe not.

"She doesn't dabble. There is a definite darkness surrounding several of the women in the family and one of the men—Aunt Trudy's grandson, Raymond. Even though it's mostly about nature and doing so-called good, the women around here are serious about this craft. That's what makes it so much more dangerous. They hold gatherings in the woods on Aunt Trudy's property, which isn't that far from your property.

"She has a coven?" I held my breath and waited for him to say no; instead he nodded.

"Essentially. And it could be she's hoping you'll be sensitive to spiritual things. Maybe join the family tradition?"

Fear trickled down my spine. "I'm not part of the family, technically, so that would make me more of a Muggle."

Again confusion clouded his eyes. Did this guy ever watch a movie? I shook my head. "It's from Harry Potter, but never mind."

"Well, anyway, in our part of the country, the old-timers believe the only way a witch can pass down the gene—for lack of a better word—is male to female or vice versa and through sexual contact."

My face warmed—what was I, twelve? "So because Jarrod and I were married, she could tag me as a member if I wanted to learn the craft?"

"Exactly."

"Well, you don't need to worry about that." I

held on to the hand brace above me as he slowed the truck at the intersection that would take us off the outer road onto the main highway. "I'm too much of a chicken to have anything to do with witchcraft. Plus, I'm too levelheaded, if you can believe that after catching me passed out this morning."

His lips twitched, as I'd intended. But he grew serious again almost immediately. "Just be careful. It's seductive. It's also easy to justify it and make it much less dangerous in your mind and heart than it is. Most of the family doesn't even give a thought to where Aunt Trudy's magic comes from. They just accept her for who she is and let her be, with her spells and moonlight gatherings."

His eyes remained on the road ahead of us, and he maneuvered the truck carefully in and out of traffic. Eli was truly troubled by all of this. I made a mental note to let Aunt Trudy know as soon as possible to take me off her list of witches in training. It definitely wasn't for me.

Four

Eli

By the time I got home, it was after nine o'clock, and my stomach felt like a cave, hollowed out. I'd offered to buy Corrie dinner in Springfield, but her stomach wasn't ready for anything solid, as I'd suspected. She waved away my suggestion.

Mom's car sat in my driveway, and my stomach jumped. Dad had passed on two years earlier, and my sister, Lynn, moved away right out of high school, so I was the only immediate family Mom had around here. I worried when she showed up late like this. She should be home, settled in for the night.

The house smelled like tomato sauce and Italian sausage, and my stomach rumbled. "Mom?" I called out. She would be absorbed in one of her nightly shows on the kitchen TV and would be oblivious to someone walking into the house. Me or a burglar or whoever. She stood at the counter chopping parsley, and as I suspected, she was watching *Law & Order: SVU*, which she always called SUV, and was clueless to the fact that I'd just called her name.

"Am I going to have to take away your key?"

She jumped at the sound of my voice, and her empty hand flew to her chest. "Gracious, Eli. Warn a person, will you? My heart is strong, but at my age I could have a stroke being scared like that."

I didn't mention that I'd called out to her five seconds earlier. Why bother? "What's all this?" I asked.

"Oh." She tossed the parsley into a bowl of other fresh greens. "I didn't figure poor Corrie would feel like stopping for food." She shook her head. "She looked dead on her feet today."

Refraining from telling her exactly why Corrie appeared that way, I leaned across the counter and snuck a piece of broccoli from the bowl. "That's thoughtful of you. You're right: she wasn't up for food at all."

"Exactly."

"What's in the oven?" I asked.

"Eggplant parmesan." She paused and looked at me. "Do you want to go wash your hands while I get this on the table?"

"Sure. That's exactly what I want to do. Be right back."

Walking down the hallway toward the bathroom, I had to smile. God love her, she tried to let her thirty-year-old son grow up, but it was hard for her. She always posed her orders in the form of a question so I wouldn't feel like a kid. I didn't mind so much, but it was probably a good thing for her to work through it. Especially since marriage had been on my mind a lot lately.

I didn't think it had to do specifically with Corrie. I knew she had just suffered an enormous loss, and I had no business even considering her in a romantic fashion. But she was cute, funny, smart—more my type than Jarrod's, I'd always thought. But he'd adored the girl, and the more I got to know her, the easier it was to see why.

I stared at myself in the mirror above the sink as I dried my hands. My mind went back to Aunt Trudy's words to me: *"She's not for you. Don't let your competition with Jarrod lead your heart down the wrong path."*

I couldn't help but wonder why she would say such a thing. It probably had a lot to do with the fact that Corrie was single now, living at the home place, and I was going to be there a lot in the upcoming weeks.

"You coming, Son?" Mom called from the kitchen. I shook my head at my reflection. I had considered moving in with Mom, or having her move in with me, after Dad died, but we'd have driven each other nuts inside a week. I figured she knew it too, because she'd never brought it up.

The kitchen table was set when I got back. Mom stood at the counter, still watching *Law & Order.* She glanced up when I arrived and shut it off with the remote.

"You can leave it on if you want," I said. "It doesn't bother me."

She shrugged and walked around the counter to the table. "It's a rerun. I'd rather talk."

After a quick prayer of thanks, we filled our plates. I waited, assuming she'd want to talk about Corrie. I didn't have to wait long.

"Did Corrie find what she needed?"

I nodded. "Cushions for her porch swing and some groceries." I slid the hot, tomato-filled bite of eggplant parmesan between my lips.

"Cushions. Good idea. They'll make the swing look better, I guess."

"They're not for decoration." My heart clenched at the memory of Corrie curled up on the swing. "She slept on the swing last night. I have a feeling she plans to do it again rather than sleep inside without Jarrod."

"I can understand that." Mom sipped her tea and stared hard at the bowl of salad. "I guess it's almost like it just happened for her, coming back here and all."

"I think she's regrieving."

"Aunt Trudy seems taken with her."

I tensed and put down my fork. "What do you think about that? Doesn't it seem like she's more interested in Corrie than she should be?"

"Hmm. Could be." Mom sipped her tea and swallowed her bite.

We loved Aunt Trudy. Her eccentricities were from being part of a very old, superstitious Ozarks family. Most of the families around these parts had at least one or two "widder women" who claimed powers. I believed Trudy actually possessed them. I trusted in God, but only a fool would turn a blind eye to the powers of darkness so prevalent in this area. Most of the folks who practiced believed their powers were for good, and despite assuring Corrie that Aunt Trudy also believed hers were for good, I wasn't so sure. She did some good, I supposed, but I thought she delved knowingly into the darkness too.

I waited for Mom to expound.

"After you left the store and we were cleaning up, she mentioned there was sensitivity around Corrie. Something that makes her special."

"Well, Corrie isn't a witch, and she's not going to be."

My mom jerked her gaze to me, and I realized I'd spoken too abruptly. "Be careful, Son. I know you're only speaking out of concern for this girl."

Mom's nerves over this were uncharacteristic. She, of all people, knew personally the people around these parts who practiced magic. She sold them their herbs and powders. Natural healing solutions that were healthy and full of vitamins and minerals the body needed to repair itself. Aunt Trudy and the like took it to the extreme and made a religion out of it.

Mom took a breath and pushed back her barely touched plate. She cut her glance to me. "Aunt Trudy believes that Corrie is like her."

"Like her? As in a witch?" I shook my head. "That's not going to happen. Corrie knows better."

Mom rubbed her temple with her fingertips. "Eli, please remember that we don't battle against flesh and blood. Try to take Aunt Trudy on without prayer and you might be in for more of a fight than you want."

She was right. I knew better than to try to fight darkness with emotion. I had to get a rein on my anxiety about Aunt Trudy's possible plans for Corrie. I had no idea where Corrie stood spiritually. Jarrod was raised in a Christian home, so I had always assumed he'd chosen a girl with similar faith. Not knowing increased my concern for her. I knew the seductive influence of magic. Too many members of my family had been deceived by it for me to close my eyes and pretend there weren't real powers involved. And what human being alive didn't enjoy the feeling of power?

I sat silently, eating and wrestling with my thoughts, until Mom shoved back from the table and stood. "I'm not feeling well. I think I'll go on home. You can take care of cleaning up, can't you?"

"Of course." I stood with her. "Migraine?"

"It's been so long I haven't kept up with my meds." She retrieved her plate and glass and carried them to the counter. After grabbing her purse and keys from the counter, she headed toward the foyer. At the door she stopped and turned. "Honey, I know you like Corrie. I can tell. But she just lost her husband. I want you to guard your heart against getting hurt."

I shoved down my annoyance and pulled her into a hug. "All these years you've been after me to go on a date, and now you're warning me off the only single girl around here with a full set of teeth?"

She pulled back, smiling, but I saw concern in her eyes. "Just be careful not to get hurt. Her heart isn't ready for a new man."

"Ma," I said, opening the door and stepping outside with her. "Don't you think I know that? Corrie and I are becoming friends because I'm the only person she knows around here. Once I'm finished with the house, I won't even see her much. So put away the worry card, and let's just put this in perspective, okay?"

She nodded, but I could see she wasn't convinced. A sigh lifted her shoulders, and her eyes closed for a brief second.

"Do you want me to drive you home? I could pick you up in the morning and bring you back to get your car." We walked down the steps, and I opened her car door.

She hesitated, then shook her head. "No. It's not far. I'll be fine."

"Call me as soon as you get home."

"That's my line."

"I know. Just be careful."

I didn't like the idea of her going home when the headache had hit her so suddenly. Briefly I wondered if it was a spiritual attack, but I didn't want to overthink it. It didn't do any good to look for demons around every corner. I prayed as I watched her drive away and remained outside until her red taillights disappeared.

Keeping my line of communication with heaven open, I walked inside, a heaviness bearing down on my heart. I didn't like feeling this way, but rubbing up against darkness always produced an uncomfortable form of warfare. And clearly there was a fight brewing. Aunt Trudy might want to believe it was between her and me, but I knew Mom was right. This fight was not to be fought by my hands. It wasn't Aunt Trudy I was wrestling. It was the darkness inside her. She thought she controlled it, but it was the other way around.

I left the kitchen the way it was, without even putting away the leftovers, and went to my living room to pray. By the time my mother called to let me know she had gotten home okay, some of the burden had lifted, but after I hung up the phone, I continued to pray.

Later, as I lay in bed, I began to suspect that today had been one battle in what I feared was going to be an all-out war for Corrie.

Corrie

After Eli brought me home last night, I put away the groceries, grabbed a pillow and blanket and my cushions, and went out to the porch. It was actually a little cool, and a few sprinkles dotted the ground, but that was okay. The quilt was warm and the cushions comfortable, and this was so much better than trying to sleep alone in that house.

My fitful drunken sleep the night before had left me exhausted, despite my long nap, and I fell asleep almost instantly. I woke up once, thinking someone had called my name, but when I sat up, I realized it must have been a dream.

I woke again to a hazy predawn world that was amazingly beautiful. I didn't want to miss sunrise, so I stepped inside and made a pot of coffee as quickly as I could. I was glad I'd invested in the BUNN coffee maker that finished brewing in four minutes. By the time I made it back from the bathroom, I could pour strong coffee into my mug and walk back out to the porch. My blanket still felt warm from the memory of my body heat.

The sun rose behind the house and flashed across the tree line, where the haze rose from the river overnight and hovered. It was an ethereal fog, like something out of a movie. The thick mist blanketing the trees gave up its hold on the ancient oaks and cedars as the sun brought the morning. The breathtaking view would never get old, and

I ached because I'd never share it with Jarrod.

I leaned against the arm of the swing and pulled my legs up. Sipping the warm, strong, sweet coffee, I watched the sun light my new world without Jarrod, and I let the tears fall.

"Jarrod," I said around a deep breath and closed my eyes. "I've been so mad at you, babe. So mad I just wanted to scream at you for saving lives at your expense. And my expense. And the expense of all the children that are never going to fill this house."

Keeping my eyes shut, I pictured him standing in front of me, holding out his palm. Lost in the fantasy, I lifted my hand and felt the warm memory. We stayed there, palm against palm, the way we'd done a thousand times.

My breathing slowed, and maybe I fell back asleep, but I felt the warmth from his cheek brush by mine. His breath floated my hair across my ear and tickled my earlobe, just as he had done too many times to count.

My stomach jumped, and I opened my eyes. I was so sure I'd find him sitting next to me, his arm pulling me close, that when he wasn't there, I nearly burst into tears of disappointment.

Instead, I saw Eli's truck coming up the road. Shaking, I forced composure I didn't feel and tried to shove away the memory of a phantom touch I could have sworn was real.

Eli had been great last night, taking me to

Springfield, putting off a day of work for me. I know it put him behind. Jarrod had been right. Eli was the kind of guy a person could count on. Fleetingly, I wondered why some lucky girl hadn't snatched him up by now.

His truck kicked up dust from the driveway as he pulled into the circular drive. Really, it was more an extension of the road than a driveway. He stepped out, carrying dishes.

"What's that?" I called as my mind slowly began the climb from the dream world to reality.

"Mom made eggplant parmesan last night." He smiled. "There's lots left. I thought we could have it for lunch if you want."

"Sounds perfect." I returned his smile. "Tell her thank you." I opened the door and held it while he carried the food inside. He set the containers on the counter, and I put them in the fridge. I nodded to the coffeepot. "Help yourself. It's fresh."

"How do you feel today?" He walked to the cabinet and found a mug. "All over the hangover?" He grinned.

"Yes, all over it," I said. "My first and last time getting drunk."

"It's just as well." He spooned sugar into his mug. "Drunk isn't very attractive."

"Now you sound like my mother." I said it as a quip, then realized I didn't like those words. I stuck out my tongue. "I thought you didn't take sugar in your coffee."

"Only in yours." A chuckle rumbled his chest.

"Aw, that's right. You're a coffee lightweight," I said, my tone deliberately condescending. "How could I forget?" But Eli was so humble, he was easy to forgive.

He grinned. "Oh, by the way. I called the electrician who usually works with me on jobs like this one."

"And?" I perked up. We couldn't put in the new central heat and air or my new ceiling fans until the electrician rewired the entire house and added a new breaker box.

"It'll be mid-June at the earliest before he can get here."

"Well, that's a relief. At least I can get the AC in before it gets too hot out."

"Let's hope."

"Uh-oh. Don't tell me he's the sort of contractor who says June but means December?"

He chuckled in his deep, comforting way. "Maybe not quite that bad, but just about."

"So I might be using fans and the window unit this summer after all?"

"Probably. But we'll have to talk about how much electricity you can have going on at once. The dishwasher, washer, and dryer all going at one time is taxing enough on this sixty-year-old breaker box. Add the window unit and fans, and we might be talking a fire hazard."

An hour later, after I arranged the breakfast

dishes in the dishwasher, I went to the hallway and started unloading boxes. By noon, the house was eighty degrees, which was pretty warm for this early in the year. It made me a little nervous, given my discussion with Eli this morning about the electrician. In mid-May, it should be in the upper sixties, maybe low seventies from time to time. Eighty reminded me of Texas. But I was dying to get outside and see if I could find that bridge Eli mentioned yesterday. A covered *Bridges of Madison County* kind of bridge.

At twelve thirty, I heard Eli's boots coming down the stairs. I had tackled half a dozen boxes, and I was sitting on the living room floor, surrounded by all the things I had yet to put away. Eli stepped carefully and glanced around at my things. His eyes stopped on my paint supplies. "You're an artist?"

"Used to be." I accepted the hand he reached out to me, and he yanked me to my feet. He didn't respond, and I sensed he didn't want to pry. Though I wasn't going to dredge up all the reasons I'd put my supplies away for years, I did feel the only way to remove the awkward atmosphere was to offer some explanation. "My sister went to medical school. I went to art school." And my mother was still hyperventilating over that choice.

I played it off as nothing, but inside I could see myself then—all those years of painting. I was good. I knew I was. "Brilliant," some reviews said after art shows during college. Fresh and innovative.

Eli followed me into the kitchen, and I pulled out the food he'd brought over. He leaned against my counter and watched me as I went about heating our lunch.

"Do you only paint for fun now, or just not at all?"

I shrugged. "Honestly? I haven't painted in ages. Not since I married Jarrod, really."

His eyebrows rose. "Why's that?"

I pulled a couple of plates from the counter and set the table. "Well, I had the choice of marrying Jarrod or accepting a position at an art gallery in Dallas where I could display some of my art. And I chose him." Besides, my mother had gotten me the job at the gallery. I'd never really wanted it in the first place.

"Yeah, I know he was relocated right after you got married, but to give up something you love?"

I smiled as I pulled the dish from the microwave and set it on the table, motioning for Eli to take a seat. "I never said I loved it."

"I'm intruding. I'm sorry."

I released a heavy sigh and lifted my gaze to his. "Okay, I did love it. I thought I would be an artist. But you know, I fell in love, and my priorities changed." I spooned some food onto my plate.

He nodded without comment, but his eyes remained on me.

I was ready to stop talking about me. "So your mom runs a natural-food store and cooks from scratch. How about your dad? What was he like?"

"Let's see. He was the sort of guy you could count on. Salt of the earth. Truly a 1950s, *Father Knows Best* type. Went to all my games during school. Took me camping. That kind of thing."

"Wow. Lucky you," I said around a cheesy, tomatoey bite.

"I take it your dad wasn't the Ward Cleaver type?"

I paused to think about it. My dad was my hero too. Only he wasn't the 1950s dad. "My dad's more '60s than '50s. Still to this day. As a matter of fact, I think he still has the lava lamp and bong he used in the '70s. A real role model."

"Hippie, I take it?"

I laughed. "Something like that. He's the artistic type, which is where I get my creative side. My mother was going through a rebellious phase when she met him at college. They eloped. And she made him miserable until I was about twelve, and he ran off with someone who 'understood' him."

"I didn't notice a fifty-year-old hippie at Jarrod's funeral. He didn't attend?"

I smiled and shook my head. "He called after Mother chewed him out over the phone. Said he really tried to come. Yada-yada-yada." I felt Eli's sympathetic gaze, and he asked the inevitable question.

"Do you ever see him?"

"Occasionally. When he thinks of it. He's killed a lot of brain cells." I laughed because, despite his negligence, I adored my dad. He was who he was, and I accepted him. I shrugged, trying to lighten the mood, and tossed the plastic containers into the sink, a little embarrassed that I'd eaten more than half the food he brought. "I think I'll take a walk by the bridge before I get back to the boxes," I said. "You're welcome to join me."

He shook his head. "I would like to, but I want to finish the floor today. Then we can start putting down the tile tomorrow."

My cell phone buzzed from where I had set it on top of the fridge. I pulled it down and rolled my eyes. "My mother . . ."

Eli stood, lifted the plates from the table, and set them in the sink. "I'll get back to work and let you deal with that."

I sighed and hit speakerphone. "Mother, we were just talking about you."

"We?" Her voice was high and controlled, as if her bun was too tight.

"Eli and me."

"Are you already dating? Good grief, Corrine, you've only been there a day."

Eli grinned over his shoulder as he headed out the kitchen door and then laughed out loud when

I scowled at him. I quickly disabled the speaker-phone and put the cell to my ear.

"No, I'm not dating. You met Eli at the funeral, Mother. He's Jarrod's best friend and cousin. Eli is doing all the renovations on my house."

"Oh, the handyman."

"Yes."

She was quiet for too long, and I realized she must be distracted by something at the office. "Did you need something?" I asked, my voice sharp. Who called whom, here? I had plenty to do without being ignored on the phone.

"Oh yes, I'm sorry, Corrine." And she's back . . . "Listen, honey. Your grandparents' anniversary is in two weeks, and I'm booking flights for you and the rest of the out-of-towners. I'm e-mailing you your itinerary. I've made your return flight a week after you arrive."

"A week! Mother, I just got here. I don't want to be away for a whole week."

"Well, how will you see everyone and get in your summer shopping without at least a week?"

By *summer shopping,* my mother meant she and Lola and I would be taking a trip to New York while I was there. We'd take the 5:00 a.m. flight, get a cab directly to the hotel, and then hit Saks Fifth Avenue. We'd have a fantastic lunch at someplace expensive, take in a Broadway show, have a fabulous dinner. Stay at The Plaza, and then fly home the next day. When Jarrod was around, I had an excuse not to go to these little family outings. Now I had no excuse that Mother would accept. I had just spent the past six months under Mother's thumb. How could she not understand that I never had any interest in her world? And even less now. I just wanted to be left alone to grieve my husband and attempt to make sense of his death.

"I have everything I need, Mother," I said. I knew I'd have to be determined to stand my ground and willing to make her angry or I'd give in.

After going round and round for a few minutes, I finally agreed to "think about it" and get back with her in the morning. Mentally, I made a note to send her an e-mail. I hated showing weakness where she was concerned, but the only way to keep my resolve was to not hear her voice.

By the time I hung up, my insides were so tight that I needed to get out of the house. I left the lunch containers in the sink and headed outside and toward the bridge. A cooling wind was starting to pick up.

I walked the path, taking in the signs of spring: green grass, squirrels running up and down the trees that lined the thin wire fence that marked off a ravine. I couldn't resist peeking over the fence, but I couldn't see anything but trees and shrubs and wildflowers. I knew anyone who fell would end up in the river. Dead or seriously hurt, but in the river either way. The path angled downward, and I walked until I reached the bridge ten minutes later. The temperature dropped a good ten degrees as I stepped onto the covered structure.

For a second I stood there, taking in the reality that this belonged to me. "Thank you, Jarrod," I breathed. I felt so close to him here, watching the water move below the bridge. I leaned against the railing and let the breeze brush across my body.

I sat down on the platform and let my legs dangle over the side, resting my arms on the middle rail, and I watched the water move high and low with the wind. I don't know how long I stayed there—it was awhile, more than an hour—imagining Jarrod. Wondering what it might have been like for him growing up around here. The solitude felt soul-healing, and I remembered a verse Mother used to quote: "He leadeth me beside the still waters. He restoreth my soul." Had Jarrod led me here? I shivered suddenly, and for some reason my fight-or-flight sense was alerted. I felt odd, unsafe, as though someone was watching me. I pulled myself to my feet, my legs stiff from dangling for so long.

I was about to head back to the safety of the house when I heard the hum of a small motor coming from the path on the opposite side of the bridge. I turned and saw a Gator coming toward me. The driver waved, and I waved back, but it wasn't until the vehicle stopped just short of coming onto the bridge that I recognized Eli's Aunt Trudy. She turned off the motor and slid off the ATV.

"Aunt Trudy," I said, walking toward her in case she needed a steadying hand. "What a coincidence."

"There are no coincidences." She showed the toothless grin that had revolted me the day before, but today I found it grannyish, and it didn't bother me at all.

"Well, I think this is a lovely chance meeting, anyway." I was a bit surprised to find that I truly meant it, despite the spooky encounter in the store and Eli's concerns over her interest in me. "What are you doing out and about all alone?"

"I sensed the need to come to the creek," she said matter-of-factly. "And I had a feeling it had something to do with Jarrod's widow."

"And here I am," I said, mostly to placate her.

"Yes, you are."

She took my arm, though I wasn't sure which of us was leading the other.

"What about you?" she asked. "Why did you come here today?"

I shrugged. "Eli told me about the bridge, and I needed a break from unpacking boxes, so I thought I'd come see what all the fuss was about."

"Or maybe Jarrod led you here."

I thought about the eerie feeling of being

watched I had experienced just before she came, and my heart rate picked up.

We stopped midbridge. She motioned toward the water. "This is where Saunders Creek began."

I had a vague recollection of Jarrod relaying the story of how the town originated, but I could see she was set on telling me anyway. "My grandparents settled here right after the Civil War. Back then, there was nothing here but woods and river." Her voice lifted with pride and a twinge of regret. But I began to wonder if there could be more. If maybe she had been designated to speak for the family or something.

"Do you think I should give the land back to the Saunders?"

Her eyes narrowed a bit as she studied me. I got the eerie feeling she was probing my mind.

"We all have to decide our own path. Who would you give it to?"

Eli's face came to mind, but I shrugged. "I guess I'd have to give it back to Fred." After all, the land had gone to Jarrod's dad before coming on to Jarrod. Guilt about Jarrod's parents plagued me. I still hadn't called or gone by to see them since coming to Saunders Creek. It wasn't right and I knew it, but I didn't have the strength to face them. They would be looking for stories about Jarrod, wondering about conversations we had that might have included them—there weren't many. Mostly, I feared their accusations. For two

83

years we lived only a hundred miles away, so why didn't we visit?

The honest answer was that Jarrod was gone so much of the time that when he was home we wanted to be together. Alone. Jarrod knew I would have gladly come with him if he'd suggested visiting his folks. But truth be told, he hadn't. On holidays, we went on vacation. That's what he wanted, though I'm sure they blamed me. What family wouldn't blame the wife for their son's lack of interest?

She nodded. "That's the right thing."

I blinked, trying to find my way back to our conversation. She went on. "I thought you were going to say Eli."

My face warmed. She had read me so easily. "He's been nice to me."

She gave the railing a little slap. "I think you ought to hold right tight to the land and the house. I was starting to wonder if you'd come back when you stayed gone for so long. And that would have been a shame."

Somehow, my heart lifted to know she was on my side. Today, out here in the beauty of this place, she didn't seem at all spooky. She was just a nice lady with a bit of clairvoyance.

A gust of wind blew through the bridge, strong enough to catch me off guard. Her hand tightened on my arm. "I best get on home," she said. "Looks like a storm's blowing in. Besides"

—she demanded my gaze and I looked up to meet her eyes—"I think I know why I came here today."

I smiled and gave her an impulsive, quick hug. The look on her face showed it delighted her.

"You're a good girl, Corrie Saunders," she said. "I know you love him still." She grew pensive. "Jarrod isn't far away. He's with you now."

I caught my breath because everything in me wanted to believe. "Are you sure, Aunt Trudy?"

"Honey, you've already felt him. He's been there even when you didn't know he was there. But other times he's reached out, and you've known it was him. Isn't that right?"

I nodded. I didn't understand how she could possibly have known such a thing, but I couldn't deny it, no matter what Eli's opinion of ghosts and demons was.

"Then he's only a whisper away."

I walked with her to the Gator, a little freaked out, but mostly fighting tears.

"You come see me sometime," she said. "We got a lot to talk about, you and me."

She fired up the engine, and I stepped back as she maneuvered the cart around. I thought she might say something else, but she lifted her bony fingers and waved, then went off as suddenly as she'd arrived, leaving me to wrestle with the significance of the encounter as I headed back to the house.

Five

Eli

I carefully placed the last plank of wood, knowing that I'd definitely made the right choice. As much as I'd wanted to tell Corrie yes and go for a walk by the bridge, I was on a deadline. The kids would start coming to camp in a few weeks, and I hadn't even started making my place ready for this year's campers. The land had to be brush-hogged and cleaned up. Plus, I was building a rock-climbing wall. It was one of the main requests we'd gotten on the feedback cards last year.

The cabins also had to be cleaned out and painted and basic repairs made. Two years ago when I built the camp, I'd decided to make the dwellings out of lumber rather than logs. I didn't want the experience to be too rustic for kids to enjoy. Still, these were army brats. Indulged because of guilt that during deployment the child had only one parent. I didn't begrudge them the right to feel a little entitled. After all, they hadn't signed up with the military, and yet they were forced to serve their country whether they liked it or not. The kids seemed to like the painted cottages, and I had to admit they were easier to maintain than logs would have been.

I nailed the last plank in place and then stood in the doorway, admiring my handiwork. Next I would tile the floor and replace the scalloped sink and the toilet. Then this bathroom would be finished.

"Corrie!" I called. "You want to come see the floor before it gets covered up?"

There was no answer, and I remembered she had gone down to the bridge. It was easy to lose track of time in the peaceful shelter over the creek. Still, I'd heard a couple of rumbles of thunder and hoped she would have the foresight to head home before the storm kicked up. I glanced at my watch and noted the time. Three o'clock. I'd been working for two hours without a break. I heard some shuffling from the master bedroom. I knew it had to be that room because there were only three bedrooms on this floor, and the other two were at the far end of the hall. I smiled. Corrie must have come home and not wanted to disturb me.

"Corrie?" I called, moving down the hall toward the bedroom. The door was open. I heard the noise again. "Corrie? You okay?" My stomach tightened, and the hairs on the back of my neck stood up.

I reached the bedroom door and was about to step inside to investigate when the door slammed. Hard. If I'd been a second ahead, it would have broken my nose. "Hey!" I said. Reaching forward, I twisted the knob and pushed the door open. The hinges protested the movement, but the door opened easily.

My heart pounded, but I forced myself to step inside. I had practically grown up in this house and knew its eccentricities and family legends. I knew these sensations. The tingling jaw line; hair on my arm standing on end. Sudden cold or sudden hot. But familiarity certainly didn't ease my tension. Something otherworldly was messing with my mind.

I blew out a breath as a blast of wind from the open double windows caught the white curtains and fluttered them up. My knees went weak, and I realized I'd been letting my imagination go crazy since the encounter with Aunt Trudy yesterday.

"God hasn't given me a spirit of fear," I said. "But power, love, and a sound mind." A sound mind. So I needed to stop imagining things.

The next gust of wind caught the door, and it slammed shut again. I jumped. It had been a long time since this house had given me the heebie-jeebies, but despite the Scripture I knew, I could feel the tingling continue down my spine, and the hairs on my arms were beginning to take on a life of their own.

I gathered a deep breath and walked to the door. I reached out, turned the knob, and pulled, but it didn't budge. It must have slammed too hard and caused the old door to jam in the warped frame.

At least I surely hoped that was all it was. I straightened up and took a deep breath, trying to force myself to stop allowing my imagination to run away with me.

I pulled again, harder. But it still refused to move. The wind behind me was growing stronger, and outside a loud clap of thunder rattled the glass in the old panes.

Okay, this was getting ridiculous. I had to get out of this room. I worked my hand, spreading out my fingers, then balling them into a fist. Twice, three times, as though warming up for a sports event. I grabbed the doorknob, determined that this was the time the darned thing would open. I was just about to yank for all I was worth when I heard Corrie calling.

"Eli!"

"In the master bedroom," I called back. "The door's stuck."

"What are you doing in my bedroom?"

My face warmed. "I thought I heard you in here, but it was the wind."

"The door's stuck?" Her voice was just on the other side of the door, and I felt ashamed at the relief flowing over me. How could I be such a coward?

"Yeah," I said. "I might need you to get the hammer and take the outside frame off if we can't get it to open. The wood probably swelled from the moisture in the air."

"Yeah, it's pretty humid. From the looks of the sky, we're in for a pretty bad storm."

A sense of urgency welled up in my chest as I stared at the white door. Painting a wooden door probably didn't help the sticking factor either.

"Hang on," Corrie said. "Maybe I can open it from this side without taking the trim off. Besides, I only have one hand available now."

My lips twitched at her words. A warped frame was a warped frame. "What do you mean by that?"

"You'll see."

The doorknob twisted. I didn't even bother to step back. I was that sure she couldn't open the door. "Okay," she said. "I'm going to shove my shoulder into it, so be sure to stand back."

"Okay," I replied, but stayed planted, grinning like an idiot. The next second I was seeing stars as the door flew open and connected with my face.

"Oh my goodness! Eli!" Corrie gasped. "I told you to stand back. It wasn't even stuck."

Blood flowed between my fingers. "Good Lord," Corrie said. "I'll be back in a second. Let me get a hand towel to catch that gusher."

My eyes watered. My nose was broken. It had to be. Corrie was back in a flash with a wet towel. "Here, put this on your face and come downstairs to the kitchen so you don't get blood all over the rugs in here. They were your grandmother's, and I don't want them ruined."

"Thanks for your concern," I said, only it sounded like "Thaksfoyocudcerd."

"It's probably not broken. I think it just popped a vessel."

"What do you have in your hand?" I asked, feeling like a fool for the absurd way my speech sounded.

We reached the bottom of the stairs, and she turned, her face glowing. "Look what I found."

My head was beginning to pound, and I could feel my face starting to swell. I squinted as I glanced at the creature she held in her arms. "A kitten?"

"Yep. I found him sitting all alone meowing at me as if he was asking me to take care of him."

"Where?"

"By the barn."

I nodded. "The barn cats have been part of the family forever. They keep the rats and field mice away from the house."

She opened the freezer and pulled out the ice bin, then grabbed a plastic storage bag from a drawer and filled it. She took a thin dishtowel from the linen drawer and wrapped it around the bag of ice. "Voilà—instant ice pack! See how good I am—all that with one hand."

"Thank you."

"Here," she said, her voice softened. She set the

kitten on the counter and took my arm. "Sit down at the kitchen table." Finally, a little sympathy. "Tilt your head back, and let me take a look. I had a first-aid course, so I'm well qualified to nurse you back to health."

I tilted my head back as she instructed, but I followed her with my eyes as she looked over my wound. She wiped away blood. "It might be broken. I can't tell. Best put the ice on it." So much for her stellar nursing qualifications.

Outside, a clap of thunder vibrated the air and shook the house. The kitten gave a loud meow. He was too little to jump off the counter. A little moan of sympathy whispered through Corrie's throat, and she hurried across the room, then gathered the little creature into her arms. She pressed it under her chin and slid her finger over his orange head.

"You know they're not really domesticated." Good grief, I sounded like I had a speech impediment.

"Well, this one is staying in the house with me." She pressed her cheek against the kitten, and it struggled to get down. "You wait and see," she said. "Within a week, all he'll want to do is sit on my lap and cuddle."

I stared at her. Completely bemused—perhaps enchanted—by this woman who had most likely broken my nose, I could well believe she could make any creature love her.

Corrie

The rain beat down so hard the rest of the day that Eli refused to let me drive him to Springfield to the emergency room. I even Googled "how to set a broken nose" and offered to jerk the cartilage back in place, but I couldn't blame him for threatening me with bodily harm if I came anywhere near his face.

I opened every window in the house. The curtains danced as the storm blew and blew, perfuming the house with the aroma of fresh rain.

We stayed in the living room. The wood floor felt damp beneath my bare feet, but I couldn't bring myself to close the window. The kitten lay nestled against me most of the afternoon. I hadn't named him yet. So far, he hadn't displayed any personality traits that would give me a hint as to what I should call him, so I called him Kitty. "You know that's not very manly," Eli said, raising himself up from the couch cushions to stare at me in disgust. At least I thought it was disgust, but I couldn't be sure, considering the swelling and bruising.

I gave a stubborn lift of my chin. "He's a baby. I don't think it matters at this stage." I eyed Eli. "Lay your head back."

As we listened to the rain, I insisted Eli lay on the couch with his head tilted back. It was the least I could do to make sure the damage was minimal until we could get him to the hospital. "Do you think it'll stop anytime soon?" I don't know why I asked Eli. He wasn't a weatherman or psychic, but I was sick of the constant rush of rain and was honestly starting to worry about Eli. I hated the idea of his nose being permanently bent. That straight, beautiful Roman nose must have been a family trait, because Jarrod had it too.

"This is what we call a Missouri gullywasher." Eli grinned around the ice pack. He'd been taking ibuprofen for the pain and swelling and keeping his nose iced. I didn't have the heart to tell him he was getting black eyes.

"You hungry yet?" I asked, glancing at the clock and noting it was already after seven. "I'm starving."

He nodded. "I hate to admit it, but yeah, I'm starving too." He took the ice pack from his nose. "How's it looking?"

"Like you've had one too many hits in the ring, Rocky."

He laughed, then moaned. "Ow, don't make me laugh."

"Sorry." I headed to the kitchen to see what I could whip up for us, wishing I hadn't been such a glutton at lunch. I probably ate enough for three people. I opened the fridge and found eggs. It would take too long to thaw out meat. "I hate to be cliché," I called, "but what are your thoughts on an extremely fancy and well-cooked omelet? I have fresh mushrooms, onions, red bell pepper, and a block of white cheddar."

"Sounds good," he called back. "You might want to turn on the radio and check the weather. I'm not really liking the way this is keeping on, and the sky has an odd tint to it. Judging from the new lightning flashing from the west, it looks like another wave is coming."

He was right, and I realized I was kind of glad Eli was forced to stay with me. Storms didn't frighten me, but I had a healthy respect for their power. And the house had electric wiring that hadn't been updated in fifty or so years. According to Eli, the lights could power off at the drop of a hat.

I switched on the radio I had set on top of the refrigerator. I had no idea where the local stations were, but soft music flowed into the room as I grabbed the eggs, vegetables, and cheese. I opened the cabinet and pulled out a nice pan.

I washed the vegetables and cut them small— the way Jarrod had always preferred. I liked them in chunks, but I never remembered that until I already had them minced. I'd been doing things his way for so long it became a habit.

Cooking usually made me happy. Cooking for Jarrod was always nice. He'd come into the kitchen, embrace me from behind, and nuzzle me. Then he'd let his hands roam until I was forced to push him away or turn off the stove and let him lead me to bed.

Jarrod never did anything halfheartedly. He ate with gusto, worked with gusto, loved with gusto. He amazed me, and there would never be another Jarrod. A sigh left me as I cracked eggs into a bowl and began to beat them to a fluffy, bubbly consistency.

I closed my eyes, fighting tears, as I dreamed of hands that would never again explore my curves and pull me close. Would never pick me up and dance me around the room. "Jarrod," I whispered.

What had Aunt Trudy said? Jarrod was as close as a whisper. I opened my eyes, knowing I had to pull myself from my grief and finish cooking Eli's meal. Then I remembered her words, as clearly as if the old woman stood in front of me. *"Jarrod isn't lost to you. Death's not the end."* Longing for him hit me so hard in the gut I lost my breath.

"Are you there, Jarrod?"

The radio went to static, and I switched it off. I jerked my head up as a clap of thunder shook the house and wind flew through the window, sending half my vegetables flying to the floor. "Five-second rule," I could almost hear Jarrod say as I scooped the veggies back into their bowl.

"No way, buddy," I said out loud, laughing. I carried the bowl to the sink and gave the veggies a rinse. I was still smiling as I walked back to the stove. Somehow, I understood how people could say they sensed the presence of their departed loved one. Jarrod was so close to me right now that I felt I could see him if I tried hard enough.

I cut two pats of butter and slid them into the pan. I lifted it by the handle and moved it around as the golden squares sizzled and shrank. My heart beat so hard I could count the beats in my ear. My skin tingled, but that could be from the wind. I knew this with my head. But I wanted Jarrod so badly I couldn't help myself. "Jarrod?" I whispered. "Are you there?"

I stood perfectly still, and suddenly I felt a hand on my shoulder. "Jarrod?"

I whipped around and came face to face with Eli's bruised and swollen face. I couldn't help myself. I screamed so loud I'm sure they could hear me all the way in town.

"Whoa! Corrie." He stepped back. "It's just me. I'm sorry."

"What the heck, Eli? You shouldn't sneak up on people like that." I was so disappointed that the hand on my shoulder had been his and not Jarrod's I practically growled. I'd been so sure he was there with me. "You should be lying down. I was going to bring dinner to you so you didn't have to get up."

"Sorry. I heard something fall."

"The wind knocked over the vegetables." I set the pan back on the burner and poured the egg mixture into the butter. The sizzle made me feel a little better for some reason.

"I thought you were going to turn on the radio so we could catch the weather."

I pushed the egg around and added the vegetables. "I did. But it went all staticky."

"So you just turned it off?"

"Yeah." I shrugged. "Static wasn't going to tell us anything about the weather." I was embarrassed to admit that I had been preoccupied and forgot all about the storm for a while.

"Maybe I can find another station." He shook his head and switched it on just as the announcer's voice broke in. "A tornado warning has just been issued for Stone County in Missouri. Again, a storm with rotation has been detected by Doppler radar, moving east and north along Highway 65 in Missouri. It has just crossed over into the Branson area."

"Is that us?" I asked, swallowing hard.

"Not far from us. Can I use your laptop to check out the weather track? There should be a radar showing somewhere."

"Help yourself." I motioned toward the table, where I left it open most of the time.

"Thanks." He nodded toward the stove. "Smells good."

"Hopefully it'll taste as good as it smells."

"Hmm." Eli clicked the keys on the computer, so I waited for him to elaborate.

I slid our omelet from the pan, slicing off the more generous portion of the five-egg masterpiece onto his plate. I grabbed two forks, carried the plates waitress style, and set his down by the computer before sitting across from him.

"What?" I asked when he didn't say more. "And eat before it gets cold."

"Looks like we're in the path of the tornado."

"The guy said Branson. That's forty miles."

He nodded, but kept his focus on the computer.

Tornadoes, or at least threats of them, were common in the Ozarks. I'd discovered that in the two years Jarrod and I lived at Fort Leonard Wood, which was about one hundred miles or so to the north and east. I had stopped ignoring the threat when the base was hit a couple of years earlier. I was lucky enough to be in a house on the other side of the base from where it touched down, but plenty of the families I knew were affected.

He exhaled a heavy breath. "You could be right," he said. "But I'd rather not take a chance. Can I use your cell phone? Mine's in the truck."

"Of course," I said. I even got up and grabbed it off the refrigerator, where it had been sitting since my mother called this morning.

He took it and shook his head. "You have six calls and ten texts."

I didn't doubt that. Well-meaning friends and family still "checking on me."

"I'll take a look later."

He grabbed his fork and then wolfed down two bites as he held my iPhone with his left hand

and punched the touchscreen with his thumb. He glanced up at me as he tasted the food, and his eyebrows rose in what I interpreted as an acknowledgment of my culinary achievement. That was enough for me.

"Mom," he said into the phone. "Are you keeping an eye on the weather? Good. I'm at Granny's with Corrie."

I smiled inside. Would this house ever be mine in the family's eyes? Probably not. Even Jarrod had always referred to it as Granny's house. "When we move into Granny's house," he'd say. "Granny's house needs a new roof." Always Granny's. Honestly, it didn't bother me. What bothered me was the thought that they begrudged me the home. I thought back to my encounter with Aunt Trudy at the bridge, and my heart lifted once again. Even if no one else believed I belonged here, she did, and so did Eli.

"Yeah," Eli was saying. "I just checked the weather on Corrie's computer." He paused. "She doesn't have a TV, and she had the radio on the wrong station." He glanced at me and smiled, but I could see worry clouding his eyes. "Should I come over?" he asked. Alarm seized me. He was thinking of leaving me alone in the path of a tornado?

"I haven't checked the cellar here since we started working. There's been a lot of other work, but I'll take a look."

Cellar? I didn't know I even had one.

"No, Ma," he said. "I didn't know I was talking funny." He cast a glance my direction.

I blushed and winced. I left him talking and went into the living room to retrieve Kitty, who was curled up on a chair. He didn't seem at all happy to be picked up, but after a few seconds of coaxing, he relaxed and let me hold him.

Eli was saying good-bye when I got back to the kitchen. "Do you need to go to her?" I asked.

He shook his head. "Aunt Liz is there."

"Oh, Jarrod's mom?" Of course he meant Jarrod's mom. How many Aunt Lizzes could there possibly be in one family?

Of course, there were three Joans and half a dozen Billys, named after the granddad they all called Pop, but I'd never heard of more than one Liz, so I had to assume.

Eli swallowed the last of his omelet and nodded. "Yeah. She doesn't have a basement or cellar, so she always heads to Mom's in bad weather. Mae and her kids are there too, and I imagine she dragged Uncle Fred. They're all hunkering down in the basement with a game of Yahtzee and the TV and radio dialed to the right stations."

I almost felt bad about the relief rushing through me when I realized that Eli wouldn't be leaving me until it was all over. But I had to admit I kind of liked the idea that he'd called to check on his mom.

Eli stood and then grabbed the table, as though the room had started to spin. I jumped up and took hold of his arm. "Okay?"

"Just a little dizzy. I got up too fast."

"You need to go back to the living room and lie down."

He shook his head, staring at me with his eyebrows up. "Have you forgotten we're in the path of a tornado?"

"No, but have you forgotten you have a broken nose?" I knew better than to discount this one, considering how nervous Eli seemed, but I also knew he was injured and that his nose could start a gullywasher of its own any second if he didn't get his head back.

But clearly, Eli wasn't inclined to tempt fate. "I'll be fine. Just stood up too fast." As if to demonstrate his point, Eli let go of the table and stepped toward the doorway. "I need a flashlight. Do you have one?"

I nodded. "In the Jeep. I'll be right back." I thrust Kitty into his arms. "Hold him for me, please."

I ran out to the Jeep and back and was breathing hard when I got back inside. I handed it over, and he relinquished the cat. "Where's the cellar?" I asked. "I didn't know I had one."

"It's right outside the back door."

"Really?" Surprised, I followed him through the hallway to the mud room and onto the back porch.

"What did you think this was?" he asked, pointing to a wooden door lying almost flat on the ground.

I shrugged. "I never noticed. I haven't really been here much, you know."

The rain had let up to almost a sprinkle, and I was beginning to wonder if our worry was much ado about nothing. I knew for certain I wouldn't be going underground if I didn't have to. A nice finished basement with a family room was one thing, but a cellar was not nearly so people friendly.

Thunder crashed, and Kitty sprang from my grasp, scratching my skin as he went. "Kitty!" I called after him and started to follow, but Eli grasped my wrist. "You're not going after that cat in this."

"This? It's barely sprinkling." The wind had come to a full stop. "It's not even blowing anymore."

"Ever heard of the calm before the storm? Look at how green the sky is. It's getting ready to hit." He yanked open the cellar door. "Here, take the flashlight and climb down."

I hung back. "You first."

"No. You first. I have to close the door." He pointed to the west. "Look!" The sky opened up and poured as I noticed the dark cloud headed toward us. I grabbed the flashlight and hurried down the steps.

Eli got inside and closed the door just as hail began to pelt the earth.

Six

Eli

The cellar was everything I remembered from childhood. The air smelled musty and felt damp and cool. Cobwebs lined the ceiling until Corrie insisted I knock them all down. We had been in the cellar for an hour, and the tornado still hadn't passed. I figured it must have switched directions, but I hated to leave the shelter until I knew for sure. It was going on nine o'clock, and after my early start today, not to mention my broken nose, my head ached. All I wanted to do was crawl into my bed and sleep.

I glanced at Corrie. "Did you bring your phone?"

She shook her head. "I'd have grabbed it if I'd known we were going to be stuck down here."

"Well, what did you think was going to happen when I asked for a flashlight and started toward the cellar?" I shook my head. It felt like a tornado had touched down on my face.

"I don't know." Her legs were stretched out in front of her on the floor, her back resting against the concrete wall. "Why do you want my phone?"

"I wanted to check the weather. I think the brunt

of the storm turned before it got this far, or we would have heard it go over."

She breathed out her relief but shook her head.

I stood up in the cramped space and then made my way to the steps.

"What are you doing?" Corrie asked. I could hear the fear in her voice, and I hated to be the cause of any more emotional upset for her, but we had no choice.

"I'm going to open the door and take a look outside."

"Do you think we should wait a few more minutes?"

For a woman who hadn't even wanted to come to the cellar in the first place, she was pretty storm-spooked all of a sudden. Besides, I didn't think a few minutes would make a difference. I hadn't heard the wind or hail in quite some time, so I was pretty sure the threat was over. "Come on," I said, holding out my hand. "Let's be brave."

Her face relaxed and a smile surprised me. She slid her small hand into mine, and I felt like a million bucks. Aunt Trudy's smoke-husky voice came back to me. *"She's not for you."*

Well, what did she know? Something was happening to me that had everything to do with this girl, and whether Aunt Trudy approved or not, I wanted to know exactly what it was.

I held Corrie's hand while we walked across the cold concrete to the stairs. I felt her hang back as I started to ascend. Loosening my grip, I allowed her hand to slip out of mine. "I'll go first. Shine the light so I can unlock the door."

"Be careful."

I nodded, hurrying up the steps. I opened the door and saw that my feeling was confirmed. "It's fine," I called down.

Relief covered her face, and she walked up the steps. As I climbed out of the cellar, I saw that we'd sustained more of an impact than I'd imagined. The new roof might need a few shingles replaced, and a couple of small trees were uprooted. The clothesline was down.

"Well, it definitely could have been worse." I turned at the sound of Corrie's shaky voice. "You think that's it?" she asked.

"Yes, it's all passed by now."

She smiled at me. "Then you should have no objection to me taking you to the emergency room to see about that nose."

"I'll go tomorrow," I said. "I promise."

She was shaking her head before I finished the sentence. "I won't feel right unless I get you there. You told me earlier that if it wasn't storming I could drive you to the hospital. Now it isn't."

My head ached, and now that the threat had passed, my whole face felt like it had connected with a door.

"Okay," I said. "Fine."

Fifteen minutes later, we were in her Jeep

Wrangler, inching our way down the steep hill from the house. I looked at her askance and rolled my eyes. "If you think you can go any slower, we could probably get there by morning."

Keeping her eyes on the road, she lifted her chin. "Better to go slow and get there later than go faster than I can handle on this road and end up flipping the Jeep. I might break a lot more than your pretty little nose."

"You think my nose is pretty? I'm flattered."

"I think it *was* pretty until I opened a door on it." She shook her head. "Too bad, too. I happen to think that nose is just about your best feature. It was Jarrod's too."

I might have thought she was flirting with me, but the breath she released seemed weighted, not light and teasing like a girl joking about a man's broken nose. I figured she was thinking about Jarrod now, so I respected her silence while we drove. Her phone rang. She glanced at me. "Will you answer it? I'm not wearing the earbuds."

I grabbed it from the cup holder and glanced at the caller ID. "It's my mom. She must have just dialed me back because I used your phone earlier."

I answered the phone. "Mom? Everything okay over there?"

"We're fine," she said. "I'm checking on you and Corrie."

"She had minor damage, but all in all, not bad."

"That's a relief. Eli, the weatherman says another one is coming."

"Another what, Ma?"

"A tornado. What do you think?"

"Another tornado?"

Corrie frowned and glanced at me. "What is she talking about?"

My mom must have been listening to the TV, because she'd checked out of the conversation. "Yes, they're showing the radar right now on KY3. Are you still in the cellar?"

"No, actually, we're headed to the hospital."

She gasped. "What do you mean? I thought you two were fine."

"I banged up my nose before the storm. I think it's broken. Corrie's driving me to the hospital."

"Wait. I think you best get back inside." She paused. "Here's what the meteorologist is saying. There were two storms. One that turned north and fizzled out and another right behind it that popped up out of nowhere. It's headed our way. Just southwest of Saunders Creek. Where are you, Eli?" My mother wasn't given to panic, but the rise in her voice sounded like just that. "I don't care what's broken. You need to get yourself to shelter."

Corrie reached over and tapped my arm. "What's wrong?"

"Another tornado." I was kicking myself inwardly for not checking the weather report before leaving the house.

"Should we turn around?" she asked, her tone tight and a little higher pitched than normal.

The radio emergency broadcast system blared into the Jeep. "All right, folks," the announcer said. "Weather spotters west of Highway 65 around the town of Saunders Creek are reporting a tornado on the ground traveling east and north around fifty miles per hour. If you're in the path of this storm, take shelter immediately."

"Ma," I said. "You might have just saved our bacon. We need to go."

Corrie slammed on the brakes at the end of the long driveway. "Turn around or don't turn around?"

We could turn left and go to my mother's. But I dismissed that. I knew they were all in the basement, and I didn't want her to have to come up the steps to open the door for me.

"Turn right. We'll go to my place."

"Your place?" Corrie made a sharp turn, gunning the gas pedal in her panic. The Jeep fishtailed, then she righted it and started down the gravel road. "Where is it?"

"Just a couple of miles," I said. "It's quicker than trying to get back up your road and into your cellar."

"Okay, you'll have to direct me," she said, her foot getting heavier on the accelerator. I was starting to get scared she was going to kill us before the tornado got the chance.

The floodlights came on around the house as soon as we pulled into the driveway, and we jumped out. The wind had picked up considerably, and the rain hurt when it hit.

"Ow! That's hail." Corrie slammed her door and ran around to the front of the Jeep. I grabbed her hand and ran with her to the house.

Lightning zigzagged from a black sky to a dark earth and lit an eerie path through the field beyond my house. Hail was unrelenting. I unlocked the door and shoved her inside. Outside, I heard the telltale roar of a mean, crazy storm, and I yanked Corrie by the arm and pulled her down the hallway.

I opened the door to the basement. "Get down there!" I yelled. My ears popped from the air pressure, and I heard glass breaking. The door fought back as I tried to shut it, and real fear shot through me until I finally got it to close.

I rushed down the stairs to find Corrie standing in the middle of the room, shaking and looking lost. I pushed her to get her moving and directed her into a small storage room where I kept all my old books. She clung to me. The house shook, and I heard more glass breaking upstairs as we sank to the floor and waited it out, holding each other and praying.

I shouldn't have noticed how good she felt in my arms. I knew I shouldn't, but her arms had slipped around my neck, and her soft, warm breath moistened my throat. Somehow I was holding her like a lover.

I adjusted, trying to set her aside, but she pressed herself in closer and tightened her grip. "Don't, Eli. Don't let me go."

"Okay." I drew her closer, keeping a tight rein on my feelings. This could be dangerous. In a dating situation, I'd have waited until at least a third date before kissing a woman, and only if I really felt like there might be a forever kind of connection. I didn't allow myself intimate situations where I might be tempted to go too far. And as much as Corrie and I had spoken on the phone and e-mailed back and forth, it had been mainly about the house and Jarrod. There was never anything that hinted of romance. Not on her part anyway.

"This is what I miss the most."

I stayed quiet. I knew what she meant. The holding, the closeness. A man, a woman, alone. I missed it too. It had been three years since my fiancée and I had broken off our engagement. Even though we hadn't been right for each other, there were times I missed her.

"I'm sorry, Eli," Corrie said, but she stayed pressed against me, and I felt myself slowly losing resolve. "I just miss his arms so much."

"I know, honey." I trailed my fingers along her spine. "It's okay. I'm here for you."

She pulled back and looked me in the eyes.

"You're so good. I'm glad your nose is all swollen."

I smiled, stretching my face and causing a burning, bruising kind of pain. "Well, congratulations, I guess, since you did it."

She laughed. "I just mean this is a very intimate situation. Don't you think?"

I looked into those gorgeous blue eyes, and I swear I'd have kissed her anyway, regardless of the pain, if not for Jarrod and the knowledge that this woman, this desirable woman who was much more suited to me than my cousin, was still madly in love with her husband. She couldn't possibly handle anything romantic.

"It is a very intimate situation." I laughed, trying to bring a little levity to the moment, especially considering all the chaos going on outside this house. "So it's a good thing I look like Frankenstein."

"Oh, Eli, that's not what I meant. Besides, your beauty is in your eyes and your heart. And your broken nose can't cover up those two things."

"That's a sweet comment, Corrie." I treasured the observation, but it further proved my point. This girl was too good for Jarrod. In life, and definitely in death. And considering my train of thought over the last few minutes, she was clearly too good for me as well.

"Don't you want to know why I'm glad you have a broken nose?" she whispered, her eyes softening as they settled on my lips. I had to force myself not to move in.

We were on dangerous ground, fueled by my taking care of her yesterday, her taking care of me today, and the volatile situation of being so close to danger. All our senses were on overdrive.

I had no choice but to end this before I did something we would both regret thirty seconds after it was over. And I didn't mean kissing. I was a man, after all. My dreams about this woman didn't stop at kissing. Not even close.

Corrie

I hadn't been in a man's arms this way for so long I'd almost forgotten how warm and secure it felt to be pressed against a strong chest. I felt safe in Eli's arms, and as much as I didn't want to leave them, I was starting to get cramped from sitting on the floor. I could only imagine how a big guy like Eli must be feeling. I pushed back from him.

"I don't hear the storm anymore," I said. "Do you think it's passed now?"

"Let's go see." He stood and reached down to help me up.

I followed him up the steps, keeping several steps between us. He opened the door, and I heard the crunch of glass on the floor as he stepped into the hallway. I walked in after him. The pictures from his walls had crashed to the floor. Eli's eyes were roving from beams to windows to the ceiling, looking for structural damage. Always a contractor.

He gave a low whistle. "Doesn't look like it's as bad as it could have been. The roof is still here."

"All the windows are gone." I stared in utter disbelief at the carnage on his floor and couldn't believe how calm Eli was as he shone the flashlight around the room. Jarrod would have been freaking out, ranting, wanting to sue someone—God, if no one else. He most certainly wouldn't be calmly looking around.

"They can be replaced," he said. "Electricity is out. Can you go get your phone out of the Jeep so I can check on my mother and Aunt Liz? My house phone is a cordless, so it'll be useless. I forgot to grab my cell phone from the truck before we left your place."

"Yeah, I'll be right back."

He responded with silence, and I suspected that perhaps the damage to his home was beginning to sink in. After everything that had already happened today, I was on overload. I couldn't even imagine how poor Eli must be feeling.

My Jeep was surprisingly unharmed, although I thought it might have been shoved a little farther away from the house than where I'd parked it. It had all its windows, and there wasn't so much as a branch or leaf on it. I grabbed my phone from the cup holder and retreated back to the house.

I glanced at my phone. Call after call from Lola. She must have seen on the Weather Channel that the Ozarks were under the gun tonight. I sent off a quick text as I walked just to let her know I was fine and I'd call her as soon as Eli contacted his mom.

She wrote me back, "You better be glad you're not dead. I was getting really worried."

The house glowed with oil lamps and candles by the time I got back inside. Eli's head was bowed. At first I thought he was upset. Then I realized he was saying a prayer. I forgot he had gone to seminary. Jarrod hadn't thought much of his cousin's decision, but I thought it was noble.

He looked up, and I saw peace on his face despite the glass on the floor and the swelling around his nose. A smile curved his lips. "Prayer might not change the immediate situation, but it changes the way I feel about it. Just knowing God's aware of things helps."

I handed over the phone, feeling a little awkward, the way I usually did when someone exercised a faith I lacked. Not that I didn't know about God. I believed in Jesus, and Mother was a full-fledged board member in the Baptist church she'd dragged Lola and me to every Sunday when we were growing up. When I was sixteen, I somehow found the strength to bump up against my mother and tell her I wasn't going anymore. The whole idea of an absent God just never quite

115

clicked with me. I guess it was a bit too much like my absent father. I knew I was like the guy in the Bible who couldn't believe without touching the holes in his hands, but I needed to see to believe. And so far, I hadn't seen much to give me the kind of faith I saw in men like Eli.

While Eli made his call, I wandered into the kitchen to find the broom. I figured the least I could do was help him sweep up the glass and cover the windows before we went back to my place. My stomach dropped at the thought of what I might find when I got back.

I found a little utility closet by the french doors that led outside. Somehow the glass in the doors had remained intact. I was glad, because french doors were my favorite, and the thought of these in particular all over the kitchen floor seemed sad. I opened the closet and found a broom and dustpan. I grabbed the trash can and took it along to the living room with me.

Eli was saying good-bye when I returned. He smiled at me.

I set the trash can in the middle of the wooden floor. "She made it through the storm, I take it."

"Yes. The tornado never even made it to that side of the road."

"Then my house . . . ?"

"Mom was in the car when I got hold of her just now. When she couldn't get in touch with me, she drove to your place to make sure we were okay." He took the broom from me. "You're a lucky lady. The only damage she mentioned was what we saw earlier. A few shingles from the roof and a few small trees."

I nodded, looking around at his place. "Do you have plastic or something to put over the windows?" I was grateful that my home had fared so well but felt a little bad for Eli. He was working so hard to get my house renovated, and now he had a mess to clean up here. I knew he was hoping to get to work on his campground soon.

He brushed the floor with the broom. "My mom is bringing over some plastic and a tarp she has."

"Oh?" I swallowed a little and bent down with the dustpan. He swept a pile of glass into the little tray. "Did you by chance mention your . . ." I pointed to his nose. "You know . . ."

"Did I mention to my mother that you broke my nose?"

I stood with the dustpan and dumped its contents into the trash. "She's going to make you go straight to the emergency room. Plus, it wasn't my fault, really. I told you to stand back."

He chuckled and continued sweeping. "You're right. You did."

I frowned and stopped, staring at him as I thought back to earlier in the day. "Why didn't you get back when I told you to?"

He shrugged. "I didn't figure you'd get the

door open. I tried several times and assumed the frame was warped."

But it had opened without any catch whatsoever. "Weird."

Headlights, presumably from his mom's car, illuminated the front yard.

"Good Lord, Eli," Mrs. Murdock said as soon as they got inside and she could see Eli in the dim light of the house. "What did you do to your face?"

"I told you I was going to the hospital." He angled his gaze at me. "I ran into a door."

"Well, you've definitely broken your nose. We'll need to get you to the doctor before it sets that way."

"Exactly what I told him," I piped in, just in case my opinion counted for anything.

She turned to me. "I'm glad you're here. I need a favor."

"Oh?"

"The storm sent my salesgirl, Britt, into labor two weeks early. I have a girl starting as soon as she graduates high school, but she obviously has classes now."

"And what is it you'd like Corrie to do, Mom?"

She frowned at him. "I'm getting to it." Then back to me. "Do you think you'd be up to helping out in the store for a month or so? I pay eight dollars an hour, but I suppose I could swing ten for you."

"Ma!" Eli said before I could open my mouth. "You can't ask Corrie to work right now. She just got here."

"I thought it might help." She gave me a tiny smile. "When Eli's father died, work was the only thing that got me through most days."

"Well, Corrie isn't used to that."

I gathered in my breath. "Eli, since when did I hire you to do my speaking for me?" I asked. Normally, I wouldn't talk to a guy like that in front of his mom, but good grief.

"I just thought . . ."

"Well, think for yourself, buster. We women have had the vote for a century now. I'm pretty sure I have a few original thoughts."

I was gratified by a chuckle coming from his mom. I gave her my attention. "Sounds like just what I need. Is tomorrow good?"

"Oh no. I think we'll close up shop tomorrow and check on the neighbors. How about Monday? That'll give you four days to try to get things back in order after the storm."

I smiled, feeling more relieved than I'd felt since word came of Jarrod's death. Between the ample life insurance policy Jarrod left me and my own trust fund, I didn't have to look for work until I decided exactly what I wanted to do to support myself. But having a purpose, even for a month, felt like a beautiful gift. The best part was I'd have a good excuse for getting out of the trip home for my grandparents' anniversary party.

Later, I left Eli in his mother's capable hands and went home while they headed to the emergency room to see about his nose. My house stood as it had when we left, and I walked up the shaky steps, filled with gratitude. I heard a tiny meow close by.

"Kitty?" I walked the length of the porch, but with the cloud cover, the night was too dark to see anything—especially a tiny kitten. I called for him a few more times and walked around the house once, but the meowing stopped and I gave up, making a mental note to search the barn area first thing in the morning if he hadn't returned.

I opened the door. My electricity had come back on, and I walked into a well-lit room.

I dropped my keys onto the table, just as the phone rang. I smiled to see Eli's number. "How'd you get your phone?" I said.

"Mom got it out of the truck when she stopped by there."

"Oh. Makes sense."

"I just wanted to make sure you got home okay."

"Yep. Just walked in the door. Everything's exactly the way we left it."

"Good. I'll see you tomorrow, then."

"Good night, Eli."

I grabbed my blanket and pillow and padded to the porch, grateful the tornado had moved away from me and left my porch swing alone. The cushions were damp, so I went back inside for an armload of towels to dry them off.

I stepped onto the porch and bit back a scream as a figure loomed before me.

"It's okay," the man said. My heart pounded in my chest. "Don't be skeered."

"W-who are you?" I asked, glad Eli's truck was still parked in the driveway. "I'm not here alone. My-my cousin is just inside. All I have to do is scream."

"No he ain't." The man took a step toward me, and I saw he was young, about my age. "Eli's headed up to Springfield to take care of his nose."

"How did you know that?"

"I'm Ray. Aunt Trudy's grandson. She asked me to come check on you."

Relief washed over me like a warm shower. "Oh. I think I met you at the funeral."

"Yes ma'am. I reckon you did."

"Well, thank Aunt Trudy for worrying about me, but I'm fine. I was actually just about to go to sleep."

"On the swing?" He nodded toward the bedding.

"Yes."

"That ain't safe."

I gave a laugh. "Why not? Who's going to come all the way up here except for family?"

"Lots of folks do, Corrie." Ray's eyes grew serious. "I reckon you ought to get yourself back

121

inside." His commanding tone bumped up against my stubborn streak.

"Well, thank you for your concern, Ray," I said firmly. "But I make my own decisions."

His gaze narrowed, and he stared down at me from his lofty Saunders height. "Suit yerself."

He turned and left as quickly as he'd come, firing up an old pickup that I had no idea how I'd missed hearing. A shudder went over me as he sped down the hill.

Still, I gathered up my bedding and went back inside. I stretched out on the couch, glad the storm was over. I closed my eyes and dreamed of twisters, Eli, and Jarrod.

PART TWO

He guides me in the paths of righteousness
For His name's sake.
Even though I walk through the valley
of the shadow of death,
I fear no evil, for You are with me;
Your rod and Your staff, they comfort me.

Seven

Corrie

Before I turned around, it seemed, two weeks had gone by. During those two weeks, rain pelted the land almost daily, but without threat of violence, and I worked for Eli's mom in the shop.

The morning of my thirtieth birthday began just like every day had since I moved to Saunders Creek. I sat on my swing with Kitty stretched out next to me, just out of arm's reach, which he still seemed to prefer. I watched the fog lift off the river and sipped my too-sweet coffee. I had brought my phone outside because I knew my family well enough to know they'd be calling one at a time. Sure enough, my grandparents called, then my mother called. She was not at all happy that I'd decided not to go home for the anniversary and the shopping trip. I'd used the storm damage as an excuse rather than my job. I knew Mother would balk about her daughter working in "retail," so I chose not to bring it up at all. Why borrow trouble?

Finally the birthday greetings concluded with a call from Lola. "Happy birthday, little sister! Am I the first to call?" she crooned into the phone.

I smiled. "Not even close, but it's definitely the best call."

We small-talked for a while, and I was still sitting there an hour later when Eli showed up.

"Lola, Eli's here. I better go."

"Oh?" she said in a higher tone. "Eli, huh?"

"Lola . . ."

"Okay, fine. You're not interested in anyone but Jarrod. I get it. Make sure you do something nice for yourself today."

"Your call was just the birthday gift I needed. Everything else will be a disappointment."

She gave a short laugh. "Sure it will."

My attention had shifted to Eli. He got out of the truck and lifted out a flat, rectangular package.

"Thanks for calling, Lola," I said. "Love you."

I stood to get a better look as Eli waved and walked toward the house.

"What's that?" I called.

He grinned, climbing the steps. His nose had a little crook to it since the night it was broken. I had to admit I found it a little rugged and cute. It had healed nicely, and only smudges of bruising were noticeable under his eyes. "What's what?"

I rolled my eyes. "Very funny."

He handed me the flat rectangle wrapped in brown paper. "For you. Happy birthday."

"I don't know what to say." I took the bulky gift. "How'd you know it was my birthday?"

"Mom told me. It's on your employee information at the shop."

"Ah. That explains why she insisted I take the day off."

Eli nodded, his eyes bright with anticipation as he glanced at his gift in my hands. "Are you going to open it?"

I walked to the swing and sat. I knew by the size and shape it had to be some sort of painting. I ripped off the paper and turned it around, held it up, and studied the white canvas on my lap. "Thank you," I said with poorly disguised confusion.

He chuckled. "I wanted to get you a painting for your birthday, but not knowing what sort of art you enjoyed, I decided you might like to paint your own."

"I don't know what to say." I looked up at him. "That was incredibly thoughtful."

I didn't have the heart to tell him all my paints were old and unusable. They'd followed me from one storage unit to the next as Jarrod and I moved from base to base over the years. As it turned out, I didn't have to mention it anyway.

"Jerry Wright, at the art store, said to come in and pick up anything you need. He's charging it to me."

My surprise must have shown on my face, because he looked even more highly pleased with himself. "Do I seem like the kind of guy to just buy a girl a blank canvas for her birthday?"

"I didn't know Saunders Creek had an art store."

"Well, it's also a bakery, but I checked with Jerry to be sure the art supplies were good ones."

I laughed. "Well, only the best for me."

"I agree."

I was kidding, of course, but Eli wasn't. I caught my breath at the intensity of his tone. I shifted my gaze back to the canvas and cleared my throat. "So this bakery art store. Where exactly is it?"

"Two blocks past my mom's store, next to the coffee shop. You can't miss it. There's a big blue sign that says 'Jerry's.' He's expecting you today."

I stood, lifting the canvas with me. "Well, I have the whole day off, so I think I'll go into town and check out this art supply store."

"Corrie," Eli said, halting me with his hand on my arm.

Turning to him, I lifted my gaze with difficulty. "I'm sorry I made you uncomfortable."

"It's okay, Eli." There was no point in denying the truth, so I nodded. He deserved honesty from me. "We're friends, right?"

"I like to think so." He smiled. "And friends buy friends gifts on their birthdays. Don't read anything else into it, okay?"

Relief went through me. "There I go over-thinking things again."

"It's okay. It must be your advanced age."

"Hey!" I gave his arm a light punch.

He chuckled and let go. "There's something I need to run by you."

"Yeah?"

"I'm hiring a couple of guys to help finish the work here. With the tornado damage at my place and the work I need to do on the campground, I'm afraid I've overextended myself." He seemed a bit embarrassed by the admission, which I thought was sort of macho-sweet. "They're going to start on the back deck tomorrow. With both of them working on it, they should be finished inside a week, and then they'll start on the porch next, if you say it's okay. I ordered the bricks, but it'll be a few days before they come. You're sure you don't want concrete for the front porch?"

Two questions at once. "Yes, I'm sure I want the porch to be brick. And yes, you can hire anyone you need to." I flashed him a grin. "I pay by the job, not the manpower."

He smiled back. "I know. I just wanted to make sure you wouldn't mind the extra people around here for a few weeks."

"I don't mind." As long as he didn't hire his cousin Ray. The creeper. I still hadn't gotten over his visit.

"Okay, I'm going to work on your bedroom floor today if you're good with that. You won't be able to sleep in there for a few nights."

"It's fine. I don't sleep in there anyway."

His eyes narrowed. "Still?"

I shook my head and moved toward the door with my canvas tucked under my arm. "Do whatever you need to." The wood floors had been refinished during an earlier remodel years ago, but now they were warping, and a few boards needed to be replaced. I hated the idea of using new wood with the antique wood, but I knew Eli would make it beautiful anyway. "Help yourself to coffee," I said as we stepped inside. "I'm going to go make myself presentable and head into town."

By nine, I had showered and dressed. I pulled my hair up into a clip and applied just enough makeup to be presentable. It wasn't like Mother was around to shame me into a Mary Kay nightmare.

I drove down the steep road with the doors off and the warm wind blowing through the Jeep. My straw cowboy hat covered my head, and I felt pretty good for a girl who just turned thirty. My size six Levi's still fit comfortably, and I wore a sleeveless shirt with confidence. All in all, today was a good day.

A horse and rider cantered toward me as I reached the intersection at the end of my long drive. I expected them to ride past so I could move forward toward Saunders Creek, so I did the polite thing and waited. Instead, the woman waved and turned her horse toward me.

She was pretty—no, more than pretty. The kind

of woman that made normal, decent-looking women feel dowdy even in their Sunday best. Dark brown hair touched sun-kissed shoulders, and suddenly I wished I had on sleeves. "Hey, there," she said, bright-eyed, with a big smile.

"Hey."

"I'm looking for Eli Murdock. Is he up at the home place?"

I hated to admit it, but my curiosity was piqued. I'd been in town for two weeks and had never seen her before, and yet she was relaxed and comfortable, like one of the locals. "Uh, yeah. He's working on the floor."

"You must be Corrie." Her eyes went sober. "I'm sorry about Jarrod. We grew up together."

"Thank you."

"I'm Ava." She reached down and offered her hand. I shook it.

"Nice to meet you." I studied the brown mare. I knew nothing about horses, but this one was shiny and sleek and beautiful. "Pretty horse."

By the widening of her smile, you'd have thought I complimented her baby. "Thank you. I don't get to ride often, only when I come home to visit my mom."

I hated the way my heart lifted at the knowledge that she was only visiting, so I tried to be extra nice.

"You said you're looking for Eli?"

"Yeah, I just got here today. Thought I'd stop

131

in and say hi." She frowned. "The two of you aren't . . ."

"Dating?" I shook my head. "No. Just friends."

I wasn't sure if it was my imagination or not, but I thought her face relaxed.

The encounter was beginning to feel awkward, and from the way her gaze kept darting toward the house, I was pretty sure Ava felt the same way. "Feel free to go upstairs when you get there. Eli should be in the master bedroom working on the floor."

"Thanks. Hope to see you again." She nudged her horse and took off at a gallop up the hill.

I moved the Jeep forward at a crawl, wrestling with the sudden emotions I hadn't felt in a really long time. I pictured Ava throwing herself into Eli's arms in a hearty hello. I'd be lying if I said I wasn't attracted to Eli. Any living, breathing woman would be. He was tall and really good looking in that understated way that came with a five o'clock shadow, ripped jeans, and a T-shirt. I enjoyed my status as his obvious crush, although I tried hard not to lead him on. Another woman entering the picture hadn't been a consideration. I didn't think of him that way. Or did I?

Eli

I had another surprise for Corrie and hoped I could finish it before she got back from town. My mother was supposed to call her in the next half hour and insist on taking her out for a birthday lunch. That would give me more time to work.

Rather than purchase new lumber to replace the warped boards, I made a deal with a local family to salvage flooring from an old home on their property. I'd been pulling up flooring and anything else I could save for months. It saddened me that descendants would choose to build new homes and leave the originals to fall into disrepair, but I understood, and in this case, I could use it to my—or, more specifically, Corrie's—advantage.

I yanked up the six warped boards and was just about to carry them outside and bring in the replacements when I heard the door open. My heart sped up. Was Corrie back already?

"Eli?" called a female voice that was definitely not Corrie's.

"Hang on," I called back. "I'm coming down." I held on to the boards and headed down the steps. I knew that voice. Ava.

She smiled up at me, gorgeous as ever. "Nothing as appealing as a guy doing manual labor."

"Hey stranger." I ignored the comment. No sense starting something I wasn't willing to finish. "When did you get to town?"

"Yesterday." I got to the landing, and she stepped out of the way. "Need a hand?"

"You could open the door."

"Got it." She stepped ahead of me and stood

on the porch as I maneuvered the long boards outside. I dumped them on the ground by my truck so I could salvage what was usable and burn the rest later.

"So what are you doing home?" I asked. "It's not a holiday."

"Way to state the obvious." Ava laughed, following me to the truck. "I had a couple of days off, so I came to help Mom do inventory and rearrange her store. She's expecting a lot of business with summer solstice just three weeks away."

I tensed at the mention of the pagan holiday. Ava's mom catered to more commercial forms of the craft: tarot cards, palm reading, and the like. Her little shop in the oldest part of Saunders Creek generated business from several towns in a seventy-mile radius. Although Aunt Trudy and her kind considered Mrs. Lancaster's business to be little more than smoke and mirrors, I knew better. She claimed to be a pretty powerful medium, and even Aunt Trudy seemed to give her some credit for that. Despite her disdain for back-room palm reading.

I began pulling the new boards from the truck. They were oak and heavy, and I'd have to carry them two at a time to make sure I didn't bump up against anything and hurt the wood.

Leaning against the tailgate, Ava shrugged, clearly realizing I wasn't going to be sucked into an argument about her mother's practices. This was a point where we agreed to disagree. "Anyway, I'm going to help with some organizing and advertising, and then I'll be back during the holiday to help her with the onslaught of customers she expects." She said the last with a facetious smile. "She's hoping to remodel her kitchen with the extra money from the rush. Who knows, she might even call on you to do the job."

Clearly, Ava wouldn't take a hint that I wanted to keep working without distraction. I was raised to be a gentleman, so I followed her example and leaned against the tailgate too, the extended boards between us.

"I'd be happy to give her an estimate, but I can't start on anything until fall. My house is still a work in progress after those storms, and we have camp coming up."

"Oh yeah. Camp."

I had just started kicking around the idea of starting one right before our breakup. Ava had never been gung-ho about it. I never really understood why.

"So what kind of damage did the storm do to your place? I drove by and saw the windows boarded up."

I nodded. "Mostly loose shingles and broken windows. The new windows are going in later today. Several trees I'll have to cut down and chop up. Your folks need any firewood for this winter?"

"I'm sure they'd appreciate it. Daddy can't do much physical labor since the stroke last year."

"Tell them to count on a couple of truck loads anyway."

Her face brightened with a smile that showed off straight teeth and a little dimple at the edge of her mouth that I once loved to kiss. "Why don't you come by for supper tonight? You can tell Daddy yourself. They'd love to have you over. Mom always says she doesn't see you enough since we broke up."

My gut tensed at the thought. I didn't want Ava getting the wrong idea. I was formulating a polite refusal when she scowled. "Honestly, Eli. It's one meal with old friends. Or do you have plans?"

The way her voice lilted on that last word, I had no doubt she was implying something about Corrie and me. My defenses rose. "No. I don't." I stood and grabbed two of the heavy boards.

Ava followed me as I walked toward the porch. "Well, then?"

"I don't know, Ava. I'll think about it."

She emitted a soft sigh. "Well, I have to get back to the store."

"I'm sure your mom appreciates the help." I nodded at the door. "Get that before you go, will you?"

"Oh yeah." She stood and held the door while I passed by, straining with the boards. She smelled faintly of Ralph Lauren Blue. I only knew the scent because I'd bought her at least five bottles of the stuff over the years for one event or another. My memory liked it.

"So, I met Jarrod's wife."

"Oh?" I tried to keep my tone nonchalant. The last thing I wanted or needed was Ava zoning in her radar on my feelings for Corrie, especially when I wasn't sure about them myself. "When did you meet Corrie?"

"On my way here. She seems nice."

"She is."

"She said the two of you are just friends."

I scowled at her, irritation zipping through me. "What'd you do, interrogate her?"

"Of course not, Eli." Her tone dripped with irritation. "She told me you were here. I asked if you were dating, and she said you were just friends."

"Well, she's right, and I'm not talking about it." I started up the steps. Predictably, she followed. She didn't seem in any hurry to get back to the store, after all.

"Wow, Eli, you're really fixing this place up." Her boots clicked on the wooden steps behind me. "It's a labor of love, isn't it?"

I shoved out a breath. "I told you we're friends. Nothing more."

I set the two long boards on the hallway floor and straightened up to find her smiling, her eyebrows raised.

"What?"

"I was talking about the house, the past, your grandparents, Jarrod. But obviously you have more feelings for Corrie than you're copping to." She stepped forward and put her arms around me. We had known each other for so many years, my natural reaction was to pull her to me and accept the hug. She drew back. "I'll let you get back to work. I just wanted to say hi."

"Will you be around on Sunday?" I asked. "I'm preaching at the little church."

"I'm driving back to St. Louis Sunday afternoon, but I might stop by to hear you preach before I go."

"I hope you do." I watched her descend the steps, her long legs striding gracefully, her slender fingers sliding along the banister. She stopped at the bottom of the steps and looked up at me. "Don't kid yourself, Eli."

Her words jolted through me. I knew exactly where she was going with that loaded comment. "It's a renovation, Ava. Nothing more. Don't read more into it than there is."

Reaching for the door, she gave a throaty laugh. "I may not have my mother's talents, but I think I can read people pretty well. You are smitten with the new girl."

Corrie

Delicious aromas of rising yeast and baking chocolate greeted me as I stepped into Jerry's.

138

Beyond the bakery section, to the far right, I could see a door leading into what I assumed was the art store. Paintings stood on easels and hung on the walls. At first glance, I didn't recognize any of the painters. A few of the more abstract pieces caught my eye, and I wondered if these were local artists.

The man behind the bakery glass had a round face and an equally round belly. He couldn't have been much taller than I was, and his face lit up when he saw me. "Hiya, Corrie Saunders. Happy birthday!"

I couldn't help but return his wide grin. "Thank you." I hesitated, trying to remember if he'd been in Sam's shop while I was working. "Have we met?"

Waving his pudgy hand, he shook his head. "Nah. Eli Murdock described you to me. I'm Jerry. I own the place. You here for your paints and supplies?"

"I am." I motioned toward some of the paintings on display. "These are good."

He nodded, and I sensed pride. "My son Billy painted most of these. Gets all his talent from his mother. I sell them here. 'Course most folks 'round here have already bought his work, so these have been here awhile." He grinned at me. "You want one?"

Of course I would get one, if for no other reason than to support a man who so unabashedly promoted his son's talents. Besides, I was a strong believer in supporting local artists.

"Sure," I said. "Let me take a look at them." They were stills mostly. Foliage in the autumn; the river in spring or summer. A beautiful red barn set against rolling, snowy hills. I was leaning toward the river picture when Jerry pointed toward the far wall at the end of the counter. "You might recognize that."

I walked to the painting he indicated. "My house."

"Yep. Looks exactly like it, don't it?" He practically beamed as he took it off the wall and handed it over.

Resting the bulky painting against my thighs, I studied the technique. Jerry's son had good raw talent but could benefit from training, though I'd never presume to say something like that.

I tilted my head to one side and concentrated on the story the artist was trying to tell. The lines were a bit off here and there, and he'd used too much gray in the dingy white, but it was definitely my house, painted against a cloud-ravaged night sky. I shuddered. It looked haunted. Was this the way Jerry's son saw my house? Something scary and Halloweenish?

"What is that in the attic window?" I asked. The double windows had some sort of shadow standing behind a candle.

A shrug lifted meaty shoulders, and he averted his gaze. "Just something the kid saw that night.

Said he thought it might be a ghost or something. I don't believe in that hooey, but kids these days believe in everything. Billy sat in his car sketching the whole thing on a pad before he came home and painted it.

Intrigued, I squinted, unable to look away. "When did he paint this?"

"Let's see." He moved in front of me to the back of the painting. "Says here November 12."

My stomach did a little turn, and my fingers weakened so that I almost dropped the painting. I recovered it in time.

"All right." I handed it to him. "I need to look at the art supplies, but this is the one I want."

I was a bit unnerved as I went into the art room to look at their selection. Jerry followed me, carrying the painting. A short, plump fortyish woman greeted me as warmly as Jerry had moments before. "You must be Corrie," she said. Her eyes smiled, along with her lips. If it were possible for a whole face to grin, hers would. Immediately, I was drawn to her. She held a cloth in her hands and wiped at the paint on her fingers. "I'm Verna, Jerry's wife."

Jerry's chest puffed out, and he slipped his arm around the darling woman. I swear, if they'd introduced themselves as Mr. and Mrs. Claus, I would have believed them. "Verna paints too."

"It's lovely to meet you, Verna." I walked to the canvas she seemed to be working on. Now I knew where the abstracts originated. I related to the painting of a flock of geese surrounded by reds and golds. "This is nice," I said.

"That's so sweet of you to say." Her face glowed red. "It's a pastime, really."

I didn't believe that for a second. This lady had talent and vision. Clearly, she loved what she did here. "Only a pastime?" I asked, then regretted my impulse. I tried to stay out of other people's business. Besides, I had no room to talk. I hadn't colored a canvas in eight years.

But I'd already opened the window, and she nodded. "I gave it up when I married Jerry."

"That's right," he said. "I'm a full-time job."

She laughed and patted his cheek. "You sure are, hon." She focused her attention on me once more. "I picked it up again as a hobby a year or two ago, after our Billy graduated high school and went on to college."

"Well, you're quite good," I said. "This is impressive work."

"Never seen a red goose before," Jerry said. "But my girl sees things her own way."

The front bell dinged. Jerry grinned and tipped his cap. "Customer. Make sure you come see me before you leave."

"She'll have to go through there to get out anyway, Jerry," his wife reminded him.

I spent the next twenty minutes rummaging through the store for supplies. I grabbed so much it was as though I'd never seen paints and brushes before. I knew I was racking up a monster bill, and I had no intention of allowing Eli to pay for it all. But when I got to the register, Verna refused my payment. "Eli threatened never to do another day of business here unless I let him buy it all."

"But it's too much. I can't let him do it." I held out my credit card again. "Can't you just ring up a few things for him and let me buy the rest?"

She shook her head. "He said you'd probably try that, and I was honor bound to keep my word."

"Good grief." I snatched up the two bags she'd already tallied. "Fine." I'd just slip a little extra into his check when he got around to billing me for labor at the house. "How much for Billy's painting?"

She named a price I thought reasonable, and I nodded.

Her face softened. "Thank you for supporting him."

"He's pretty good." Finally, she accepted my card. "And it is my house."

When the transaction ended, she picked up the painting. "I'll carry this out to your car for you. And Jerry has something for you from the bakery too."

"Oh?"

Jerry was waiting on a customer when we walked through the door. He glanced up. "Ah, the birthday girl is finished shopping. Looks like you got yourself an armload."

"Your wife knows how to stock an art supply store." I was sincerely pleased with my purchases and doubted I could have found much better in the city. It was clear she knew about paints. "I'm afraid I broke poor Eli."

"Now, you let him get you that birthday gift. A girl needs pampering now and then."

The customer paid, grabbed her bag of goodies, and left. Jerry lifted a box from the shelf behind him and set it on the counter. "These are also from Eli."

"These?"

Grinning, he opened the box, revealing a dozen cupcakes.

My mouth watered. "Red velvet with cream-cheese frosting?"

"Yep. Said he called your sister and asked her your favorite."

"He must have jacked my phone when I wasn't looking," I said, mostly to myself.

A red candle poked through each cupcake, and I was taken aback by Eli's thoughtfulness and generosity.

"He must like you a whole lot to go to all this trouble for you," Jerry said, chuckling.

"Jerry!" Verna shook her head and frowned.

"What?"

"Mind your own business, that's what."

I couldn't help but laugh. It must be wonderful to grow into a plump older couple and still be so much in love.

Jerry carried the cupcakes outside while Verna followed with the painting. I had to admit that so far Eli had given me a very special birthday. Now I was off to do a little shopping until lunch with Samantha Murdock.

I waved as I drove away, leaving my two new friends standing outside their shop, arm in arm, waving back. At the stoplight, I glanced at the painting, which was wrapped up to protect the paint. November 12. Billy saw the shadow of something he thought was a ghost in the window the very day Jarrod died.

Was it possible Jarrod had left his body and come back to the home he left me? Hope poured into me like warm liquid, and I could almost feel his love for me. Maybe I had been right after all, that Jarrod was the one leading me back to this place.

Only, if it was true . . .

"Jarrod," I whispered. "I came back. So where are you?"

Eight

By noon my stomach had reached a new low. I hadn't put anything in it except coffee this morning, and it wouldn't stop reminding me. I walked into the café where Sam and I were to meet for my birthday lunch feeling like I could eat my weight in food.

Sam had already arrived and waved at me from the far end of the room. I walked over and slid into a red vinyl booth. "Happy birthday," she said, her face lit with the same smile I'd seen a hundred times on Eli's face.

"Thank you. Am I late?"

"Right on time. How's your day so far?"

I relayed my morning phone calls, Eli's gift, and the art-store-slash-bakery, leaving out the ghost-in-the-window painting of my home. "Oh," I said. "And I met Ava."

"Ava Lancaster?"

I shrugged. "I didn't get her last name. Are there lots of gorgeous Avas around here?"

Her eyebrows rose, but as the server approached our table, she didn't comment. I ordered sweet tea and opened my menu. It felt awkward because, as much as I was dying to hear about Ava, I didn't want to appear interested. Luckily, Sam spared me the conundrum. "I assume she was riding?"

I nodded. "She was looking for Eli, so I sent her up to the house."

"They've been friends forever. She grew up with the boys."

By "the boys," I assumed she meant Jarrod and Eli. I wondered if Ava had dated one or both of them through the years. Again, Sam seemed to read my thoughts. Aunt Trudy had nothing on her. "All the little boys had a crush on her, but she set her sights on Eli and never wavered. They were good friends until high school, then started dating in their junior year."

Something akin to relief washed over me, as I assumed she and Eli were nothing more than friends turned childhood sweethearts turned friends again. The server returned with our drinks and took our order. When she walked away, I met Sam's gaze. "Did they break up when they went to college?"

"Yes. Then a few years ago, they both moved back to Saunders Creek and took up right where they left off. They dated awhile, then got engaged."

I hated to sound nosy, but she had opened up the conversation. "What happened?" Then it occurred to me that maybe she was the reason Eli never showed up with a girl. What if they were still engaged and their relationship was confined to weekend visits? I hadn't noticed a ring on her finger earlier, but then again, I never looked.

"They were a fairly good match. I didn't object to Ava. After all, I've known the girl her whole life and enjoy her very much. I think it came down to a fundamental difference in how the children would be raised."

"How so?"

"Well, Eli has deep convictions about God as He is portrayed in the Bible. He believes in absolutes and doesn't have patience for anything that he feels contradicts the Bible."

"And she doesn't believe the same way?"

Sam shook her head. "Ava's mother is a medium and wiccan. You'll find quite a bit of that around here."

"I've noticed."

She smiled. "Ava's mother has a little shop that sells a lot of potions and dream catchers. Supernatural paraphernalia. It's mainly tourist trinkets and the like without much, if any, power. Aunt Trudy and her kind don't care much for it. They tolerate each other at best."

"Ava's mother isn't part of Aunt Trudy's coven, I take it?"

"Heavens, no. Aunt Trudy isn't in it for profit, and she believes she has much more power than Ava's mother does."

"Sounds like a rivalry."

"It's more than that. Aunt Trudy believes she has a calling, every bit as much as Eli believes that about himself. She would no more open a booth and read palms than she would start a psychic hotline. She's the real deal."

I listened to Sam, intrigued that she seemed to accept the idea of witchcraft so easily. "What about you, Sam? You sell herbs and things that they use in potions and ceremonies. But you're a Christian, right?"

"Now you sound like Eli." She shook her head. "He believes I should close up shop since some of my customers are buying the herbs for what he considers ungodly purposes. But as you've seen since working with me, I only order the natural things all my customers want. St.-John's-wort might be used to honor a goddess to the wiccans, but for others it's a calming agent and has nothing to do with spells and potions. If I closed my doors, as he seems to want me to, I would be depriving the community of a valuable health-food store."

I could see logic in both arguments, but as much as I'd come to admire Eli's single-focused mentality, I sided with Sam.

"So back to Eli and Ava," she said with a short laugh. "They broke off the engagement three years ago, and Ava took a job at an ad agency in St. Louis. They rarely see each other."

Our food came, and we changed from talk of Eli and Ava to my family. I told Sam about my grandparents and Lola, skirting the issue of my mother as much as possible. "And your father?" she asked.

"He's a wanderer," I said. "Lola and I just accept him as he is and enjoy the rare occasions when he visits."

She seemed to sense my desire to let it drop, and as she looked away, her eyes widened in recognition. Smiling brightly, she sent a hearty wave toward the door. I followed her gaze, and my stomach did a flip-flop as Fred and Liz, Jarrod's parents, walked to a table in the middle of the room. It would have been rude not to acknowledge them after Sam's greeting, so I followed her example and gave a polite wave of my own, along with as much smile as I could muster. They nodded and smiled in return. Not a bright "great to see you" kind of smile but cordial enough. The server came up to their table, and their attention turned away from me. I felt sufficiently dismissed.

Feeling Sam's focus on me, I forced myself to meet her gaze. She studied my face, her eyes full of compassion. I could tell she was refraining from whatever she wanted to say. As she looked from me to Jarrod's parents, I realized she expected me to go to them. My stomach tightened at the thought, but I knew one of us had to make the first move. Jarrod would expect it to be me. "Excuse me," I said, sliding from the booth.

My legs felt heavy as I forced my steps toward

the table, imagining everyone's gaze following me. Fred and Liz both turned before I reached the table, watching me with guarded expressions as I approached.

"Hello," I said and reached out to shake Fred's hand.

A grunt left him as his work-roughened palm met mine. "We heard you'd come back to town."

"Yes sir." My throat tightened around the words. "A couple of weeks ago."

He turned my hand loose, and I reached out to Liz. "I hope you're both well," I said, drawing on my polite upbringing to force out anything that might sound cordial.

"As well as we can be." She squeezed my hand. "All things considered."

I stood next to the table, unsure of the next phase of conversation, as they exchanged glances and Fred cleared his throat before sipping water from his glass.

At an utter loss for words, I swallowed hard. "Well, I'm having lunch with Mrs. Murdock, so . . . It was really nice to see you two."

"You too, hon," Liz said, in a barely audible voice.

I turned, and the walk back to the table seemed like miles. My insides trembled as I slid back into my seat.

"That was good of you, Corrie. They're still grieving so deeply," Sam said, her voice soft and filled with sympathy. "The three of you really should get together."

"Probably."

She reached over and covered my hand with hers. "I'm sorry. I shouldn't have butted in."

After I assured her it was okay, we finished our meal but never returned to the lightheartedness of our earlier conversation. I glanced at Jarrod's folks a couple of times, but they never once looked my way. My heart ached for them in the same way it ached for my own loneliness. But the last thing I wanted to do was spend time with them. Maybe because if I acknowledged their grief, offered and accepted comfort, I'd have to acknowledge Jarrod's death with a finality I wasn't ready to accept. Quite simply, I wasn't ready to let him go.

The clock on my dash said two o'clock by the time I finally returned home. My birthday had been an unexpected day of joy for me, but I was ready to put an end to it and settle in. Maybe I'd take a walk by the bridge.

Eli's truck wasn't parked in the driveway, so I walked into an empty house. I went straight to the kitchen to deposit the cupcakes and bags. I'd have to go back outside for the painting. On the middle of the table sat a bouquet of daisies that hadn't been there when I left this morning. My heart lifted at the sight. They were my favorites. I couldn't remember if I'd told Eli that or not. Somehow he'd managed to reintroduce me to my artistic side—or at least point me to the start arrow—ordered my favorite flavor of cupcakes, and now this? I walked toward the flowers, but hesitated. I appreciated Eli's thoughtfulness, but was this a bit much? Had I given off some vibe that I was ready for another relationship? Because God knew I wasn't. Rather than reaching for the card, I headed back to the Jeep for my painting. By the time I returned, I was ready to read the card.

My worry turned to tears as I looked down at the writing. "Happy birthday from Fred and Liz."

Jarrod's parents had remembered. I reached for my bag to retrieve my phone, but again I stopped. After the painful exchange at the café, I couldn't bring myself to talk to them on the phone, even to thank them for the lovely gesture. A thank-you in the mail would have to do for now.

I grabbed my paint supplies and headed up to the room I had decided would be my studio. I smiled as I walked inside to find my birthday canvas already set up on the easel I had unpacked a few days ago and left on the floor leaning against the wall in my room. I could only assume Eli had brought it in here and set it up. We would have to move it when Eli was ready to work on this room, but until then I could store my paints and brushes here. The double windows on either side of the far corner would bring in a good amount of natural light.

The room was a bit musty, though, and could use some airing out. I walked to one of the windows and raised the sash, looking out at the rough-hewn barn that had been around as long as the house itself.

My heart tapped a double beat as movement by the barn door caught my eye. A man emerged from the barn, stood there for a second, looking up at the house, then walked off, away from the house and barn, into a patch of pine trees that lined a stretch of field. The tall figure reminded me of someone. Fear tightened in my stomach, and I remembered Ray telling me it wasn't safe to sleep on the porch. Ray! It was a crazy thought. Why would he be in my barn? My body crawled with goose flesh as I remembered his steely eyes and towering form the night of the tornadoes. I would mention this to Eli tomorrow, but in the meantime, I planned to make sure every door and window was locked. Too spooked to leave the second-story windows open, I closed them tightly and headed back downstairs.

A horn began to honk as I approached the kitchen. Eli must have come back. I'd assumed he'd knocked off early, but perhaps he'd simply gone into town for a late lunch or supplies. Another honk drew me to the front door, and I stepped onto the porch. I didn't recognize the

SUV in the driveway. Then the door flung open, and I gasped.

"Happy birthday!"

"Lola!" I rushed down the steps. "What are you doing here?"

My sister held me tight and laughed that infectious, generous laugh of hers. "After hearing your voice this morning, I got so lonesome I cashed in a few vacation days."

"What about your patients?" It wasn't like Lola to leave work. I'd seen her pass up trips to Hawaii and cancel concert plans.

"I have them covered. I found a flight into Springfield—you know it's only an hour or so from Dallas to Springfield by plane—grabbed a bag, and rented a car at the airport. And here I am!"

"But why didn't you let me know? I could have picked you up."

She slid her arm around me, and we headed for the house. "I wanted to surprise you. And I can see it worked."

"Should we get your bag?" I asked just short of stepping on the porch.

She shook her head. "We can get it later," she said, moving ahead of me.

I watched her open the door, and as glad as I was to see her, I wondered about the real reason my sister had decided to come visit. She was definitely welcome, but I wasn't buying that I was her only reason for leaving Dallas.

"Coming?" she asked.

As I climbed the steps, my mind wandered back to the barn and the man I'd seen come out of it. Did he know I'd seen him? If so, would he be back? I shuddered, glad to be going inside.

Eli

After three text messages from Ava, I finally agreed to come to dinner at her parents' home. I left Corrie's place early to meet the window guys at my house and worked for a couple of hours replacing loose shingles while they installed the new glass. I knocked on the Lancasters' door at six and was greeted by Ava's dad. "Eli," he said, accepting my hand. He'd never much cared for me, despite Ava's insistence that her parents missed seeing me, but he'd never been deliberately rude.

"Ava!" he called. "Eli's here."

She appeared in the doorway almost immediately, as though she'd seen me pull up and just hadn't gotten here fast enough to open the door for me. "I knew you couldn't resist an apple-smoked pork roast." Her face was flushed, and I realized she'd been by the smoker. Probably since she left me this morning. I felt a little guilty.

"You didn't need to go to the trouble."

"Well, we have to eat, with or without you." She grinned and motioned me into the kitchen.

I walked past the statue of some goddess or another and felt the hair on the back of my neck stand up. I always felt uncomfortable with religious icons that didn't profess Christianity. A deck of tarot cards sat on the kitchen counter, and charms and herbs were everywhere.

"Don't worry. Momma's not going to cast a spell." Ava laughed. "We'll eat in a few minutes."

I took a seat on one of the wooden bar stools while she sliced the meat. My stomach grumbled. I'd wanted to get the boards replaced and sanded before I left to meet the window guys at my house, so I'd worked through lunch.

As though reading my thoughts, Ava asked, "Did the window guys show up?"

"Yeah. Didn't take them long."

"That's good." She beamed. "I haven't told Daddy about the firewood yet. I thought you could do that while we eat."

She was making more of it than it was. After all, the damaged trees had to be chopped into wood anyway, but I nodded. "That's fine."

She opened the refrigerator and pulled out two salad dressings. She also grabbed a can of Coke and handed it to me.

"Thanks. How's work going?" There had been many reasons Ava and I didn't work, but one was her lifelong desire to live in the city. She wasn't cut out to be a country girl. Funny when compared to Corrie, who had grown up in the city and

157

seemed to prefer the simplicity of Ozarks life.

"Great. I'm working on a new campaign now. If all goes well, I'll end up with a promotion."

"Congratulations." I truly meant it.

"You didn't ask if I'm dating anyone." She flushed and smiled a little. Clearly she was.

"Are you?"

"Yes, I am. And I think he might be the real thing."

"I'm happy for you." But cautious. Since our breakup, Ava had dated lots of men who were supposed to be the "real thing." At any rate, it was a relief to know she hadn't come back to try and reconcile with me. She had tried in the past and left mad. And I always felt like a jerk. This time, we could be friends like we were long before we ever started dating.

After dinner, we went for a drive in Ava's convertible. Twilight had fallen and the air had cooled, but we were comfortable with the top down and the breeze blowing. As we approached Corrie's road, I glanced up and could just make out the lights in her windows. Ava stopped the car and followed my gaze. "Aunt Trudy told my mom that Jarrod came back."

Irritation flashed through me, and I shook my head. "You know that's nonsense."

"No, *you* think it's nonsense. I've seen too much that proves otherwise. And so have you."

I rolled my eyes but didn't contradict her.

"You're not going to deny it?" She turned to me. "Remember the time we went upstairs to get something for your grandma and the doors slammed?"

They had slammed like they did the day of the tornado. I'd been trying to make myself believe that had been nothing but wind, but doors slammed a lot in that house.

"I remember the incident."

She was laughing at the memory now. "We went running down the stairs without whatever it was your grandmother had sent us up for and told her about the door."

Granny had accepted that there was a presence in the house. She called it her friend and refused to believe there was any malevolence intended toward her or those she loved. As a child, I had decided to believe her and rarely felt anything that scared me. But as an adult, I knew better than to believe it was a friend.

"Have you seen or heard anything since you've been working there?" she asked.

"Not really." I shrugged. "Maybe, but I pray while I'm in the house, so I think it keeps the thing at bay."

"Do you think Corrie has seen anything? Aunt Trudy seems mighty sure that Jarrod's back and interacting with Corrie somehow."

Her words alarmed me. I thought back to the morning after Corrie arrived when she'd asked me about ghosts. She'd thought my footsteps were Jarrod.

I glanced back at the house. Everything in me wanted to charge up the steps and talk with Corrie. Get a sense of what she was seeing, hearing, or feeling and try to give her some spiritual guidance. But she hadn't asked. She hadn't even brought the subject up again since that day. I shrugged. "I wouldn't know."

"She hasn't said anything to you?"

"No. So maybe whatever it was moved on."

A truck pulled up behind us, and Ava put the car in gear. We moved forward.

I had a feeling it was a demon that slammed the door to scare us when we were kids and it was still lurking in the corners of that house—still slamming doors and now pretending to be Jarrod.

Nine

Corrie

The early morning breeze was likely the only cool air we'd find today. Once the sun began to warm up, it would burn off the dew. Forecasters called for ninety degrees and high humidity, which, while unusual for early June, certainly wasn't unheard of.

We'd be baking in a Missouri oven by noon. But for now, the air was comfortable, just right for a morning walk. Lola and I stood on the wooden bridge, leaning our forearms on the railing, looking out at the still water below us. Lola had been at my house for a week and still didn't seem to be planning a return to Dallas anytime soon. I had asked her a couple of times but stopped when it became evident that Lola was having either man problems or career problems. I knew my sister couldn't be pushed, so I let it ride, knowing she'd open up when she was good and ready.

"I can't believe it's been seven months since Jarrod's funeral," Lola said softly. "I never thought I'd miss the big jerk, but I do."

"Yeah." I breathed slowly, gathering in the sights, sounds, and smells of rural Missouri. "I still feel like I ought to be in mourning garb. The world is going on around me and time is passing, but the hole is still big."

Lola let out a small laugh. "Yeah, I can really see you in widow's weeds like the old days."

I shrugged. "Maybe they had a good idea back then. I mean, a woman who lost her husband could take time to heal without pressure. No one expected anything from her."

"Oh, please. You mean tuck herself away and sleep for a year."

"Sounds pretty darn good to me."

"Then why did you take a job?" She turned to me and rested her elbows on the rail behind her. "In a health-food store, yet."

"Oh, well, excuse me for not being a doctor."

Lola rolled her eyes. "Give me a break. You don't have to be a doctor, Corrie. But at least be what you always said you'd be."

I laughed. "An artist?"

"Why not? Someone has to paint beautiful pictures. Right?"

"I guess."

"Mimi paid for art school. The least you could do is use your education."

I groaned. "Don't even bring up her name. You know Mother still won't forgive me for missing the anniversary party and trip to New York?"

Lola grinned. "I know. She canceled the New York trip anyway. Why do you think I got to sneak away to see you?"

I couldn't help but laugh at the teasing glint in her eyes. Lola heard more of Mother's lectures and "advice" than I did, being the one there in Dallas.

"Well, after all," Lola said, a smirk playing at her lips, "Mimi DID pay for your education."

Yes, I'd heard it all. Every time Mother wanted me on a guilt trip, she reminded me that my grandparents paid for the education I had squandered.

"I'm sure it really set her back to do that." My

grandparents were so wealthy they probably didn't even know their own worth. A little thing like a four-year education wouldn't make a dent in any of their bank accounts, and I refused to feel guilty over the fact that I chose art instead of law or medicine. My grandparents hated the idea that I wanted to pursue art. That made me a little too much like the former son-in-law they wanted to forget ever existed. But they had promised to pay, and I wouldn't budge about my major.

"Well, even if they could afford it, you love art. When was the last time you picked up a brush?"

"Forever ago." I thought about my art room at the top of the steps. I hadn't shown Lola the room. Somehow I was afraid she would make more out of Eli's generosity than I wanted verbalized. And it seemed wrong somehow to go back to painting—or anything that had seemed fulfilling before I met Jarrod. I had traded my passion for painting for a new passion: my husband. And I'd never looked back. "Seven years flew by after I married Jarrod. I just forgot to care about painting. There was the military and dealing with his needs."

"Oh, honey. I know you loved him. But why stay here now that he's gone? I mean, really. What's here for you?"

"This house, for one thing. Besides, he's not really gone, you know." I could have bitten off my tongue the second I let those words fly. I didn't feel like he was lost to me, but one person's comfort was another person's crazy, and I knew Lola's thoughts about the afterlife and one's ability to contact the dearly departed. I just hoped Jarrod would behave himself during her visit. But then, Lola would never have guessed I meant literally.

"I know it doesn't feel like he's gone for good. You've been separated so much the last five years anyway, but he's not coming back this time. I bet if you spoke to a psychologist, she'd tell you the best thing you could do for yourself right now is to look inside and find something you love, just for yourself."

"I love to eat." I grinned. "How about if I just start eating from morning to night and get really fat and sassy like Gramps?"

Lola rolled her eyes. "There goes all hope of ever finding another man."

"Hey now, you never know." I tossed out a grin. "Some men like a little something to hang on to."

Laughter hung in the air between us, then faded. Lola looked at me with her "let's cut to the chase" eyes.

I frowned. "What?"

"Seriously, what are you doing keeping this place, Corrie?"

"You mean the house?" The question took me aback. "Why wouldn't I? It's my house."

"Is it? I mean, really?" She breathed out and shook her head.

"What are you trying to say, Lola?" I turned to face her, leaned my elbow on the rail, and put my other hand on my hip, as indignation roared through me like a freight train. "I should just run back to Texas and live with Mother?"

"Don't get defensive." She let out a short laugh. "No one needs to live with our mother. All I'm saying is, why not let these people have their family land back and get on with your own life? You can live with me. We could be roomies."

Maybe I was deliberately being defensive, but I stared at her in what I'm sure looked like disbelief. "These people? Do you mean my husband's family? Or are you referring to the fact that they're country people and not refined like the blue bloods of Highland Park?"

"Come off it, Corrie. Don't put words in my mouth."

"Okay, then tell me what you're saying. Because it truly sounds to me like my big sister is telling me to abandon my husband's family because they're not 'our kind of people.' "

"Okay, fine. You want me to be honest? I'll just be honest. I don't think you were raised to live in a freaking run-down farmhouse in Podunk, Missouri. Come on, half these people can't even read, I'll bet. They're backward, and that's the way they like it."

My defenses rocketed at her assessment of my neighbors and members of the community where Jarrod and Eli were raised. "Eli isn't that way. And neither is his mother. Have you even met her?" Plus, I was a little offended by the way she called my house run-down. I loved the way it was shaping up. How dare she?

"I agree. Eli's mom is lovely and smart and accomplished," she said before I could continue with my indignant response. "I shouldn't have generalized. But you have to admit these people aren't like you—they don't want a better life."

"There you go generalizing again." My mouth twisted in a wry smile. "Maybe they don't think there could be a better life, Lola. Some people are actually happy with the way the dice were rolled." I sighed. "You know, I never pictured getting married right out of college and spending the next seven years of my life dedicated to being a wife. But I'm glad I did. So sue me. What is wrong with having a gorgeous piece of land and a house I love? Even if it is in small-town Missouri?"

"Because you were raised for more." Her calm assurance irritated me. I wasn't sure if that was because I knew she was right or because I knew she was completely wrong. All I knew was that in my home I felt Jarrod, and nothing would make me give that up. But Lola was like a dog with a squeaky toy. She wasn't about to let it go. "You weren't wired to do nothing and have no one. You're thirty years old. There's still plenty of life ahead. A husband, kids." She sighed. "Stop burying yourself in the hills, and start thinking about living again."

"I'm not buried, and I don't want a husband and kids. I had my shot. It's over."

"Maybe not right now. But in time, I'll bet you will. Besides, you are a brilliant artist letting your gift go to waste. You know if you come back to Dallas, you could get work in a gallery right away, especially with Mimi's influence."

That'd be the day. "Can we please drop it? What about you?" I was just ticked off enough with her to turn the tables. "When are you going to tell me why you're really here?"

She scowled and turned her head back to the scene playing before us. Rippling water, leaves on the bank below blowing gently in the breeze. Every now and then a bass jumped and made a splash. All these things were good distractions for a girl who didn't want to come clean. "If you don't tell me, I'm calling Mother."

"Don't use the *M* word, please." A groan escaped her lips. "I suppose I have to talk about it someday. Guess who is the latest casualty of the recession?"

My mind searched to figure out who she meant. Then it struck me she meant herself. "Lola. You were fired?"

"Downsized. With references." She gave a wry, humorless smile.

"Oh, man. What did Mother say?"

A laugh, without humor. "That she'd make a few calls on my behalf."

"Oy."

"Yeah, tell me about it." She pushed back a strand of hair that had blown into her face. "I said thanks but no thanks, but did that stop our mother?"

"Not a chance."

"The question was rhetorical, but you're right. She called three clinics and had me a job within fifteen minutes."

"And yet you want me to let Mother 'make some calls' for me?"

She tilted her head and gave me a quirky grin. This one I believed. "Misery loves company?"

I laughed with her, because really, what else was there to do? "Poor Mother. We must be such a disappointment."

"Well, Dad would be proud of us for not bending to the status quo. I should call him and invite him to go to Africa on a medical mission. He'd love that. At least I'd have one parent's approval."

"Dad approves of us no matter what."

"Yeah, I always thought that was cool until I grew up and realized that apathy and not uncon-ditional love is what made him that way."

I hated for her to talk that way about him, but truth be told, she nailed it. "I guess it was a lot easier to live and let live than try to guide us in any way."

"Poor Dad."

"So, you're here indefinitely, then?" I asked.

She shook her head. "I've had about enough. I'm headed back next week. I'm paying a fortune for that rig I rented."

"Yes, and now that you're unemployed for about five minutes—because we both know you'll find a job as soon as you go home—you can't be too careful with funds."

Neither of us mentioned the trust funds we hadn't touched. I never used it because Jarrod wanted to support me. We had talked of using my trust for retirement if we had to, but until then, we kept it tucked away where it had always been. Lola simply hadn't needed the money. She was a great doctor, after all, and pulled in plenty to support herself.

We turned and walked back up to the house. As we got close, I heard the high-pitched whine of the electric saw, but there was no sign of Eli's truck. As he had mentioned on my birthday, he hired two guys and put them to work on my place the very next day. Tim Scott, a freshly graduated teenager who was trying desperately to save up for his first semester of college, and Joe MacGregor, a thirty-five-year-old out-of-work contractor Eli

169

knew from church. And unless I was mistaken, Joe had his eye on my sister, poor guy. Lola, an up-and-coming ob-gyn in Dallas, wasn't likely to be attracted to a contractor who hadn't gone to college. She wasn't a snob exactly, but to her, social status did have some bearing on compatibility.

Joe looked up from where he was sawing two-by-fours and nodded at us as we passed.

"Besides," I said, looking askance at my sister and picking up the part of our conversation where she told me I needed a life, "at least I've had my man. You keep picking Mr. Wrong—on purpose. Some might say it's so you don't have to commit."

"That's ridiculous. I work all the time. I don't have time for a relationship."

"But you have time to leave a string of broken hearts across the Dallas-Fort Worth area. And unless I miss my guess, you've already made a date with my handyman."

She glanced back at Joe, then at me again. "Hardly a handyman. More like a swarthy contractor. With big dreamy muscles." She shrugged and gave a sheepish grin. "It won't hurt to go out to dinner with him," Lola said.

"Why do you want to give poor Joe false hope?" I asked. "He's a great catch for a girl around here. Good looking . . ."

"*Really* good looking . . ."

"Right. Okay. Really good looking. Kind, smart—"

"Which is a nice bonus."

"You're such a snob."

"No. I just want a guy I can have a decent conversation with."

"Really? I had no idea. I thought you were just looking for a man with good genes to father your two point five children."

"It's one point eight now. Didn't you know that?"

"I guess I missed that memo." I laughed at my sister.

Lola laughed back at me. "Get with the program, sister dear."

Unlike me, Lola had her life plan firmly in place, and she had since her tenth birthday when she watched a live birth on some documentary. Mother was mortified to discover she'd watched it, of course, but Lola knew at that moment what she would do with her life.

Over the years, she broke more than one heart in her determination to not marry until she graduated, got through residency, and set up her own practice. And she'd done it—except for having her own practice. With a little help from our mom, of course. Financially and then by recommendation. The elite women of Texas bared it all for my sis. But Lola wasn't too proud to take it. Or she hadn't been the first time around. I guessed pride was an issue now.

We stopped next to a bed of daisies, and I bent to clear out a few weeds.

Lola knelt beside me but kept her manicure out of the dirt. She sighed. "Now all I need is my husband. Well, a job and a husband. But like you said, I'm fairly certain another position will present itself soon."

"How does going out with Joe and breaking the poor guy's heart fit in with your life plan?"

"And you call me a snob?"

"Come on."

"Okay, you got me. I can't resist those shoulders. We'll have a good time while I'm here and that will be that."

"Poor Joe. All that false hope."

"Dinner, a little conversation, a nice wine. That's not false hope. It's called a casual date. And most men want that."

"Not salt-of-the-earth men." Oh well. I glanced at my watch. "I have to dash. Are you sure you don't want to come to town with me?"

She gave me a little pout. "Can't you stay home today? We could go shopping or something. Besides, why work for now? You don't have to."

What was supposed to be a month-long job at the Nature of Things had turned into a full-time gig for as long as I wanted it. The teenager who was supposed to work had gotten a better offer— a month-long vacation in Florida. Who could blame her? But it did leave Samantha in some-thing of a lurch, and I had felt more than a little obligated, especially after she bought me lunch on my birthday and gave me the dish on Ava.

"I like it," I said as we turned to walk back toward the house. "It keeps my head occupied with things besides Jarrod."

She looped her arm with mine. "I know. It's a good thing. I'm just being selfish. Oh, look, there's Joe again." She waved and the contractor, whose hands were full of wood for my new porch, nodded his acknowledgement. They were going to build a frame and lay brick, the kind of porch I always wanted. No concrete for me. Joe wore a tank top that showed off deeply tanned arms and neck. His dark sunglasses hid a pair of "dreamy"—Lola's word—brown eyes.

"Hi, ladies," he called out. "Have a nice walk?"

"We sure did. The only thing missing was you." Lola had invited him to go along, but of course he had declined. That was work ethic for you.

"I'm sure it was my loss," he said. "Next time."

I left Lola standing outside while I quickly dashed inside and upstairs. I grabbed a fresh change of clothes. Then I showered, dressed, and ran a brush through my hair. I'd never worn much makeup, and now I wore less, but a brush of a mineral base and a little mascara kept me from scaring off the customers.

Lola's upbeat demeanor had changed by the time I came downstairs. She now sat at the breakfast table staring pensively out the window.

I poured myself a to-go cup of coffee but

hesitated before walking away. I'd worry all day if I left her with that troubled expression, creasing her flawless brow.

"Everything okay?" I asked, absently sipping from the thermal mug.

"I'm not sure," she said without looking at me.

I glanced through the glass, following her gaze. "Something wrong with Joe?"

"There has to be." She looked up at me. "You don't think he's gay, do you?"

I nearly spat my coffee across the room. With difficulty, I kept my composure and swallowed hard. "Gay? Joe?" Laughter bubbled up in my throat. "He's the town Casanova. Every single girl between the ages of twenty and forty has either dated him or desperately wishes she could."

"Hmm."

"Oh, Lola. What's wrong? Doesn't he seem interested?" She had been peeking out the back window while the two men worked on the deck all week. "I guess you'll have to keep worshiping from afar. At least you can sit at the table and be a more comfortable Peeping Tom while he works on the front porch."

"Don't mock. This is tragic." She frowned and looked back outside. "I invited him inside for lunch later. I was planning to cook shrimp scampi with my own hands, and you know what he said?"

"I'm guessing he said 'no thanks'?"

"Exactly. He packed a sandwich and a Pepsi and is going fishing by the river."

"You could always go with him." I felt a little sorry for my poor perplexed sis. She was usually the evader in a situation like this.

"I actually invited myself to go. Me! Fishing."

"Well, then—"

"Corrie, he said, 'No offense, hon, but I spend my lunch hour with someone else.' "

"Ouch."

"Yeah, ouch. I'm this close to canceling my dinner with him tomorrow."

"Well, I have to dash." I grabbed my to-go cup of coffee and headed toward the hallway. "Don't do anything just because you're embarrassed. He probably just needs the time to clear his head."

Lola, being an extrovert, didn't understand anyone with that sort of personality. Even me.

She shrugged. "Maybe."

"What are you going to do while I'm gone?"

"I'll probably lie in the sun on your new deck and read the new Emily Giffin book." Eli knew I needed a place to sit outside in the mornings and evenings, so he'd made sure the new deck was built at the back of the house before he started tearing out the front porch. Apparently that project was going forward today.

"Good plan." I glanced at my watch. Eight thirty. "Okay, I have to go now. I'll be home around two."

She was already staring out at Joe again.

"See ya, Joe!" I called as I walked to my Jeep.

He grinned and nodded. "Have a good day at the store." He motioned to the porch. "This will all be out of here when you get back. You'll probably have to go inside through the back for a few days."

"It's okay. It's worth it."

I smiled as I drove off down the steep driveway. I wasn't nearly as nervous about the road after driving to town four days a week for Sam Murdock. I saw a lot of Eli's mom these days, more than I did of him.

She was swamped by the time I got there, even though it was ten minutes before nine. "Thank goodness you're here," she said. "Can you take over on the register?"

"Sure." I tossed my purse under the counter and greeted the next customer in line.

Within thirty minutes the air inside the little shop had grown warm and sultry, and my forehead had begun to bead with sweat. I hated to say anything, but some of the customers were complaining in their polite southern manner.

I smiled and handed a young woman her women's formula probiotic multivitamin, then closed the register, twisted the key, and slipped the stretchy band over my hand. The door opened as I started over to Samantha, and I glanced up to find Eli standing against the blinding sun.

"Whew," he said. "Mom was right. It's like a sauna in here."

I should have known Sam would be on it whether she kept me posted or not. And I had to admit it was nice to see Eli. It had been several days. "Are you the cavalry?" I asked, smiling up at him.

"We'll see. I told Mom she needed to put in a new air-conditioning system last year, but she wanted to get another year out of it."

Samantha joined us, her breath a little heavy, probably from the excess heat. "Corrie, honey," she said. "Can you do us a favor and drive Aunt Trudy to the grocery store? I was supposed to do it, but with the air acting up, I hate to leave just yet. I need to get some fans going, and besides, I need to be here to reassure my customers."

Eli scowled. "What she means is she wants to look over my shoulder."

"What a bunch of nonsense," she said, but sent me a wink that belied her objection. "What do you say, Corrie?"

Eli spoke before I could. "Maybe Aunt Trudy could just call Ray or one of the girls to drive her."

My stomach did a little turn at the thought of spending alone time with Aunt Trudy. But I was intrigued with her insight that Jarrod wasn't gone for good. That perhaps he was trying to contact me or reveal himself to me.

I nodded, my nerves a strange combination of

anxiety and anticipation, as Aunt Trudy walked into the main room from the storeroom. "If you're sure you don't need me here," I said to Sam, then I glanced at Eli, who still frowned. "I don't mind driving her wherever she needs to go."

Aunt Trudy imposed herself into the very atmosphere of the room but was unaware that she was the controversial topic of our conversation. She carried a couple of herbs with her, and she held up the bundle. She gave a cryptic and, I thought, goading smile when she saw Eli. "Milfoil for a love potion. You better watch yourself. Some girl just might come to me with just the right price in her pocket to convince me to mix up a potion."

"I'll take my chances against your magic charms, Aunt Trudy. That's why I ask God's protection daily."

I drew my breath at his flip answer, anticipating the offense it might cause. As I suspected, her eyes narrowed and her brow creased into a deep frown. I could see she was indeed offended by his comment. "You need protection against me? Let me tell you something, Eli. God gave me these gifts. How else would I have gotten them?"

Thankfully, Sam stepped in to diffuse the situation. "Aunt Trudy, you know as well as I do that Eli didn't mean to hurt your feelings." She slipped an arm around her aunt's thin shoulders. "Now, he needs to come back and look at the air conditioner. Do you mind if Corrie drives you to the store instead of me? I hate to leave with the air broken."

She gave a grudging nod. "Keep an eye on those herbs. They'll lose potency if you let them get too hot."

"I'm going to put a fan on them in a minute."

Eli grabbed his great-aunt and wrapped his arms around her. "Aunt Trudy, you know I love you."

She scowled at him as he let her go, but she patted his arm. "One of these days you'll see how much good I do for folks around here. And maybe you'll stop being so high and mighty."

"Maybe so." He winked as he passed her, heading for the back of the store.

She stared after him, and I wondered what thoughts swam in her head. As I watched her, she turned to me sharply, and her eyes seemed to reach inside me, drawing me in. "You're taking me to the store and then home?"

"Yes ma'am. If that's okay with you."

She gave me a slow smile. "I've been wanting a little time to get to know you better, anyhow."

I couldn't look away from her as I tried to dissect her words. Did she feel the same way I did? That perhaps she was the key to connecting Jarrod to me?

A shiver ran up my spine.

She turned to Sam. "Keep those herbs from wilting, please."

"I'll do my best. Hopefully Eli can fix the unit quickly. But I'll put the herbs in the coolers in back if it gets too hot."

"You'd best get a new one like he suggests. It's not like you don't have the money."

"Good grief, Auntie."

I hid a smile. Polite southerners didn't discuss money issues.

"Oh for goodness' sake," Aunt Trudy said, waving her hand dismissively. "We're all family here." And I almost felt included.

Sam rolled her eyes and gave Aunt Trudy a hug, then looked at me. I'm sure I looked a little lost about the whole situation. But Aunt Trudy intrigued me. Maybe I should have been more cautious, especially knowing she practiced folk magic, but something in me was drawn to her. Perhaps Jarrod had something to do with that.

"Thank you for doing this for me, Corrie," Sam said.

Aunt Trudy gave a huff. "Never knew I was such a bother."

"Corrie." Eli took hold of my arm. "I want to talk to you for a second, if you don't mind."

With his mom looking on, I really had no choice, although I felt just a little annoyed. For all his talk about Aunt Trudy wanting to add me to her so-called coven of witches, I'd heard nothing about it, and Aunt Trudy had been nothing but kind.

"I'll be right back, ma'am," I said and allowed Eli to pull me into the office.

"Don't close that door!" his mom called. My face burned, thinking she meant because she didn't want us getting romantic in there, but Eli grinned.

"She means because the window air conditioner is in here. Not that it does any good out there."

"Oh." I couldn't hold back a sheepish grin. "So what do you want? We shouldn't leave Aunt Trudy in all that heat for much longer."

"I just want to remind you about her. She's the real deal." He took a deep breath, and I could sense he wanted to say the right thing. "You're physically safe. She wouldn't hurt you. But don't forget how seductive witchcraft can be. It truly is disguised as light."

I could see how concerned he was for me. He believed my soul was in danger, and I took that seriously. Still, he had to trust my ability to figure things out for myself. "I'll be okay. Don't worry." I refrained from referring to *Star Wars* and being "turned to the dark side," because so far all my TV and movie references had bombed, and I figured he wouldn't get it anyway. Also, I didn't think a joke would make him feel any better. Instead, I gave him what I hoped was a reassuring smile. "Don't worry about me. I have good instincts and will be cautious. Besides, isn't worry a sin?"

He scowled at me. "She's got a lot of power."

A frown creased his tanned brow, and I wanted to ease his mind. "She's frail and speaks softly, but her power is very real, and she's not afraid to wield it in a way that you might have trouble resisting."

"Trust me." His troubled expression never wavered, even under my reassurance. "Come on, Eli. I'll be careful."

"Do be. But I'm also going to pray with you before you go."

He didn't give me much choice, but I didn't mind. Truth be told, I felt a little nervous that she might want to discuss my sensitivity to spirits and the possibility of studying wicca or joining the family coven. I knew she couldn't and most likely wouldn't even try to force me into a life I didn't want, but I didn't want to disappoint a powerful folk witch either.

Aunt Trudy narrowed her gaze and watched us with serious, even stern, eyes as we came back into the room. "Took you long enough."

"I'm sorry, Aunt Trudy." I reached for the bag she had filled from the store. She relinquished the weight of it to me. I motioned her toward the door and hung back to allow her to go first.

Without warning, a sense of foreboding hit hard, tightening my stomach, and I was suddenly very glad Eli had prayed. I knew I had a way-too-vivid imagination, and I could probably talk myself into believing Aunt Trudy had cast a spell on me, even if she hadn't. I attributed it to my artistic soul.

"You have nothing to fear from me, Corrie," Aunt Trudy said. "Eli doesn't believe I'm good. He believes all magic is evil." She seemed hurt. Truly hurt, and my heart reached for her.

"I'm sorry, Aunt Trudy. I know he loves you and would never want to hurt your feelings."

"I know. He's simply deceived. That's all."

I nodded, for want of anything to say.

"Tuck in your arm," I said gently. She did and I closed the door. As I walked around to my side, I thought about her words *"He's simply deceived."*

Funny. Eli had said the same thing about her.

Ten

I kept my nerves in check as I drove Aunt Trudy to this place and that. I ignored her complaints about the open Jeep. Eli's comments the day after I arrived regarding Aunt Trudy's coven made me nervous, and I wanted to steer clear of that topic —provided he had read her right in the first place. But I did want to talk to her about Jarrod. She might actually help me hear from Jarrod. Just to hear him say, "Your face was the last thing I saw when I carried that boy bomber away from the crowd." Or "I'd give anything if I could have come back to you, to have grown old looking at your face every single day of my life."

Those thoughts drove me, and I was anxious to hear more about life after death and the ability of souls to remain tethered to a place or a person. Did Jarrod have unfinished business here? Was that the reason I sometimes believed he was so close to me, trying to get into my head?

Eli might be dead set against the idea, but I had to know for myself.

I wasn't sure how to bring up the topic, and every time I thought I might have drummed up enough courage, Aunt Trudy wanted to make another stop. Finally, after I helped her in and out of the Jeep at least five times, she said she had nowhere else to go and asked would I please take her home.

Relieved, I inched out of the parking space and headed out of town. Did I want to ask about Jarrod? Eli's voice in my head told me to leave it alone, but something gnawed at me. A desire stronger than reasoning. Turns out, I didn't have to make the decision after all. Aunt Trudy adjusted herself in her seat, and I heard her gather breath.

"You have questions about contacting Jarrod." She said it in such a way that I wasn't sure if I was just obvious or if she could sense it with her gift. Either way, I wasn't going to deny my curiosity.

I gathered a deep breath of my own and plunged ahead. "I've been thinking about our visit at the bridge that day."

For some reason, I'd neglected to mention our meeting to Eli. He seemed so concerned about Aunt Trudy's intentions toward me, and I felt a little defensive that I couldn't write her off as easily as he seemed to.

I was trying to reconcile myself to the idea that Jarrod might be looking for a way to contact me. So far, I hadn't sensed him again since the night of the tornadoes, when I was almost sure he was there. Lola's presence in the house kept me from even trying to reach out to him.

She waited, her veined hands clasped in her lap.

"It's just that I'm not sure what I'm feeling. Sometimes I'm almost sure Jarrod is right there and if I turn really fast, I'll catch a glimpse of him. Does that sound crazy?"

A little cackle rose from her. "If you ask half the folks around here, they'll tell you I'm crazy as a loon. When folks aren't sensitive to the spirit world, they want to dismiss those of us who are."

"So you don't think it sounds crazy, then." The words came out as a statement, not a question.

"I do not. As a matter of fact, your experience sounds about right. Often we catch glimpses. We can't see into the spirit realm with the natural eye, but every so often, if the departed wants to get to us bad enough and the live person is willing, they can show themselves as shadows or light."

My mind shifted to Billy Wright's painting and the shadow in the attic window. "So you think when I sense him and have that instinct to turn around, it's actually Jarrod trying to get through?"

"That's what I believe." She peered at me with those all-knowing eyes. "It's what I've experienced countless times."

The question lingering in my mind frightened me, and I didn't want to ask. It was almost as if there was a line between Aunt Trudy and me, and if I asked, I'd be crossing into the very territory Eli had warned me against.

"You have something else to ask?"

It was on the tip of my tongue, but something held me back. Fear? God? Or more likely, Eli's warning voice in my head.

"No. That's all."

I checked for traffic on the all-but-deserted road and made the left turn.

"You're not ready." She reached out and touched my arm. "But when you are ready to contact him, I can help. All you have to do is ask."

"Do you mean like a séance?"

She stared at me without apology. "Yes, that is precisely what I mean."

I forged ahead, if for no other reason than to sate my curiosity.

"How would that work exactly?"

"I would bring in two or three colleagues with

strong links to the other side, and we would create a calm, welcoming atmosphere to help him communicate."

She pointed to a modest cottage-style home on the right. "This is me."

I hid my surprise. I'd expected something a bit more ominous looking. I nosed the Jeep into the narrow gravel driveway and pulled to a stop in front of her house. She held my arm again as we walked to the stairs, and I wondered why she was so frail. After all, she was only seventy-five years old. Mimi and Gramps were older and were still full of vigor. She shuffled along, grunting as she took each step, leaning heavily on the porch railing, but she didn't let go of me. Her large black bag hung from the crook of her arm.

"Do you need help finding your key?" I asked when we reached the door.

She shook her head. "Ray's home. It shouldn't be locked."

I tensed at the sound of his name. She didn't seem to notice as she reached forward and twisted the knob until it gave way. I definitely didn't want to see him. I was almost sure he was the guy in my barn that day, but not sure enough to bring an accusation. I hung back as Aunt Trudy stepped inside. "I'll get your things unloaded from the Jeep."

"Ray!" she called out. "Come help Corrie bring in the bags."

"No, that's okay," I said. "There aren't that many."

"Nonsense."

Ray appeared at the door. A bit unkempt, his hair unruly, shirt unbuttoned, too thin for his incredible height. "Hey, Corrie," he said, brushing past me.

"Hi." I followed him, and we grabbed all the bags in silence. Thankfully, we only needed one trip. I'd never been one to shrink from confrontation, but something about this guy made me steer clear of mentioning my suspicion that he'd been in my barn that day. It was too weird to even think about. If he'd been trying to steal from me, the barn was the last place he should have been. The only time I went near it was to get Kitty, so there was definitely nothing of value in there.

Aunt Trudy's house smelled of jasmine and cigarette smoke. I kept my distance as I followed Ray into the kitchen and set the bags on the counter. Silently, he exited the room, leaving me with Aunt Trudy, who had already plopped down in a kitchen chair, her feet propped up, puffing away on the longest cigarette I'd ever seen. Not that I was an expert.

"Would you care for some sweet tea or coffee, dear?" she asked, pointing me to the refrigerator. "I could answer any more questions you have about contacting Jarrod."

Nothing could have induced me to stay with Ray in the house. The way the guy appeared and disappeared gave me the creeps. But of course I couldn't say that to his grandmother. "Thank you for the offer, but I should get back to the store and see if Sam needs me."

"Wait just a second. I want to give you my number." She reached for a tablet sitting on the table. Resting her cigarette in her mouth, she scribbled on the paper, ripped it out, and handed it to me, squinting around the smoke puffing upward. "Call me if you need me."

Even though she didn't say Jarrod's name, I knew what she meant. If I wanted her to conduct a séance. I took the number and tucked the paper into my pocket, with a mental note to add it to my contacts list on my phone.

Aunt Trudy didn't get up as I said good-bye and then walked through the dining room to the door. I hoped Ray had gone back to wherever we'd pulled him away from.

As I drove back to town along a deserted gravel road lined with maples and pines, I wondered how many times Jarrod had driven this same route. Did the beauty of trees and fields and blue sky give him the same desire to breathe it all in so deeply?

Did he miss his Ozarks home, or was he still here waiting to be invited into the conversation?

What if Aunt Trudy honestly was able to contact him in a real way? What if I could communicate with him, and he could speak back to me?

I had never been one of those girls given to Ouija boards and séances at sleepovers. To be honest, I'd always been afraid, thanks to my mother, who always said Ouija boards let demons speak and that those who contacted the dead were an abomination to God. As much as my mother drove me crazy, I never wanted to take a chance she might be right.

But that was before my husband died, before I began to sense his presence, and before I met someone who might actually be able to help me.

I wrestled with the two sides of the issue all the way back to town, and by the time I turned onto the street that would take me to Sam's store, I was no closer to an answer than I had been when I opened my eyes this morning. I just didn't know.

Eli

A blast of cool air finally made its way through the vent, but I couldn't feel good about it when I knew I'd be back in a week or two to fix it again.

"There," Mom said, nodding with satisfaction. "I told you there's no point in getting a new one. This one works fine."

"Have it your way. I have to get back to work on my house." I lifted my hand in farewell. "Go easy on that unit. You can't turn it down to sixty-five and expect it to last."

"Well, I can't expect my customers to bake in here either."

Without bothering to respond, I walked into the spring scorcher. Dad had always maintained that he'd married the single most stubborn woman in the world. And in my thirty years, she hadn't given me any reason to disagree with his wisdom.

Corrie's Jeep pulled into the parking space a couple of cars away. Finally. Her face was flushed from the open Wrangler, and she seemed nervous. Aunt Trudy must have upset her.

I set the toolbox in the back of the truck and waited for her to glance my way and wave. Instead, she seemed lost in thought. I stepped up from the curb and cut her off on the sidewalk before she could enter the shop.

She gasped and jumped back. "Oh sheesh, Eli," she said, her palm on her chest. "You scared the heck out of me." She backhanded me on the arm and showed a crooked grin. "What are doing sneaking up on people?"

"Sneaking up?" I laughed. "How could I sneak up on you when I walked right toward you from the front?"

"Whatever. I wasn't paying attention."

"So, how did your afternoon with Aunt Trudy go?"

She gave me a sly grin. "She hates my Jeep."

"I imagine. A ride like that isn't exactly an old lady's speed."

"I guess I should have taken your mom's car." She glanced toward the shop window. "Did you get the air conditioner fixed?"

I nodded. "For now. But it'll go out again in a

couple of weeks, and I'll be back here to patch it up again."

"She doesn't want to buy another one, huh?" Her eyes gentled with compassion. "How are the house repairs coming along?"

"Not too bad. The house is almost done. It's the yard and rest of the property that's taking the most time." As a matter of fact, I was beginning to wonder if I'd ever finish repairs in time to accomplish the work on the camp that had to be completed before the campers arrived. "How are you getting along with Joe and Tim?"

"I like them a lot, actually."

"So they're doing a good job?"

She nodded, smiling. "Joe finished the back deck yesterday. Today he says he's getting rid of all the boards on the porch and building the new frame. He told me I'd have to use the back door for a while."

"I'll stop by later and take a look at things."

"Do you want to come for supper? My sister, Lola, is here for a couple of weeks." She smiled. "She's got a major crush on Joe, so you don't have to worry about her dumping any love potions into your drink."

I laughed. "Did Aunt Trudy make you stay while she fired up her cauldron?"

She smiled. "No. I took her to the grocery store, and then she asked me to stop by Dollar General for the nonfood items, because they're cheaper there. By the time I got her all the way to her place and helped her unload her things, three hours had gone by." She sighed. "I left my phone inside, which is why I didn't call. I just hope your mom doesn't think I blew her off the whole afternoon."

I grinned and opened the door for her. "Mom knows Aunt Trudy. She even mentioned you probably had to go to several places before you took her home."

Her face relaxed. "Good." She turned to me before heading inside. "So what about dinner? We're throwing some lobsters on the grill."

"Lobster, huh?" My eyebrows rose, and I couldn't resist teasing her a little. "You must be some highbrow chick."

"I'm related to a highbrow chick. They're actually lobster tails, and I think she cleaned out the little fish market in Springfield, because we have way too many. You'd be doing me a favor if you said yes."

She smiled with her eyes, and her dimples flashed. I knew I'd be going to dinner at her house.

Corrie

"Oh shoot, Corrie. I wish you'd called first." Lola looked gorgeous in a blue summer dress that showed off her deeply tanned legs and perfectly toned arms that made me jealous. She slipped on a pair of three-inch Jimmy Choo shoes. She was beautiful enough to take any guy's breath away, but she was definitely not dressed for firing up the grill.

I glared at my sister. "I told you I left my phone at the shop all day while I drove a crazy lady all over the stupid county." I felt a little guilty for calling Aunt Trudy crazy, but I couldn't believe Lola was ditching me at the last minute.

She walked out of the room, and I followed her up the stairs to the guest room. "And you can stop pouting about me going out," she said, sliding in a pair of silver hoop earrings. There wasn't a hint of regret or apology in her tone. "Joe asked me to go with him to a concert tonight, and I know you don't want me to call and cancel on a guy like that."

"What am I supposed to do about Eli?"

She turned to me and gave me a look. "Well gee, I don't know, Corrie. Cook the man a meal, perhaps?"

"If I grill lobsters and serve dinner out on the deck, it'll look romantic."

She shrugged. "So? You can't pretend you haven't thought of Eli that way."

"I don't have to pretend. Eli is a friend and my late husband's cousin. That's it." And I didn't want to give him the wrong impression. "Lola, he's going to think I invited him to dinner under false pretenses."

Her silver bracelets jangled as she waved aside my concern. "Look, if it bothers you so much, just call him and reschedule for tomorrow. Wait, not tomorrow. Joe and I are going to dinner tomorrow. Make it Wednesday. The lobsters will last that long if we keep them in the crisper and ice them."

I couldn't believe her audacity. "Eli has church on Wednesday, and I'm so happy you came all the way from Dallas to visit my handyman."

She grinned. "Well, you're the one that hired him."

I walked across the bedroom and grabbed Lola for a tight hug. "Have fun with Joe." I left her and went to the door, then turned back. "You know what I think would be really funny?"

She looked away from her gorgeous reflection and looked at me. "What?"

"If you fall madly in love with my handyman."

Eleven

Joe picked Lola up at five thirty so they could grab a bite before the concert. The house heated up quickly in the late afternoon and early evening hours, so I cranked all the ceiling fans and turned on the window unit. Eli hadn't installed the outside unit yet because the electric wiring in the house wouldn't support it, so the house stayed warm despite my best efforts.

I had considered calling Eli and canceling, but if I were truthful with myself, I would have to admit that I'd missed our chats over the last week and I didn't want to cancel the dinner.

I expected him by seven. Should I finish cooking early and take time to shower off the smoky smell of the grill? Or should I get ready and be grilling when he arrived, thus smelling like charcoal all evening? I finally decided to wait to cook. He wouldn't be getting close enough to be bothered by the smoke anyway.

The thought of spending the evening alone with Eli sent my nerves reeling. I didn't try to analyze my unexpected feelings as I showered, blew my hair dry, and brushed makeup over my face. I dressed in a pair of jeans and a pullover top. All I knew was that Eli was coming over, and my stomach had butterflies because of it.

Eli knocked on the back door at two minutes before seven. I grabbed the lobster tails on my way out and smiled. He wore a pair of khaki shorts with a button-down shirt slipped on over a T-shirt that said "Still Waters Camp." A pair of flip-flops finished off the outfit.

I motioned to the shirt. "Is that the name of your camp?"

"Yes. It seemed fitting." He smiled and lifted the lid on the grill for me. "You should come out and see it sometime. It's not quite up to par just yet, but we're working on it."

"And your place? No wonder I barely see you these days." I smiled, sliding the tails onto the rack. "And I'd love to come see your camp. Thanks for asking me."

"Well, you really didn't have to wait for an invitation."

I'd come close to walking over there more than once this past week, but I hated to impose when I knew he was pushing to get it finished. I couldn't bring myself to actually go. "Good to know." I motioned to the outdoor table. "I thought we'd eat out here, if that's okay with you. It's not much cooler inside."

"That window unit's not much good," he said. "Especially in this kind of heat."

I smiled. "I'm sure the last thing you want to talk about is an air conditioner."

He held out my chair for me as I sat, then took a seat catty-corner from mine. "I'll be up and down checking the grill, so don't plan to hold my chair every time. I'll understand."

"Duly noted." He glanced toward the house. "Is your sister joining us?"

"Oh." I scowled and stood up again, then walked to the grill. "She threw us over for a concert with Joe MacGregor."

Eli lifted his chin in acknowledgment. "He mentioned the concert, but he didn't say he was taking anyone."

I shrugged. "It was last minute, I think." I turned

the lobster tails. They were starting to smell good, and my stomach gurgled in appreciation. I'd missed lunch while I was running Aunt Trudy here and there, and I hadn't wanted to spoil my dinner by grabbing a bite when I got home, so I was ravenous.

"I have to get a couple of things from the kitchen," I said, walking toward the back door. "I'll be right back. Do you want some ice tea or a soda?"

"Tea sounds perfect. But I can get it."

I shook my head. "I have to get the vegetables for the grill, anyway."

Eli followed me inside despite my protest. "I'll get the drinks while you get the vegetables," he said.

Eli's very nature and presence in the house made me feel feminine, and I had to admit it felt good to make a meal and share it with a wonderful man. I was a little embarrassed at the direction of my thoughts, and even more so that the narrow nineteenth-century hallway necessitated that we walk single file in order to reach the kitchen.

"Thanks, Eli," I said, opening the fridge. I grabbed the pitcher of tea and handed it to him. I waved toward the cabinets, but there was no need to state the obvious when the doors were glass. I pulled out a covered platter that contained vegetable kabobs and the salad fixings—lettuce, tomato, cucumber, and a vinaigrette dressing I'd made earlier. I actually preferred creamier dressings, but I thought this went better with lobster tails and sweet potatoes. Besides, Mother had always believed it was tacky to serve blue cheese, ranch, or Thousand Island to guests. I never knew why, but it must have made a mark somewhere in my psyche, because here I was serving a dressing I didn't much like.

Eli finished getting the drinks and went outside to watch the grill while I put the salad together.

Fifteen minutes later, we sat down to an alfresco meal. A nice breeze flowed over us, drying the perspiration we'd both acquired during the few minutes inside the sweltering kitchen. I dipped a bite of lobster tail into a finger bowl of clarified butter and slid the bite into my mouth.

Movement by the door caught my attention, and as I swallowed my bite, I looked up. The curtain moved, and I could have sworn someone's silhouette appeared in the window. My face must have shown my confusion.

"Everything okay?" Eli asked.

The shadow remained, and I nodded toward the door. "I think someone is in the house." The slightest hint of a thought made me consider that it might be Jarrod, but I had never seen him or felt him other than the hairs on my arms or neck going up. I had been nervous about an intruder ever since Ray showed up on my porch the night of the tornado, and my anxiety had only grown after the incident at the barn. Only Lola showing up that day and sleeping in the house with me had kept my nerves from getting the better of me. This house wasn't exactly burglarproof.

"Do you think they decided not to go to the concert?" Eli asked. "Maybe it's Lola."

He had tensed up, though, and was poised to go inside.

"Lola would have called me if they were going to be home early. She would have wanted me to save her a lobster tail."

He nodded. "Stay here while I make sure it's not an intruder."

Some part of me—the part that was all coward —wanted to allow him to be the big, strong hero while I sat back and let him take care of me. But I had played that role for too many years with Jarrod, and then I got left alone and suddenly had to learn to take care of myself. As much as I loved Jarrod, I wasn't ever going to be the damsel in distress again. I got up at the same moment he rose from his seat. He frowned. "Well, at least let me go first," he said.

"Gladly."

He smiled as he walked to the grill, his limp more pronounced than usual, and grabbed the tongs. He held them like a weapon. Carefully, he opened the door and stepped inside. I stayed at his elbow. Any closer and I'd be piggyback.

Nothing looked disturbed. But it was a big house, and I knew what I'd seen.

We walked through, room by room, upstairs and down, and as we stepped over each threshold, I felt myself relaxing a little more. We made our way back down the steps and through the house. When he opened the front door, I moved into the kitchen. I walked toward the hallway but stopped short in the center of the room. Something seemed different. I looked around, first toward the cabinets, then the fridge, stove, and table. I did a complete three-sixty and was standing with my hands on my hips when Eli entered the kitchen a minute later.

"What's wrong?" he said.

I shook my head, frowning. "I don't know. There's just this feeling I get when something isn't quite right."

"You have that feeling now?"

"Yeah. But nothing seems out of place or anything." I shook myself to get rid of the sense of foreboding and motioned my head toward the hall. "Let's finish eating."

"Good idea."

"You don't think I saw anything, do you?" I preceded him down the hall and through the mud room.

"I don't know if you did or not." He leaned around me and opened the door. "It's enough for me that you think you saw someone. It's always better to be safe than sorry."

I loved the way Eli made me feel validated

instead of foolish. Anyone else would probably have said I imagined it. I stepped onto the deck, and my stomach sank as I looked at the table.

Eli's plate was turned over, his food strung across the table and on the ground. His glass was toppled, and his tea soaked the tablecloth.

"Interesting," he said.

"Interesting?"

"Your plate is exactly the way you left it."

It was. My heart sped up as I examined the table. On his side of the table, it looked as though someone had deliberately upended things. My half-eaten plate of food looked exactly the way I'd left it, as Eli had noted. My glass sat next to my plate, and even my napkin hadn't moved.

I frowned and glanced at Eli. "Why would someone do this?"

And where was he? Had someone come into the house, waited for us to investigate, and come around to the back just to tip Eli's plate?

"It was probably a gust of wind that hit my side of the table just right. Yours was probably protected by the house."

I rolled my eyes because of how unlikely that sounded. He shrugged and gave me a wry grin. "I got nothing here. It's a quandary for sure. Raccoon?"

"Ever heard of a raccoon that knocked over a plate but didn't eat the food?"

"What about that cat you took in?"

I considered it for a second, then shook my head. "Kitty wouldn't have tossed the food off the table. He would have just jumped right up and started digging in."

He pursed his lips in thought. "Well, that's it. I'm out of suggestions."

"Random one-sided wind and raccoon? Those are our options?"

"Now you know why I went to seminary instead of the police academy. No instincts."

I laughed, but my mind turned to the shadow I'd seen in the window. That shadow was real. I had seen something. I shoved aside my feelings for the time being. "I'll clean this up and get another lobster tail. It doesn't take but a few minutes to grill."

"You have extra lobster tails just sitting around in your fridge?"

I hated to sound pretentious, and I was afraid I somehow had. "Blame Lola. She always over-buys. I don't know why. It's not like we ever did without as children."

"I'm relieved to hear it."

"Do I sound like a rich girl without a clue about real people?" I had lived on a budget for seven years, and none of my friends had a clue I was raised in an affluent family. To them, I was just frugal Corrie who could stretch a dime into a dollar with coupons and bargain shopping.

Eli smiled and shook his head at my question.

"You are the most down-to-earth woman I know. Rich or poor."

"Then you know I'm not one to keep expensive food lying around my fridge."

"I was kidding."

I exhaled. "Sorry. I'm sensitive about my upbringing. Anyway, my theory about Lola's obsession with cooking too much is that Mother always made more food than we needed. She said you never could tell when company would stop by." I grabbed my plate and glass from the table. "You want to grab the rest of the dishes? I'll take up the tablecloth and grab another from inside."

The door was still open, so I carried my food and drink inside, through the hallway, and to the kitchen table. Eli followed closely behind. "Put everything in the sink, even the tablecloth," I said. "I'll take care of it later."

I opened the drawer and took out another tablecloth and more flatware. I glanced at Eli. "Want to grab the tray of lobster tails?"

"Sure." He opened the refrigerator and glanced back over his shoulder. "How many?"

On a whim, I decided to go ahead and cook the rest of them. It wasn't likely we'd fire up the grill two nights in a row. "Just grab the whole tray," I said, glad the idea to cook them all hadn't come to me the first time around. They might be on the ground.

Eli pulled out the lobster tails, and we walked back to the deck. "I'm glad you're the kind of guy who can roll with the punches," I said, giving him a little nudge.

"Why are you cooking all of these?"

I grinned as he spread the tablecloth over the table. "There are fifteen tails left here. If Lola has a good evening with Joe, she'll want to stay up talking and eating. If she has a bad date, she'll also want to stay up talking and eating. She'll eat at least two of these, you'll eat two of them, and there's always lunch tomorrow. So they won't go to waste."

"Makes sense."

"It really does. If I didn't cook them tonight, they'd most likely end up going bad."

I turned the tails, one at a time. Why was I talking about such insignificant things when I really wanted to talk about the plate and the glass and how on earth that had happened? Again, my thoughts turned to the shadow that no one could ever convince me I hadn't seen. Aunt Trudy's voice echoed in my mind: *"The departed come to us as glimpses and shadows."* Had Jarrod done this? Was it even possible? Part of me wanted to speak with Aunt Trudy. To get her opinion. I think she would say Jarrod was trying to get my attention. Was it possible he saw Eli with me and was telling me not to go there?

I felt hands on my shoulders and jumped.

"Whoa," Eli said. "I'm sorry. I didn't realize you were so deep in thought."

"Eli." I could hear the relief in my voice. "You did scare me. Sorry."

"I have an idea," he said, turning me by my shoulders until I was eye level with his chest. He tipped my chin so that I met his gaze.

"What idea?" I said, a little disconcerted by his closeness.

"After dinner, let's take a walk past the bridge and go see the campground."

"Won't it get dark?"

"Yeah, but I have a four-wheeler with head-lights. I'll get you home safe and sound." He smiled down at me, and my heart did a little dance. "It'll do you good to get fresh air, and I really want you to see the campground."

I felt honored that he wanted to show me his land. And the fact that he could see I needed to get out of the house to clear my head made me feel unbelievably cherished. I wasn't sure how he did it, but he made everyone around him feel loved. I knew it wasn't just me. He had a way about him that drew people. I'd seen it at the shop when he stopped by. Even Aunt Trudy softened when he came into the room. Despite their deep, fundamental differences, her affection for him was obvious. Eli was a kind and generous guy, and for a little while this evening, I felt cherished again.

Twelve

Eli

I didn't want to admit it to Corrie, but the incident over dinner got to me. I didn't feel threatened or afraid, but I remembered things like this happening when I was a child. Things being knocked over, doors slamming, unexplained scratching noises that Granny swore was a friendly sort of ghost. Only as I got older did I question the "friendliness" of slamming doors and such.

Was the demon from my childhood playing games with Corrie now? So far she hadn't mentioned anything to me about other disturbances, but I remembered the overturned coffee cup and the stuck door, and if that destroyed table was any indication, I'd say it had returned —if it had ever left the house in the first place. At any rate, I wanted to get away to regroup and give Corrie a little distance as well. She truly seemed a little shaken.

Silently, I prayed for peace, and as we walked over the bridge and paused to listen to the shallow water rushing over the pebbles below us, my prayer was answered. Birds sang their last song of the day, and the cicadas were in full voice. The atmosphere soothed the soul and fueled the romantic feelings I'd been trying not to show.

We leaned against the railing and tossed in errant branches. "How could anyone not love this place?" Corrie asked, her voice soft and airy.

"I honestly can't answer that." I fought the urge to cover the hand she'd placed on the railing. I just wanted to be close to this woman, to touch her soft skin, to take away the sadness I so often saw in her eyes. She closed her eyes, and a smile touched her lips, and I knew she felt the wave of contentment I was experiencing. The essence of nature created by a loving God. I wanted to say something about the awesomeness of God, but I knew that sometimes it's better to let Him do the talking.

Her eyes opened and she turned to me. "Do you think I should give up the house?"

The words slammed into me like a wave crashing into the side of a ship. I felt tossed. Not because I thought she should give it up, but because I wondered if someone had been cruel enough to suggest it.

"Why would you ask that? Has someone in the family been giving you a hard time?"

I knew family members mumbled about Jarrod leaving her the land and the house rather than stipulating it had to stay in the family. But Corrie was his family, and Jarrod never intended to die before he built a life here with his wife and children.

She shook her head. "Not overtly. I know there is some resentment, but that's not what I'm concerned about."

"That's good. What made you ask my opinion, then?"

"Lola." She paused for a brief second and then continued. "She thinks I need to give it back and go home. Get on with my life, take a job in an art gallery, and definitely start painting again. Find a nice guy and remarry."

Again, I felt tossed. But I sensed I needed to tread carefully. I couldn't begin to know what God had planned for this woman. It wasn't my place to speak from my own heart. She had to make that choice. "What do you think you should do?"

She drew in a breath and released it slowly. "I don't want to go. This is where I feel Jarrod." She glanced at me. "You know? I'm afraid that if I go somewhere else, he'll be lost to me forever."

Jealousy rose up. I knew it was ridiculous. I was jealous of a dead man. I thought I'd left that part of me behind long ago. I thought I'd matured. But clearly I had more growing ahead of me.

"Then I suppose that's your decision."

"But what about you? Do you resent that I got the place? Your mom told me that you spent most of your weekends and practically all summers here with your grandparents while you were growing up."

"I did grow up here and would have loved if it had passed to me." I nodded as memories raced back, creating that familiar sense of nostalgia. "But it was Granny's choice to make. And Granny inherited the land from my Pop. Land that had been in his family for years. She was the 'you' in that era."

"With the notable difference that your grandfather didn't die young and childless, so his brothers and sisters didn't consider your granny an interloper."

"That's true, but it doesn't change anything. Keep the land or don't, but not because of pressure or guilt. Do what's in your heart. It's yours, and you deserve to keep it if you want."

She smiled, and before I could react, she slipped her arms around my waist and pressed her head against my chest. "Thank you, Eli." She pulled back, still wrapped around me. "You're a good friend."

An adorable dimple flashed in her cheek, and I couldn't help but smile. But that was all of her arms I could stand without being forced to try to convince my heart we were only friends. I pressed a quick kiss to her forehead and disengaged. A crease flashed between her eyes, and then smoothed out. "Was that hug out of line? I didn't mean to make you feel uncomfortable."

If only she knew how my feelings were growing, she'd probably turn and run the other way. "You didn't make me uncomfortable."

Her eyes still held concern, but she turned and motioned with her head toward the other side of the bridge. "Okay," she said. "Let's go see that campground of yours."

I felt like an artist showing off a new work as I opened the gate and she walked through— nervous, excited, hopeful. I wanted her to see the potential here, even without me having to share step by step how I planned to get it all fixed up by camp time.

"You don't lock the gate?"

"Your land adjoins mine. You planning on breaking in and trashing my cabins?" I laughed at the notion.

"Well, I don't know," she said, continuing the banter. "They look pretty nice, and if my house doesn't get finished soon, I might be looking for some new digs."

I sobered at her comment, though I knew it wasn't directed at me or my workers. "I promise it'll be done by fall."

"I know. I was only teasing. You're all doing a great job, and I appreciate it." She tilted her head and caught my gaze. "It's actually shaping up really nicely. My bedroom floor is beautiful."

I could tell by the gentleness in her eyes that she was sincere, but I wanted to reassure her just the same. "The camps will all be over by the end of July, and I'll have time to come back and oversee things. With three of us working, we'll have it finished in no time."

"That'll be nice." She gave me a nudge. "But I'm really not being impatient."

"Sure you're not."

A shrug lifted her shoulders. "Maybe a little."

We entered the boys' cabin area. There were four cabins that would hold six boys each, two on either side of the path. "We hold six camps during the summer, starting in mid-June."

"So you have two weeks?"

"Give or take a couple of days."

Tension hit my stomach. I wasn't sure I'd even be ready. As I looked around, I made a quick decision that I would definitely set aside the remaining repairs to my house and spend a little more time here, beginning first thing tomorrow. Brush and debris removal had to be first on the list. The tornado hadn't done a lot of damage, but there was enough that I'd need to start there. I also needed to finish the rock-climbing wall and clean and paint the cabins.

"What needs to be done to the cabins themselves?" Corrie asked, as though reading my mind. We walked into the first cabin. "Definitely sweeping, and cleaning the windows."

"Definitely." I glanced around, almost overwhelmed at the idea that each cabin would need the same overhaul this one obviously needed. In truth, that part of the preparation had been the last thing on my mind. I needed to do a few minor repairs to some of the buildings, and that concerned me most, but I also had to get rid of the growth since last year and tackle a few other projects I'd planned. "I haven't focused much on what needs to be done cosmetically."

"Like cleaning and painting?"

"Definitely cleaning, but painting too if we have time."

"Well, you know, I'm pretty handy with a paintbrush."

"Are you offering your services?"

Her eyes lit up. "I'd love to help."

"You would?"

"Of course. I work for your mom until two, but I'd be happy to come over afterward."

"What about your sister?"

She shrugged. "She ditched me for a guy tonight, and she has a date tomorrow. She'll spend all afternoon primping. Trust me, Lola isn't going to care if I come here after work and do some painting."

I loved the thought of spending the afternoon with her, working side by side. "Sounds like a great plan, then. Don't plan dinner at your house. I owe you one."

"You owe me more than one, if I recall. I made you my world-famous omelet."

"So you did." I brushed a cobweb from her hair. "Then I guess I owe you two."

"Don't think I won't take you up on it." We headed for the door. "Eating is one of my all-time favorite pastimes."

"Eating is a pastime?" I closed and locked the door behind us, and we moved down the path.

"Eating can be a lot of things." She tossed me a grin. "Before Jarrod, I dated a guy who worked his way through art school as a competitive eater."

I narrowed my gaze at her. "I don't believe you."

"No, really. And guess what?"

"What?" I chuckled.

"I could outeat him when we had meals together."

"You should have joined the competition. You could be famous right now."

"Mock me all you want, but I'll have the last laugh." Her eyes smiled, teasing me. "You're the one feeding me."

"On that fine note"—I motioned to a white building in front of us, the largest one on the property—"this is the chow hall."

We walked inside the long wooden hall. I really loved this building. Every morning we had a devotional before breakfast, and then the place came alive with laughter, fun, even the occasional food fight, which I allowed as long as it didn't get out of hand and the kids cleaned up their mess.

"What kind of camp is this?" she asked. Her feet shuffled along the concrete floor. "Bible?"

"Not really a Bible camp like you'd find sponsored by a church or Christian organization. We want the kids to come and learn team-building skills, burn off some steam, that sort of thing. If they feel God while they're here, so much the better."

She nodded. "I see."

"We do have a chapel. Before breakfast we have a quick devotional, usually led by a camper, and we pray before our meals."

"Sounds like a Bible camp to me. Not that there's anything wrong with that."

"Let's just say we are open about my position as an ordained minister, and the co-leader, Major Machaelson, is a chaplain in the army. But we don't have church services, except on Sundays between camps. Our chapels consist of a short skit, followed by an object lesson and a Bible reading. They last thirty minutes at the longest." I followed her into the kitchen. It was dark, so I reached around to the wall and flipped on the light. "Other than that, the days are filled with ball games, horseback riding, and rope swings. And I'm building a rock-climbing wall."

She shuddered. "I'm scared of heights."

"Well then you probably wouldn't want to rappel off the thirty-foot deck either." I grinned at her. "But some of the kids really learn to face their fears on that."

"I don't have any fears."

"Other than heights."

"Exactly."

I laughed. "At night we have bonfires and late-night swims in the pool. Sometimes it gets pretty loud, so you might hear us every now and then. Will that be a problem?"

She rolled her eyes. "I'll try not to call the cops."

"I'd appreciate it." I leaned against the counter, staring at all the unopened boxes of canned goods that still had to be put away. "Hey, do you want some coffee?"

She shook her head. "Coffee'll keep me up all night."

"I have a bottle of wine tucked away."

Again she shook her head. "I haven't touched alcohol since the night I got here. The thought of it makes me want to hurl."

"Water?"

She smiled. "That I might take."

I walked around the counter and grabbed two bottles of water from the refrigerator.

She clucked her tongue. "These are horrible for the environment."

"Would you rather have tap? I keep these for when we're working away from the kitchen."

"Nah, I'll lower my standards this once."

"That's big of you." I handed her one of the bottles.

"It's the least I can do for a friend." She laughed.

"Why didn't you ever tell us about this place? All this crazy physical stuff would have been right up Jarrod's alley."

I sipped my water and nodded. I didn't want to lie and pretend I'd never asked Jarrod to be part of the camps, but I didn't want to snitch on a guy who had died for his country either. What was the point of that?

"Never play poker." Corrie tilted the water bottle, keeping her eyes on me, while she swallowed a mouthful of water and set the bottle on the stainless-steel counter.

"Hmm?" I raised my eyebrows, trying to look innocent.

"Oh, please." She shook her head. "You look as guilty as a puppy that wet on the floor."

"Okay, fine, Sherlock Holmes." I leaned across the counter on my forearms, facing her. "After I got approval to do the camp, I invited Jarrod—and you—to join me in the venture. I thought he might enjoy taking on the horseback riding or even the rappelling."

"I'm surprised he turned you down without at least discussing it with me." She frowned. "It really does sound like the kind of program he'd want to contribute to. Maybe not for all six camps—he did have duties at the fort—but one or two." She shrugged, but I could see the information confused her.

"It's old news, Corrie," I said. "You can't hold it

against the guy when he isn't here to explain himself."

"It's not old news to me, but I suppose he had his reasons. I'm just surprised he never told me about it."

Silence filled the air between us, and I was sorry I told her about it. I had to wonder what my motives were in the first place. Was I trying to vilify my cousin to her, somehow show her he wasn't everything she believed him to be? I cringed at my own pettiness. I didn't want to win Corrie's heart by default. I wanted her heart to heal from Jarrod's death, the way the living always heal and move on after a loved one dies. And then if I was a lucky, lucky man, she might turn her eyes to me.

But first I needed to try to undo the damage I had done. "Hey," I said. "You know Jarrod would have told you if he'd thought it mattered. He probably just knew there wasn't time."

"Probably." We drank our water and watched the sky grow darker and darker. She glanced up at me. "I guess you'll have to use the four-wheeler to take me home."

"I'll take that as a hint that you're ready?"

"It's too dark to see the rest of the camp, isn't it?"

I grinned and shook my head. "Hold on." I walked into the utility closet and flipped the lever at the back. Outside, the camp lit up.

"When I was a kid going to summer camp, we had to use flashlights to see at night. Those are nice. But I wonder . . ."

My stomach tightened. Was there something about my favorite project that she didn't like?

"What?" I asked, holding my breath. I cared a lot more than I should have about her opinion.

"Well, I just wonder how the kids are supposed to sneak out and go skinny-dipping in the river with all these lights."

Relief flooded my suddenly fragile ego, and I gave her a light punch on the arm. "Remind me not to let you near those impressionable teen-agers."

"And I was going to volunteer to be a counselor."

I wanted to ask her if she was serious, because I could really use another helper out here, but I didn't want to put her on the spot.

As we walked back through the dining area, I pointed to a bare wall at the back of the long, rectangular room. "Eventually I'd like to see a mural up there."

"What sort of mural?"

I shrugged. "Ideally, something that can give the kids comfort in knowing that, even though one or more of their parents is deployed, God sees them all. I don't know. Got any ideas?"

She shook her head. "Not really. My art is more abstract."

"Oh, subject to interpretation. Modern stuff."

"Something like that."

The sun had completely set by the time we mounted the four-wheeler and headed back to Corrie's house. She wrapped her arms loosely around me, and I couldn't help but wish the distance between my camp and her house was longer. The ten-minute ride went by way too fast as far as I was concerned.

Joe's car sat in front of the house. "Looks like Lola invited Joe inside," I said. "They must be hitting it off."

"Yeah. Lola's the queen of vacation romances. No pressure to commit." We walked around to the back deck.

"She's met her match in Joe," I said. "He's the most confirmed bachelor I know."

She laughed. "Oh, please. He's got nothing on you, Eli."

I frowned and opened the door. "What's that supposed to mean?"

"I think you can figure it out."

"Oh, you think I'm a confirmed bachelor. Afraid of commitment?"

"Aren't you?"

"No." I grinned. It wasn't about commitment. "I just haven't found the right woman."

"Classic line for anyone with commitment issues."

"Touché." I laughed.

We walked through the mud room into the hallway. Joe and Lola sat in the kitchen, eating the leftover lobster tails.

Lola waved. "These are fantastic, Corrie. You did great. Why'd you cook them all, though?"

"So you could have a midnight snack, obviously." Corrie rolled her eyes and motioned me to a seat as she headed for the refrigerator and pulled out a pitcher of tea. "How was the concert?"

"It was great," Joe said. "An Australian praise band was playing at the JQH Arena."

Corrie's eyebrows went up, and she stared at her sister. "You liked that?"

Lola shrugged. "It wasn't bad, actually. It felt good."

Corrie set a glass of tea in front of me. "Hungry?" she asked.

"I could eat again."

Lola shoved the platter of lobster tails across the table. "Have some."

"What do you mean it felt good?" Corrie asked, setting two plates on the table, one for me, one for her. "Like it feels good to get a new dress or have a facial, or you actually 'felt' something?"

Lola frowned. "I don't know. Why?"

"Just wondering." Corrie sat and reached for a lobster tail. It felt very bohemian, all of us using our hands and eating cold lobster. I liked it, but it had a sensuality to it that unsettled me as I watched Corrie's slender fingers break the lobster tail and pull out the meat. She tore off a piece and dipped it into the clarified butter.

I looked away before she slid it into her mouth.

"It felt good to me too," Joe said. "There's just something about five thousand people praising God that feels good. You can't explain it. You just have to experience the sensation."

"When you say you felt a sensation . . ." Corrie paused. She was clearly not ready to let it go. She glanced at Lola. "Sorry. I just . . ." Her gaze slid back to Joe. "Did you feel a physical sensation, or are you speaking in terms of something more ambiguous, like 'I feel loved,' or 'I feel joy'?"

"Good grief," Lola said. "Leave the guy alone. He wasn't being literal."

"Yes I was." Joe put a piece of lobster into his mouth.

I dared to glance at Corrie. "Why do you want to know?"

Her face turned a pretty pink, as though she'd been caught. "I just wondered if people could feel spiritual things in a physical body."

"How so?" I was beginning to think Corrie had more than a passive interest in the topic. My mind shot back to the years just after Pop died. I stayed with Granny a lot, and she welcomed his "spirit" back into the house. At first I even believed it was him. The feeling was so comfortable. I could sit on the porch and smell his pipe. That's how well the demon knew my Pop. It knew exactly how to act and smell to draw us in. I wasn't ever sure if the "friendly ghost" from mine and Jarrod's earlier childhood masked itself as Pop later on, or if more demons came—after all, they were clearly welcome. All I knew was that eventually I wised up to spiritual truth and stopped believing they were friendly or "Pop."

Clearly, Corrie had questions that involved supernatural phenomena. Was she being visited the way Granny and I had been?

I thought it—or they—left when Granny died. But what if I was wrong?

Thirteen

Corrie

I got up before Lola woke and took my coffee to the deck.

The conversation the night before had tossed me a major curve ball—one I hadn't anticipated and definitely couldn't hit. Joe felt a physical, tangible sensation when what he considered the presence of God entered a room. Mostly, according to Joe, this happened when he prayed or worshiped, the way they had at the concert.

But I knew my sister hadn't prayed or

worshiped at the concert. She had the barest understanding of God in the first place and had problems even believing what we'd been raised on in the Baptist church. Besides, her purpose for going to the concert was strictly to spend time with Joe. There were definitely no religious motives. And yet, she'd felt something too.

I sipped my coffee, looking at the horizon, where the sun was peeking over the back hills. I'd need my sunglasses soon. I missed my front porch swing. The bricks were going down today. In a few days, my front porch would be my sanctuary again. I could hardly wait.

By the time the sun made its brilliant presence known, Lola made hers known as well. "Sheesh. That's an obnoxious sunrise." She stumbled onto the deck wearing a light blue, midcalf, terry cloth robe and carrying a twenty-ounce coffee mug.

"I know." I moved my feet from the chair closer to her and motioned for her to sit. "You have to bring sunglasses in the morning or it's unbearable."

She grinned and turned the chair to face me. "Or you could not look at the sun."

"That defeats the purpose of rising with the sun." I gave her a rueful smile. "So, you and Joe, last night. Looks like you hit it off."

She shrugged. "He's great. A little religious."

"Oh-h-h."

"What?"

"You have that pout that says, 'I didn't get kissed.' "

"I know, right?" She frowned and sipped her coffee. "Must have been all that lobster. My breath was fishy-garlicky."

"It probably was awful." I couldn't help but laugh. Lola wasn't used to men not giving her what she wanted. I took a great deal of glee in giving her my opinion. "But garlic-fishy or not, he probably wouldn't have kissed you. Guys like Joe aren't going to do anything against their religion."

"Kissing is against his religion?" Lola asked, incredulity in her voice.

I laughed. "Probably not. What I meant,"—I paused to find the right words—"guys like Joe won't let things go too far. Come on, Lola. You know what I mean. You and I were raised in the same church." I was beginning to wish I'd never brought it up in the first place.

She nodded. "When you say 'guys like Joe' "—she swallowed another sip and looked up at me—"you mean guys like Eli."

For some reason, her words struck me like a slap. I think I might have even jolted a little. "I suppose so, yes. They're cut from the same cloth."

"I bet I could change Joe's mind." Her eyes blazed with humor.

I knew she was kidding, but something about

it irritated me—alarmed me, really. "Leave him alone. You'd hate yourself if he went against his faith and gave in to you."

A scowl darkened her face. "You're right. But doggone it. He's the best-looking guy ever. Can I help it if I'd like to make out with him? We wouldn't have to go all the way."

I couldn't resist a laugh at her junior-high description of sleeping with a guy. "For you, that might be easier than for him."

"Don't bet on it," she mumbled. "Hey, are you okay today?" She reached out and laid her hand over mine. "I heard you crying last night, all the way upstairs."

My mind scrambled back to the overnight hours. I'd slept like a rock. I shook my head. "I took melatonin. I didn't wake up at all last night. You probably heard Kitty. He's been coming around the last couple of days."

She glanced around, as if looking for the cat. "I don't see how you can call him your pet when he doesn't want to be touched."

"We have a special relationship that works for us. So leave Kitty and me alone. He loves me from a distance."

"Whatever." She shook her head. "I could have sworn it was actual crying, though. It didn't sound catlike."

"Well, it wasn't me, so what else could it have been?"

"Beats me. It's your house." She sipped her coffee. "So what was all that about last night? Hammering Joe about what he felt or didn't feel?"

Now that she had brought it up—even jokingly—I wondered if I should just tell Lola that I thought Jarrod might be here.

"Well?" Her eyebrows went up as she waited for my response. "Come on, Corrie. It's not like you to pursue a topic like that."

"I don't know. I just wondered if God's a spirit and you could feel the essence of His presence, like people can feel something from other types of spirits."

"Are you kidding? Like ghosts?"

I swallowed a gulp of coffee and nodded, looking at her over the rim of my cup. Her eyes were wide, as though she couldn't believe what she'd just heard. "Well, why not?" I asked.

"Okay, seriously, Corrie." She set her cup down on the table and leaned forward. "You need to come home. I swear I didn't get it until this second. You came to this godforsaken hole in the world looking for Jarrod's ghost, didn't you?"

Anger rose in me, and I felt my defenses rise along with it, creating a wall between us. "Of course not."

She slung herself back in the chair and folded her arms. "Look, I'll be the first to admit I find the idea of ghosts fascinating, and you do have a deliciously ghostworthy house. But to come looking for one? Admit it, Corrie. That's what you're doing in this town."

"Fine," I said. "I'll admit I came back here because I wanted to be in his world. His child-hood home would have more memories than I hold. More of Jarrod." Tears burned my eyes as I fought to hold them back.

"Corrie, listen to me." Her tone softened. "Jarrod is gone. Forever. He's not coming back, and you're going to have to accept it and move on with your life."

"I am moving on with my life." Tears slipped out unbidden and rolled down my cheeks.

"Are you? Then why do you have a studio set up with all the paints still in the bag and an empty canvas on the easel?" So she had been in the art room after all. Normally I wouldn't have cared at all. But now wasn't the right time to yell at her for snooping.

"I got those the day you came, and you're still here."

I hated the way I sounded. Defensive and hateful. Those weren't my normal emotions, and they felt foreign to me, especially when directed at Lola, who had always been my closest friend.

She nodded. "Okay, then let's say I'm not leaving until I see you painting." She smiled.

"You can't just force me to sit down with a brush and come up with something."

"Yes I can. In art school you had to, didn't you?

You had assignments and couldn't wait for the muse to hit. You just had to put the brush in the paint and the paint on the canvas. That's all I'm asking, Corrie."

Fear clutched my stomach. "What if I can't do it anymore?"

Compassion softened her face. "You are a brilliant artist with more talent in your pinky than most people have all over. Will you try?"

It wasn't that I didn't appreciate the vote of confidence, but I had never been able to quite believe the hype about my work. I saw more flaws than brilliance. But try to convince Lola I was less than ubertalented. I rolled my eyes. "And you'll go back and do your own brilliant work if I do?"

She made the motion of crossing her heart. "Scout's honor."

I laughed. "Those are truly mixed signals."

Lifting her coffee mug, she shrugged. "Whatever. As long as you promise to try, I promise to try too."

"Deal."

She took a sip and then stared at the cup, her eyes reflective and serious all of a sudden.

"What?" I asked. "What's that look about?"

"I just could have sworn you were crying last night. There was crying, Corrie." She frowned. "Do you think the house might be haunted?"

A shiver ran up my spine. "Five seconds ago you wanted to snatch me up and deliver me to

Mother's doorstep for suggesting that memories of Jarrod keep him more alive for me, and now you're the one thinking my house has a ghost? I thought you didn't believe in ghosts."

"I didn't say that. This house is the perfect place for a haunting, don't you think?" She lifted her hand toward the window where I was sure I'd seen a shadow last night. "I mean, look at it. It's a hundred years old. There's no telling what kinds of crazy stuff went on in this house through the years. What if the crying I heard was the spirit of someone who had a great tragedy?"

"The house is one hundred and fifty years old," I said offhandedly. "Eli and Jarrod's great-grandmother lived here and served as a healer and medium, so there might have been some crazy stuff."

"Have you asked around? If there's enough history in a place, people are bound to have heard rumors. I think we should find the oldest person in the family and start asking questions."

Aunt Trudy would be that person, and I already knew what she thought.

For the tiniest second, I considered telling my sister about my encounters with the elderly lady. I opened my mouth to try, but something else came out, something deep inside me clearly responding to unnamed fears: "Lola, I think there are things we aren't supposed to understand." I stood, no longer able to enjoy the coolness of morning. "And it's stupid to think a howling cat is a crying ghost. I swear, with your imagination you should be a writer, not a doctor."

"Maybe I will be someday. *The Spirit of Corrie's House.*"

I rolled my eyes. "Sounds riveting. I'm going for a walk by the bridge. Want to join me?"

"Give me five minutes."

At ten minutes before nine I walked into the store and breathed a heavy sigh. Poor Eli. The place was like a sauna again. Samantha looked up from the counter and waved toward me. "I know. Don't say it. I'm not even going to bother Eli about this. I'm ordering a new unit."

I wasn't sure how Eli would feel about his mom doing that without his input, but I'd discovered a couple of things about those two. Eli took on way too much responsibility, and Sam was way more capable than he gave her credit for. Like any good mother, she didn't want him to feel unimportant, so she allowed him to take care of her. Still, I knew that if she could get the best deal on a great unit, it would be a relief for her son.

"Are you sure?"

"Yes." Her voice trembled, and I peered closer. Her eyes were actually misty.

"Is everything okay, Sam?"

"That air conditioner was the first thing my husband ever installed." She smiled. "He was a terrible handyman. I have no idea how Eli ever became so good at working with his hands. But his father was livid at the thought of paying extra money just to have someone install it after how much it cost to purchase the unit in the first place."

Now I got it. "So that's why you can't bear the thought of letting it go."

She nodded. "It feels like I'm throwing him away." She waved her thought aside. "I know that's silly."

"It's not silly. I'm sure if you explained it to Eli . . ."

She offered a tiny, crooked smile. "It's been fixed so many times the repair guys won't even come out. That's why I've had to get Eli to do it the last couple of years. It's time to let it go."

I couldn't argue with that.

"Can you gather up the herbs and put them in the refrigerator, please?" Sam asked. "Aunt Trudy will pitch a fit if I let her plants wither."

"Aunt Trudy grows them?"

"Yes." She smiled. "She's an expert at using herbs for healing and whatnot."

It was the "whatnot" that gave me pause. Sam must have noticed my hesitance. "What's bothering you, Corrie?"

Carefully, I gathered the tender plants and placed them in a bin. "I'm just surprised you would encourage her. Eli is so against the folk witchcraft that I guess I assumed you felt the same way."

She narrowed her gaze, and I had an uncomfortable feeling I'd offended her. "You have to under-stand how things are in this part of the country," she said. "Within families there are mediums and witches, who are usually one and the same. But not always. There are healers; some rely on magic, some on the name of Jesus. Christians, for the most part, condemn the magic as evil, though family members like Aunt Trudy swear her gift is from God. She considers her calling and Eli's calling to be from the same source. It offends her that he is openly opposed to witchcraft. Even so, we are family, and we love each other. And as the Bible says, 'Love covers a multitude of sins.' "

"I see."

Sam seemed to understand my bewilderment with the contradictory relationships. "We know that we don't wrestle flesh and blood." She walked toward me, her voice kind. "Aunt Trudy is my blood. I would no more turn my back on her than I would Eli. She isn't born again, and that keeps me in constant prayer."

I nodded. "I can understand family loyalty." My hippie dad flashed across my mind. Even though he'd disappointed us over and over when we were growing up, I knew Lola and I both wanted to see him. We'd welcome being part of his life.

"We don't choose the way our family behaves. Only how we respond to their behavior."

She sent me a wink. "Exactly."

"What if she did get angry, though?" I asked. "Or someone like her?"

"In what sense?"

"I mean, if she decided to sock a spell on someone or something. I don't know. I've never really been around this sort of thing."

"Are you worried about Aunt Trudy? Has something scared you?"

I shook my head. "Not really. I just wondered."

She pursed her lips, as though trying to formulate just the right response. "We know we don't wrestle flesh and blood, so we don't fight spiritual battles with physical weapons."

I was lost already. Sam seemed to notice and smiled. "Were you raised in church, Corrie?"

"Yes, but no one talked about this stuff. At least not to me." I gave her a sheepish grin. "I stopped going when I was a teenager."

"All right. Then this is what I want you to remember. No matter what you see on TV or hear in those movies with exorcisms and such, there is one Name that's above all that. And if you believe in Him, you have all the power you need to resist the devil and his demons."

"You mean Jesus, right?"

"There. You said it. Don't you feel better already?"

Honestly, I wasn't sure how I felt. "Well, let's hope I never have to put it to the test."

"If you're alive and a believer, you can be sure you will in some form or another."

"Well," I said, "I guess I'll get to those shelves now." I moved away to restock the natural shampoo and conditioner. There were no customers right then, so Sam followed me. Thankfully, the topic of conversation changed.

"How is your sister's visit going?" she asked.

"Good. She went to a concert with Joe last night and plans to go to dinner tonight."

A smile touched Sam's lips. "Ah, the hearts that have been smashed in two by that man."

I returned her smile with a dubious twist. "Trust me. He's met his match in Lola."

She looked at me, her eyes pensive, studying me for a split second. "How are you doing, Corrie?"

"Fine," I replied, my voice small.

"I was married to Eli's dad for more than thirty years before he passed away." She sighed, and somehow I understood her need to hang on to that air conditioner for so long. "If you need to talk," she said, "I'd be happy to listen. No one understands the pain of losing the man you love like another widow."

My instinct was to thank her politely and tell her I would call on her if I needed to talk. Instead, words rushed out of me like water from a faucet. "How do you learn to live without him? At the end of the day, Jarrod and I always connected. Even when Jarrod was deployed, there was almost always an opportunity to speak, at least a couple of times a week, even when he was in more remote places. That's what I miss the most. The talks we had."

She nodded. "I don't know if you ever stop missing the moments only the two of you shared. But I can say that the pain of the loss eases over time. And I suspect for a young woman like you, another love may eventually find you."

I wondered briefly if she was thinking of Eli. The fact was that I liked him a lot. So much that I felt guilty sometimes—when I thought about how warm and good and strong his arms felt the night of the tornado. Or when I recalled the moments we laughed together, or the way he had given me a canvas and paints and red velvet cupcakes, as if he understood that inside I was ready to live again.

"I don't know," I said. "Right now the thought of loving again makes me feel like I'm being unfaithful to Jarrod."

The door opened and she turned. My stomach tightened as Ava Lancaster breezed in and waved. "Hi, Miss Sam," she called. "Corrie. Nice to see you again."

I returned her greeting but turned back to Sam.

Sam waved at her. "You're back so soon? This is an unexpected surprise."

"Momma's been under the weather since middle of last week. Doc says she's got bronchitis and a sinus infection, poor thing."

"I'm sorry to hear that," Sam said. "Is she better?"

"On the mend, anyway. But she's been fretting over getting ready for summer solstice business, so I took a few vacation days to lend a hand."

"Glad to hear it. I'll be right with you, hon," Sam said. She patted my arm and dropped her tone so that her next words were for my ears alone. "I can understand your guilt. But when your heart is ready to love again, you'll have to be strong enough to accept it and release the guilt." A soft smile touched her lips. "Because trust me, honey, Jarrod loved you, and he wouldn't want you to pine away for him the rest of your life because of misguided loyalty."

She went to Ava, leaving me to sort out her words. I could see the wisdom in what she said. The Jarrod I knew and loved for eight years would never want me to be alone. At least that's what he told me. My mind returned to the talks we'd had before each dangerous deployment. Lying in each other's arms, we hated to sleep, knowing that soon after sunrise he would leave and be gone for months on end. "Remember," he would say, "if something happens to me, don't be alone, Corrie. Don't make yourself into a martyr for love. You have to get married again, have a bunch of kids.

Name at least one of the boys after me, maybe two of them, so you'll never forget me."

We would laugh then, and I would tell him to shut up and promise to come home or I wasn't letting him go. And he would say okay.

He only broke his promise once.

Fourteen

Eli

Even though I knew Corrie wouldn't be off work until two, I had been watching the clock all day, waiting for her to arrive. At a few minutes before two, she pulled up in front of the chow hall in a cloud of dust. She was earlier than I'd expected, but the surprise was a pleasant one.

She wore cutoffs with a pair of flip-flops and a man's old blue button-down shirt. How could anyone be that gorgeous in such a dressed-down outfit? She wasn't wearing short shorts either. The cutoffs were midthigh and modest, and I appreciated her consideration. It was difficult enough being a single red-blooded male in a world where beautiful women didn't have much of a sense of modesty and either purposefully or through ignorance gave no consideration to their effect on men.

"Hey," I said. I knew I had a stupid grin on my face, but I was glad enough to see her finally arrive that I didn't care. "You're early."

She nodded, hopping out of the Jeep. "Your mom's AC pooped out on us again. She's getting a new one."

Guilt clutched at me. "Why didn't she call me?"

Reaching into the back of the Jeep, she took the slightest second to give me a knowing glance. "She didn't want to bother you again so soon."

I reached for my breast pocket and grabbed for my phone. "I best give her a call."

Something crossed her expression, but she didn't voice her opinion.

"What?" I said. As I slid the phone back into the pocket, I realized she had gallons of paint in both hands. I reached for two. "What's with the look?"

"There was no look. Where do you want these? Your mom had me stop by her place and pick them up for you. There's at least fifteen gallons, which I don't think we'll need."

"Leave the ones for the cabins in the Jeep, and you can drive down the path. No sense making several trips carrying heavy paint." I motioned to the ones in my hands and jerked my chin to the building. "These will go in the chow hall."

She set her paint back in the Jeep. "Good idea."

"So why don't you think I should call my mom about the air conditioner?" Call me a bulldog, but I couldn't let it go.

239

"Good grief," she said with a laugh.

"You started it."

"I didn't say a word, you crazy."

"You gave me a look."

She sighed and shook her head as she climbed back into the Jeep. "Are there brooms and buckets in the cabins?"

"First boys' cabin," I said, "the one you toured first last night. I didn't know where you wanted to start."

"That works." Her beautiful blue eyes gleamed with humor as she stared at me. "Okay, here's the thing, since you won't let it go. Your mom is a young, capable businesswoman. She can buy herself an air conditioner and have it installed without your help."

The words struck me, and my defenses rose. But she raised her hand and went on before I could respond. "I think you're a great son, Eli. But we women are capable of making decisions too." She smiled and I relaxed. "Your mom will always need you, especially as the years go by, but you'll be doing her a favor to let her do what she can do for as long as she can do it. She's barely sixty, I bet."

"Sixty-one, smarty."

"See? Like I said. She's still young, and take it from another widow—doing for oneself is empowering." She rolled her eyes. "And it's only an air conditioner. She's not selling out and moving to Mexico to live on the beach."

"Well, thanks for putting it in perspective."

"No problem." She laughed. "It's a gift."

I smiled at her. "All right. I won't butt in."

"Good. Now I'm going to go work for my supper. You do remember that you're springing for supper, right?"

"I do. Ham sandwiches okay?"

"Sure. Just don't tell my Jewish grandmother."

I laughed. For someone raised with a silver spoon in her mouth, Corrie was the lowest-maintenance woman I'd ever met. "I'm kidding. I didn't figure you'd feel like going out after painting all day, but I have a couple of filets marinating, and I made shrimp kabobs."

"Oh, wow. Now I'm starving."

I shook my head. "No work, no eat. See you later."

"Fine. And you should know my grandmother is all Texan, which, as you know, is all the nationality anyone needs." She gave me a little half wave and drove off toward the cabins.

I watched the little cloud rise up around the wheels, knowing my heart was beginning to lean toward her a little too much. If I wasn't careful, I could ruin what was the promise of something really great between us by moving too quickly.

Corrie

It felt good to be needed. Sam had hired me at the store, but I had come to think she did it more to be sure I didn't bury myself at the house than out of any real need for my stellar salesmanship. Of which I had none. As I worked, I could hear the sound of Eli's truck as he rounded up branches and other debris blown around by the tornado to be burned. Something about working together on this project made me feel a connection to him I'd never felt with anyone besides Jarrod, and it scared me a little. After my talk with Sam earlier, I had to wonder, were my feelings for Eli growing deeper than friendship? And if so, what did that say about my need to discover if Jarrod was trying to communicate with me?

I scrubbed all four of the boys' cabins—mostly a year's worth of dust and cobwebs and animal droppings—and moved on to the girls', which held more of the same.

Still, I couldn't stop my brain from wrestling with these new questions. Feelings. I wasn't sure how I could sit across from Eli at dinner and not feel awkward now.

While I scrubbed the cabins, I tried to think of a graceful way to excuse myself. After all, Eli was still the same guy he'd been yesterday when I'd grilled for him. I didn't want him to know how confused I was.

I'd grown so accustomed to the friendly banter and boy-next-door feeling about Eli that romance seemed like the next step, I supposed. Again, I remembered the strength of his arms the night of the tornado. I hadn't felt attraction that night, just the need for someone to hold me and make me feel less afraid.

Two hours into scrubbing and knocking down cobwebs, I was ready for a break. I still had more cabins to clean, but I was going to die without water at the very least. I set the broom against the wall and grabbed the bucket to dump the grimy wash water outside. I opened the door and found Eli walking up the path toward me. He looked tired himself, but he smiled and held up a couple of bottles of water and a paper plate with chunks of cantaloupe. "I thought you might be ready for a break."

I smiled. "Perfect timing," I said. "I was just about to head up to the chow hall for something to drink."

"I got you covered." He handed me a plastic fork. "Mind eating off the same plate?"

"Nope."

We sat on the wooden floor, drank water, and ate cantaloupe, and I felt my strength returning.

I motioned to the window unit blowing cool air. "So you got air conditioners for the cabins, I noticed. They weren't here last night."

He nodded. "I had them, but they were stored away. I thought I'd get them out so you don't sweat to death out here."

"I appreciate it. Even with them, all that moving around worked up a sweat."

"Least I can do." He motioned to my plate. "How's the cantaloupe?"

"Sweet. Exactly the way it's supposed to be." I bit into another chunk. "So, Ava's back again."

His expression changed from a smile to a frown in a split second. "She is? She was just here a week or so ago. It's unusual for her to come home this often."

"She said something about her mom being sick and she came to help out in the store. What do you mean it's unusual for her to come home so often?"

"She just doesn't, that's all." He glanced away, as though he didn't want to talk about it. Jealousy hit me hard and fast, surprising me.

"Sorry, I didn't mean to pry."

He expelled a breath and looked at me again.

"You're not prying. We have a history together. Ava moved to St. Louis after we broke up for the last time. That was three years ago." He took a swallow of his water. "I've seen her four or five times a year since. Usually just for quick trips. That's why I'm surprised that she's come back so soon. It's a nonissue, and I doubt she'll even come around."

In a flash, I envisioned the two of them back together and eloping all in the span of two weeks. I shook the thought aside but didn't like where my mind had gone.

"Tell me about her."

He looked at me as though I'd asked for the moon.

"Or don't." I laughed.

"Do you want me to?"

I didn't mention that Sam had already given me the rundown on Ava. I was curious how he saw things. "Eli, sure. Tell me about Ava."

I braced myself as he glanced pensively toward the window. Again, I was struck by the angst I felt.

"We knew each other from the cradle, practically. There wasn't a lot of interaction between our families because we were churchgoers and they weren't. Our social community was church and family. But in school she and I became friends, and friendship naturally evolved into a crush and then romance by the time we were in high school. There's a lot of history there."

I was a little jealous of that history, I was ashamed to admit. I wanted to know all about Eli. I wanted to know what he loved and hated. What scared him and made him laugh.

I loved Jarrod. I ached for him. Still dreamed of him, felt him in my home. He was my soul mate, and we had been torn apart way too soon. Maybe that's why I felt so close to Eli. Because he and Jarrod had been so close all their lives. Maybe I just felt protective and cousinly toward him. But even as the thought crossed my mind, I realized that it was a defense mechanism. As much as I still missed Jarrod, I was also starting to have feelings for Eli, and I definitely didn't want another woman waltzing in and confusing him.

I realized he was staring at me as though it was my turn to talk. He'd said something about history. I sighed a little, stretching my legs out in front of me, leaning on my hands. "I understand having history with someone. It's nice to have someone who knows what makes you tick. Someone to talk to who gets what you're talking about."

I chided myself a little on the inside because that pretty much described my friendship with Eli.

He sat silently, jabbing at his cantaloupe with his fork. I allowed him his silence and nibbled on mine. Finally, his eyes clouded over with what I'd come to recognize as his troubled look, and I couldn't keep quiet any longer.

"What's wrong?"

Sighing, he tossed his fork onto the plate and met my gaze. "I don't know. I guess I'm just a little worried I can't get everything finished in time for the first set of campers."

Somehow I felt relieved that his pensiveness wasn't about Ava. I knew from experience that sometimes a person needs to take a break and try to stop fretting for a while. I jumped up and reached out my hand to him. "Come on," I said decisively, giving him no chance to protest.

His large hand swallowed mine up as I yanked him to his feet. "What are we doing?"

I grinned. "You'll see."

Fifteen

Eli

I stared at the creek and realized what Corrie had in mind. I was glad I'd worn cutoffs today.

"Peel off the shirt, cowboy," she ordered, unbuttoning her own men's shirt to reveal a black tank top. She snatched the rope swing from the large oak tree with overhanging branches. Jarrod and I had used this tree more times than I could count. I had replaced the rope so the camp kids could have the same fun I'd experienced as a kid, but I hadn't personally used it in years.

I grinned as Corrie wrapped her arms around the rope, backed up, and took a running leap into the water. She squealed as she flew through the air and dropped into the cool creek. I caught the rope as it swung back to my side of the creek and waited while she swam to the surface. I wouldn't want to land on her head.

"That was great!" she hollered up at me. "Get in here. It's perfect."

I followed her example, creating a splash as I landed in the water. As I surfaced, she grinned. "Let's see if you can swim with that bum leg." She took off swimming toward the other side of the river.

"That's not very nice," I said.

"Don't think playing the sympathy card is going to keep me from kicking your behind."

I caught up to her easily and reached the bank before she did.

She hung on to the rock edge and fought for breath. "Whew! I'm out of shape." She glanced back at the other side of the river and groaned. "I guess I'm going to have to swim all the way back."

"Unless you want a piggyback swim."

"Don't tempt me." Her breath was beginning to even out, and she pulled in a deep breath. "I might be too tired to paint any more today."

"Wimp."

"Wimp?" Her eyebrows rose. "You realize of course that now I'll have to beat you across the river. No more taking it easy on you."

"I appreciate it."

"I can hear in your voice that you don't believe me." Her eyes narrowed, but humor edged her tone. "Fine, mock me, but when you're eating my dust, don't say I didn't warn you."

"Eating your dust in the river?"

"Semantics."

I won easily again, and by the time she crawled up to the wooden slab Pop had put in for the grandkids years ago, I had already been there a full minute. Her words came in gasps as she collapsed on the deck. "You're not a gentleman."

I laughed out loud. "Sorry. Competition takes the gentleman right out of me."

"Now you tell me. I should have gotten a head start before challenging you."

"It wouldn't have done any good. I've always been the best swimmer around, bum leg or no."

"Well, I'll never challenge you to another race again."

"You could probably win if we were running."

She raised to her elbow, resting her ear against her palm. "What happened to the leg, anyway? Do you mind telling me?"

I frowned. "Jarrod never did?"

She shook her head, then gave me a cheeky grin. "This may come as a surprise to you, Eli, but most of our conversations had nothing to do with you. What do you think of that?"

I chuckled. I knew exactly why Jarrod had never told her about my leg. But how did I answer her question without telling too much? Other than one mentor whom I'd confided in, only Jarrod, me, and God knew the truth about that day.

"We were riding and decided to take a shortcut. But we didn't realize the ridge was so soft. He passed me and my horse lost its footing."

She frowned, and for the first time I noticed a cute spray of freckles along her cheeks. "Your horse fell on you?"

I nodded, remembering the fear and pain of that day. "We fell down a pretty deep ravine."

"Was the horse okay?"

"It was more merciful to put him down." I smiled. "Good thing I'm not a horse, because my leg was broken worse than his."

"I'm sorry," she said softly. "Yours was really bad, wasn't it?"

"It took a few surgeries to get me to where I could get around without a wheelchair, and then I had crutches."

"I'm confused, though. Where was Jarrod during all this?"

"Depends who you ask."

"What's that supposed to mean?"

Shame scorched through me. I had never set the record straight. Had always allowed Jarrod to be the hero. But this time, for Corrie, I wanted to say exactly how cowardly Jarrod truly had been. How impatient and cruel he could be at times. I never really understood how he could have been so selfish. But I guess I had supported him and made allowances for him just like everyone else. Even now, as much as I wanted to set the record straight—to make Jarrod look like the bad guy he had been in this instance, make myself the hero—I couldn't do it. I wanted to be better than that. Besides, I knew his relationship with Corrie and the disciplines of army life had changed him. The final sacrifice he'd made was proof of the fact that the Jarrod I grew up resenting as much as I loved wasn't the guy we'd buried.

"So what did you mean?" Corrie asked again. "Where was Jarrod when you were falling down the hill?"

I pushed aside the real memories and told Corrie the version Jarrod told people. "He came down and helped me get back up the ravine, then lifted me onto his horse and got me to town, where someone called an ambulance."

She sat up slowly, her hair wet and stringy around her face. She still looked pretty. She reached for her shirt, slid it on, and lifted her hair over the collar. "What aren't you telling me?"

I pulled at a frayed string on my shorts. "What do you mean?"

"Come on, Eli. It's obvious there's something you're not saying." She stretched her legs toward the river, allowing them to swing over the side of the deck. I enjoyed her ease with the outdoors. I was kind of surprised by it.

"If Jarrod were alive, I would tell you to ask him."

Something flashed in her eyes, but she turned away with a laugh. "Well, he isn't, is he? So you'll have to do the honors."

But I couldn't. I'd always protected Jarrod's reputation. I couldn't look Corrie in the eyes and undermine her memory of him.

"Hey," I said. "Are you getting hungry? That cantaloupe didn't stay with me."

"You're avoiding the topic, I take it?"

"Sorry. Maybe we can talk about it another day."

She shrugged. "I get it. Jarrod told me you dreamed of military service yourself until that day."

I gave a short laugh and stood, holding my hand out for her this time. "I dreamed about it a lot longer than that day. That was just the day I knew the dream wouldn't come true."

I pulled her to her feet, and she stumbled against me. I drew her to me to steady her. Her lovely face was mere inches from mine. "Eli," she said, "I'm sorry life didn't give you what you wanted. I know Jarrod would have done anything for it to have been him instead of you that day."

"But if it had been, he wouldn't have been there to save all those people."

She took in a sharp breath. "And I wouldn't be a widow."

Corrie

The sun had set by the time Eli and I finished our meal and I drove home, exhausted from the day's effort. Lola's rental was there, but I knew she would still be out to dinner with Joe, so I anticipated the silence as I walked around to the deck and unlocked the back door. I considered going to bed, as soon as I stepped into the mud room and kicked off my shoes, but the art room seemed to draw me. I went to the kitchen, poured myself a glass of tea, and headed upstairs.

I turned on the light and stepped inside with no idea what I might brush onto the canvas, but Lola was right. Sometimes art came, not because of inspiration, but through determination. Right now, it was more about desperation—my need to give expression to some of the conflict in my heart.

I sat on the floor and began taking the paints from the bag. I lifted a brush and removed the plastic protector from the bristles. What had once been like an extension of my own hand now felt unfamiliar. I couldn't remember how to hold it. I set the instrument down and picked up a container of yellow paint. Next, I dabbed red, blue, black, and white paint on the palette, already wishing I had just gone to sleep instead of attempting to be creative.

I held on to a breath as I stood with the palette and brush, then walked to the stool in front of the easel. Slowly releasing the breath, I sat, staring at the white, fear gripping me. What if I couldn't do this anymore? Jarrod's face came to mind, and I dabbed the brush in red and reached toward the canvas. Suddenly I was crying, great gut-wrenching sobs, tears blinding me as they poured from my eyes and dropped onto the palette to mix with the paint. "Jarrod!" I called. The bags rattled as though someone walked across them. He was there, encouraging me to do what I'd given up all these years.

Three hours later, when Lola came home, I was still in the studio. I didn't hear her come inside or climb the steps. I only stopped painting when she tapped on the door. "Come in," I said, suddenly aware that I hadn't stopped crying the entire time I'd been painting. My face was a mess, but I didn't care. For the first time in seven years, I had shared my art with Jarrod.

Lola burst into the room. "You're painting!" she said, her voice filled with joy. "Oh my gosh, Corrie. What . . . ?"

She looked from my face to the canvas. Her eyes filled with tears as she stared at what I had created. "What have you done?"

"It's Jarrod."

"Corrie, no. This isn't Jarrod."

I looked back at the painting, red with the blood he had spilled, black from the ashes left behind after the fire burned out. In my abstract way, I painted what I saw. To anyone else's eye, it didn't look anything like a human being. But the body they couldn't ship home hadn't either. Jarrod had been torn apart by that bomb, and the canvas showed the way my tortured mind imagined him.

"Let's get out of here," Lola said, her voice quivery as she reached for the palette and brush.

I relinquished them and stood, allowing Lola to lead me from that room. As she closed the door, the bags rattled again. I wondered what Jarrod thought of the work he had inspired.

Eli

I couldn't help the crazy grin that remained plastered on my face as I went about my morning, removing brush and preparing to mow the campgrounds. Spending yesterday with Corrie had been great, from eating cantaloupe on the floor to racing in the creek and finally eating dinner prepared by yours truly. I couldn't wait for her to arrive today. I knew she most likely couldn't come every day, but before driving away last night, she had assured me that she would be here to work today.

Around ten, my phone buzzed in my shirt pocket.

Caller ID said it was my mom's store. "Good morning, Mom."

"You sound awfully chipper," she said.

I laughed. I was not prepared to share the reason for my good mood. "It's a pretty day, and I'm working on the campground. What's up?"

"Have you heard from Corrie today?"

Something in her tone stole the smile from my face. "Isn't she usually at work at this time?"

"Usually. But she hasn't shown up yet and hasn't called."

"That's not like Corrie. Did you try calling?"

"No. I wanted to talk to you first." She exhaled a sigh into the phone. "Didn't she help you yesterday afternoon?"

"Yes, and she stayed for dinner." I slung a

branch into the back of the pickup and leaned against the bed, swiping at my forehead with my sleeve.

"How was she when she left? Did she seem upset at all?"

"Not that I could tell. We actually had a really great time." All the joy I had felt was gone now, replaced with worry. "I'll hang up and try to call her. Maybe she just overslept." Though that seemed unlikely with all the work being done at her place.

"Good idea. Let me know if I should be relieved or worried."

We hung up and I immediately dialed Corrie. Everything in me wanted to jump in my pickup and drive over. Had I done something to make her uncomfortable yesterday? Did something I fed her last night give her food poisoning? Or had she come down with a virus or something?

Her phone rang three times before she answered. "Corrie's phone."

I frowned. It wasn't Corrie. "Lola? It's Eli. Is Corrie okay?"

"Yes, Eli," she said, but her voice seemed strained, and I wasn't buying it. "I should have called. She's a little under the weather today. Can you let your mom know?"

How sick was she that she hadn't been able to make a call? Something was off, but if she wasn't going to be forthcoming, I didn't feel I had the right to pry. "I'll let Mom know. Please tell Corrie I hope she gets better soon."

"I will, and thanks for calling. Hey, Eli?"

"Yeah?"

She hesitated, and I wanted to ask if she was sure Corrie was okay.

"Don't worry. I'm taking good care of her." I had the feeling that wasn't exactly what she wanted to say.

"Are you sure there's nothing I can do?" I asked.

"I'm sure. Thanks again for calling."

She said good-bye and hung up. I called Mom to let her know, then went back to work, decidedly less optimistic than when I started off this morning.

Unease grabbed hold and refused to let go. *Lord, help Corrie* was my constant prayer as I moved through my day. By noon, I decided to head into town for lunch. Again, I was tempted to stop by the home place, but Lola hadn't made it sound like Corrie was up for visitors.

I could always stop by to check the progress of the workers, but the guys would be having lunch. Tim would have gone home to his mom's to eat, and if I knew Joe, he'd be down at the creek with a fishing pole, a sandwich, and his Bible, spending his lunch hour with God.

Releasing a heavy breath, I rolled on into town and parked in front of the café. I wasn't exactly in the mood for company, but I realized I was starving, and they made the best burgers in town. When I stepped inside, I wished I'd gone somewhere else. Ava sat with Jarrod's sister, Mae.

I tried to get to a table of my own before they noticed me, but Ava looked up almost immediately and waved me over. "Just in time to have lunch with a couple of hot girls. This must be your lucky day."

I felt trapped, so I slipped into the booth next to her. "What kind of trouble are the two of you up to today?"

Mae smiled. "I'm just trying to get away from kids for an hour so I can hear myself think."

Amazing how even in a town as small as Saunders Creek, a person could go months without seeing someone else, even if she was your cousin. "You deserve a few minutes to yourself."

"Thanks, Eli." She sipped her tea, and Ava took the opportunity to speak. "How are your camp preparations coming along?"

I shrugged. "Moving brush right now. I'll start fixing a couple of the roofs tomorrow. Shingles blew off in the tornado a few weeks ago. So what are you doing back in town so soon?"

"Momma needed me." She glanced away quickly, arousing my suspicions. Something was definitely up with her. I wished I could walk away and not care, but we had been friends too long, not to mention we'd been this close to marrying. I figured she would eventually come to

258

me with whatever was bothering her, and I prepared myself for the drama.

"Eli, how is Corrie doing?" Mae asked. "I know you've seen a lot of her since she got into town, which is more than I can say for my parents."

I heard the bitter undertone of her words, but the server approached before I could pursue the matter. I gave her my order, and as she walked away, I turned my attention back to Mae. "Your parents haven't been to the house at all?"

She scowled and shook her head. "They don't think Corrie wants them there. And that's fine if she doesn't, but you'd think she would have at least called or dropped by."

As if on cue, Ava spoke up. "Mae said they sent her flowers on her birthday last week and she didn't even call and thank them."

I had noticed the daisies. I knew they meant something to Corrie because she had been taking special care of them. Even as the petals began to wilt, she seemed unwilling to toss them out. But something bothered me in the way Ava jumped into the conversation. "I see you two have been gossiping about her. It just so happened her sister showed up on her birthday, so she's been a little preoccupied."

Mae glared at me. "You know, Eli, it's not so easy to watch people you love hurting so much. Corrie is their last link to Jarrod, and they'd like to see her. She was part of our family for seven years." Her volume rose with every few words, and I was aware of a few curious stares coming from the tables around us, but Mae didn't seem to notice. "So, yeah, I've been talking to my friend about it. Call it gossip if you want. I don't really care."

"Not that Jarrod and Corrie ever came around much when he was alive." Ava punctuated her words with a short laugh that grated on me.

Perhaps it was my uncertainty about how Corrie was really feeling yesterday, but Ava's criticism annoyed me thoroughly. I turned on her, letting my anger rule me as I hadn't done in a long time. "Mind your own business. You don't know the half of what Corrie has gone through."

Ava's brow rose. "Well, I guess it's easy to see why you spend so much time with Corrie."

Mae frowned and shook her head at Ava, and I didn't have to wonder what else they'd been discussing. Clearly, they'd made up their minds that I was after Jarrod's widow.

"That's also none of your business." I stood. "I'm getting my order to go." I glanced down at Ava. "If you want to talk about why you're really home again so soon, I'm working at the camp. Feel free to drop by."

"Don't count on it."

"It's up to you."

I walked to the counter and asked the server to box up my meal. I slid onto a bar stool to wait and to cool down. Ava knew me too well. She was all too aware of how to poke at my raw places. Barely two minutes passed before Ava brushed against my elbow. "I just don't want to see you get hurt."

My eyebrow lifted as I met her eye to eye. "Why would I? Corrie and I are just friends."

She tilted her head and pursed her lips. "Sure you are."

"Well, like I said . . ."

She waved away the rest of my comment. "Yeah, yeah, I should mind my own business."

"You said it, not me."

"Actually, you did say it. Twice, thank you very much." Her voice dipped with hurt, and shame washed over me. Before I could apologize, she went on, "And here's the thing. Even if we're not a couple, we've been friends a long time—a lot longer than you've known Corrie Saunders."

"Okay, I'll give you that." I forced a grin, hoping to lighten the mood and avoid the lecture.

But Ava saw through the ruse and wouldn't be silenced until she had said her piece. "I still care about you, and I don't want you to put your heart out there for a woman who is still madly in love with *and* still grieving the loss of her husband."

My jaw clenched. "Duly noted."

The server slid a takeout container in front of me. "Gotta go," I said. "And I meant what I said. Come over if you want to talk."

"Eli," she said, her tone full of the venom that I'd come to know all too often toward the end of our engagement. "Stop setting yourself up for hurt. You'll never be Jarrod."

Sixteen

Corrie

The day passed me by as I lay on the couch, not speaking, not eating. I spent the time thinking about Jarrod, sleeping, and dreaming about him. A cloud had settled over me, and I felt the weight of his death as though it had just happened.

The door opened, bringing a burst of light as the sun made its final appearance before it set. I flung my arm across my eyes. "Geez, Lola, close the door before I go blind."

She ignored my outburst and breezed in, snuggling Kitty in her arms. "Look who I found meowing outside the door. I think he misses someone."

"I forgot to put food out for him, that's all. The cat never comes near me unless I sneak up on him." I rolled over, facing the back of the couch, and tried to ignore them both. I felt the warm, furry weight on my legs and, for the first time ever, heard purring from the wretched cat that I had been trying to domesticate for weeks.

He walked up my body and curled up beside me. "See?" Lola said, triumph in her tone. "Told you he misses you."

I rubbed his orange coat, amazed he didn't immediately hop off the couch. He had always hated being touched. I wondered if the workers had been giving Kitty attention. "Hey, Kitty," I crooned. "Did you miss me?"

Lola shut the door and plopped down in the rocking chair next to the door. "Don't you think it's time to give him a real name?"

After scooping him into my arms, I rolled back over to face my sister now that the door was closed. "He has a real name."

"But it doesn't suit him. Plus, people will think he's a girl cat."

"You sound like Eli." My stomach jolted at the sound of his name on my lips. I fought the urge to duck under my covers and cry, although I couldn't understand why. Eli and I were friends. How could there be more when Jarrod was still part of my life? "What kind of name did you have in mind?"

She shrugged and pursed her lips. "How about Louis after Brad Pitt's character in *Interview with the Vampire*?"

"Why would you think of that?" I looked down at the cat, now content in my arms for the first time since I claimed him from the barn.

"He's the mysterious, brooding hero. Just like Kitty here."

I tilted my head and studied the animal. "I don't know, Lola. He doesn't look like a Louis to me."

"You could call him Louie. That's kind of cool."

Lola was clearly taking this renaming thing a little too seriously. I shook my head. "But then I'd always think of the mean dispatcher in *Taxi*. The Danny DeVito character."

She scowled. "You're a slave to your classic sitcoms. Louie's a perfect name for that cat, and you know it."

Kitty hopped down, leaving a cold spot where his warm body had been. "See," I said. "Why name something that isn't going to stick around anyway?"

The expression on Lola's face gentled. "You mean why love something that isn't going to stick around. Like Jarrod?"

"I'm not going to talk about the painting," I said. "So don't start."

Releasing a sigh, Lola stood and walked over to me. She sat on the floor in front of the couch and grabbed my hand. I had to admit a human touch felt good. "I love you, Corrie," she said, pressing our clasped hands against her cheek.

My eyes filled with tears, but I remained silent as Lola continued. "It tears me up to see you hurting so much. Maybe this is the perfect time for me to be without a job. I'll stay until you don't need me anymore."

Part of me wanted to tell her to stay forever. That just knowing someone who would always love me unconditionally was here meant so much. But something else, the part of me that held my secrets, wanted her to go so I could be alone with Jarrod's presence. Alone without scrutiny, with-out someone thinking I was losing my mind. Maybe I was.

I don't know if I would have told her to go or thanked her for staying, because a knock at the back door interrupted our moment.

Lola pressed a kiss to the back of my hand and patted it back to the couch. "I'll get it," she said, and hauled herself up. Kitty hightailed it out of the house the instant he realized the back door was open. The rejection might have hit me harder, but I heard Sam's voice greeting Lola as the two of them walked down the hall from the back door. She walked into the living room carrying a dish in her hand.

Shame washed over me like a cold rain, and though I knew better than to be rude, I wanted to hide. "Hi, Sam," I said, wishing I could fake a cold but knowing I'd never be able to pull it off.

"What do you have there, Sam?" Lola asked.

Sam handed the dish to her. "Chicken noodle soup," she said. "Nature's healer."

"Wow! Look, Corrie, we eat tonight." She

grinned at Sam. "Thank you. With Corrie out of commission, I was afraid I'd have to cook. Then we'd both be sick. Please sit down," she said. "I'll put this in the kitchen."

Guilt hit me hard. Sam believed I was physically ill. For a millisecond, I again considered faking a cough, but I couldn't go through with it. Besides, Sam was pretty savvy. I'm sure she would have seen straight through that. I decided I'd better come clean; otherwise I wouldn't be able to look her in the eye.

"I'm sorry I didn't come in today, Sam," I said, sitting up. I grabbed my pillow and pressed it against my stomach.

"Honey, that's okay. I'm not a slave driver. I appreciate any time you do come in."

I met her gaze. I know guilt was written all over my face. "I'm not really sick."

Compassion, rather than the surprise I'd expected, swept across her face. I knew Sam well enough to know she wouldn't be angry, but the sympathy took me aback. She walked to the couch. "May I?" she asked, nodding to the space next to me.

"Of course." I pulled my sheet and blanket away from the cushion. "Thanks for not being mad."

"You're welcome. You can come and go as you please."

I knew she couldn't possibly run a business that way. "You're such a nice woman. Eli's lucky to have a mom like you."

Lola stepped back into the room. "That's the truth. When we were kids and got sick, our mom barely remembered to check on us in bed."

"Lola . . ." Had Mother taught her nothing? I gave her our mother's famous we-don't-air-our-dirty-laundry look.

She dropped into the rocking chair with a shrug. "Well, maybe she didn't totally forget about us, but homemade chicken soup to soothe the pain? You know that never happened."

Rueful laughter erupted from Sam. "Now's my turn to be honest. I didn't make it either."

She would have been Wonder Woman if she had, considering she worked at the shop today. Often the ladies from her church group brought her a meal to take home. "I hope you didn't bring us your dinner."

She shook her head and waved a hand. "Not at all. Liz stopped by for some stevia, and I was ringing her up when Eli called to let me know you weren't feeling well."

The words fell upon my stomach like a punch, and I suddenly really did feel nauseated. Perhaps Jarrod's mom didn't hate me after all. Confusion swept over me. "She went home and made soup for me?" My emotions had been so raw over the past eighteen hours I teared up again, just as I had a hundred times today.

"She did. And she asked me to drop it off."

"But why didn't she just drop it off instead of

driving all the way back to town?" They lived just down the road.

"I couldn't tell you."

Suddenly I remembered the birthday flowers. My eyes went wide. I gasped, taking in too much air, and then I really did cough.

Lola sat up in the chair, ready to do the Heimlich or something. "Corrie, what's wrong?"

I recovered from the cough and slapped my forehead. "I never called and thanked them for the daisies."

Lola's jaw dropped. "The birthday daisies?"

Feeling about as small as ever, I nodded.

"Yikes," Lola said.

"It's okay, Corrie." Sam patted my forearm. "Liz and Fred probably didn't think a thing about it. They're not ones to get offended."

Not a bit mollified, I groaned. "Jarrod must really be mad at me." Too late, I realized what I'd said. I jerked my gaze to Sam's.

"You mean he would be mad at you if he were here?"

I grabbed the pillow on my lap and pulled it tighter against me. "Yes. Of course that's what I mean."

Sam's gaze demanded mine. Her face was no longer soft and filled with compassion. Now she looked determined. "Listen to me, honey. If you are feeling something . . . otherworldly in this house, I wish you would say something."

I dropped my gaze to my fingers, still clutching the pillow tight. "I think Jarrod's here," I whispered.

Adjusting her position, she shook her head. "No, Jarrod's dead. And he's with Jesus."

The door upstairs slammed and shook the house. We all jumped. Lola jolted to her feet. "What the heck?"

"It's Jarrod," I murmured.

"What are you talking about?" Lola said, planting her hands on her hips.

Sam ignored Lola's outburst. "Corrie, I don't doubt you've been experiencing some encounters with something spiritual, but—"

"Are you kidding me?"

I glanced up and scowled. "Settle down, Lola. You don't know everything. Remember that talk we had on the deck yesterday morning?"

"About ghosts and this old house being haunted? Corrie, I was mostly joking about that."

Sam took my hand and held it between both of hers. "Look at me, honey."

Reluctantly, I did so.

"There are spirits or demons who are familiar with families. They've been around so long and have been welcomed by so many, including Jarrod's great-grandmother and grandmother, that they don't go unless told to do so."

As if on cue, the chair began to rock of its own accord. Lola screeched and jumped away from it.

"You see?" Sam said. "I don't know what you've encountered"—the rocking grew more emphatic—"but it wasn't Jarrod."

My skin crawled as the hair on the back of my neck rose. "How can you know for sure?"

"Because I believe the Bible. People don't come back to live in their own homes or to haunt their living loved ones." She studied my face. "Do you believe in Jesus?"

I nodded. "I was raised to." Maybe I wasn't like her or Eli, but something had always told me Jesus was real. People were the problem.

Finally, as the rocking reached a frenzy, Sam jerked her thumb toward the chair. "We have authority in the name of Jesus to stop that and command it to leave."

The chair stopped rocking.

Lola exhaled as though she had been holding her breath.

Just as the chair stopped rocking, the photo on the table next to it slammed facedown so hard the glass broke. Immediately, the chair began to rock at its former frenzy.

I did want this to stop. But after all the times I'd sensed Jarrod's presence, I couldn't convince myself this wasn't him trying to let me know he was here.

"Corrie, for Pete's sake," Lola said. "Let her do it. This is creepy."

"I don't want Jarrod to leave until he's ready to

pass on," I said. "What if this is the only way he can let me know he's here? He's not trying to scare anyone."

The thumping lessened and settled down.

I smiled. "See?"

Sam gave a slight sigh, and I felt bad that she was disappointed. "Do you believe Jarrod loved you?"

I nodded. He still loved me, but I didn't want to antagonize her by mentioning that out loud.

"Would he want you to grieve for him forever by staying with you, knowing you couldn't heal with his presence so close?"

It felt like a trick question. If I said yes, I'd paint Jarrod as a narcissist; if I said no, then how could the presence be him at all?

Sam stood, apparently sensing my dilemma. "Call me if you need me. Remember, if Jarrod loved you, he wouldn't do anything to cause you fear or any kind of uneasy feeling. Fear and depression both come from one source, and that's the devil. Anything that robs you of peace isn't right. Like today. Seven months after his death, you're spending a day in bed hurting and depressed. The Jarrod I know wouldn't want that. His death was a selfless act. Would he be so selfish afterward?"

She bent and hugged me. I could smell the jasmine from the store clinging to her. Suddenly I wanted to grab on and ask her not to leave. But I refrained. She straightened. "I have to go. But I meant what I said. You can call me. And if you find yourself afraid or sensing that something isn't good, I want you to remember something, even if you remember nothing else."

"What?" I asked.

"If you can find the strength to so much as whisper the name of Jesus against the enemy, he will leave."

In all my years in church, I'd never heard that. But I didn't argue. I knew she meant well.

"I'll remember," I said.

Jarrod was no enemy. He was a hero and my love, and the reason he had been so forceful just now was because he was frustrated. When Jarrod got frustrated, he slammed things. I recognized his tactic.

Lola walked Sam to the back door and returned a minute later. With tentative movements, she reached for the picture that had fallen and righted it on the table. "That was intense," she said.

"Very."

"Do you think she was right? Maybe you should have let her do what she wanted with that thing."

I frowned. "It's Jarrod. I'm sure of it."

Aunt Trudy's face came to mind. "Where's my cell phone?"

Lola pointed at the table by the couch. "Who you gonna call?" She was still shaken, I could see, but she rallied and grinned. I rolled my eyes at the *Ghostbusters* reference. I had to hand it to her, she recovered pretty quickly.

I grabbed my phone and found Aunt Trudy's number in my list of contacts. I dialed her. She answered almost immediately. "It's Corrie," I said.

"Hello. I hear you're not feeling well. What's ailing you? I can brew you a tea for just about anything."

"I was faking it," I admitted. "I'm calling you about something else."

"Oh?"

"I know you can communicate with spirits."

"If the spirit is so inclined, yes."

"Well, I think Jarrod is."

She paused. "Would you like me to come do a reading?"

I nodded, then realized she couldn't see me. "Yes."

"I can be there tomorrow."

"My front porch is gone, so you'll have to come to the back. Is that okay?"

She chuckled. "I'm old, but not that feeble, dear."

We set a time, and I thanked her before saying good-bye.

Lola stared, an incredulous expression on her face. "Were you actually talking about a séance?"

I shrugged. "I don't know what they call it, but Aunt Trudy's the real deal. If Jarrod has something to say, she'll be able to get it out of him."

"After all that slamming and rocking?"

I nodded.

"You're nuts."

"You don't have to be here if it bothers you," I said, feeling defensive.

She sank onto the sofa next to me. "Well, I'm not leaving you with a bunch of crazies and a ghost. If you're doing it, I'll be here."

Jarrod didn't come to me again that night. I stayed awake, thinking of what had occurred earlier. Sam's words, *"Do you believe in Jesus?"* ravaged my already reeling mind. I lay there remembering my childhood, when I truly did believe in Him. In my mind's eye, I saw little-girl-me, alone at night and falling asleep peacefully, aware that if Jesus died for me, He must love me. It wasn't until later that I forgot all about Him.

When I finally fell into a fitful sleep around two, I dreamed I stood in the midst of a crowd looking up at a man on a cross. Blood poured from His head, and His body was so broken and bruised He barely resembled a human being. He raised His tortured head and looked through the people until His gaze settled on me. Beautiful brown eyes stared at me, and I couldn't breathe. Somehow, without words He spoke.

"I'll never leave you."

Eli

As much as I tried to shove away Ava's comment, it haunted me the rest of the day. *"You'll never be Jarrod."*

Though I was alone, my defenses went up at the suggestion that I was even trying to be my cousin. I knew Jarrod to be selfish, volatile, full of himself. Of course, in the end, he gave up his life for others, and for that I admired him. It must have taken a lot of strength for him to be willing to make such a sacrifice. He had become the hero he'd pretended to be. And perhaps that was the most bitter pill of all for me to swallow.

I supposed if I was truly honest with myself, I'd have to admit that I was still envious that Corrie had loved him so deeply she gave up her interests to be solely his wife.

My thoughts drifted to Corrie—her smile, laugh, humor. Her beauty was incidental. I'd have been attracted to her even if she were not so pretty. I wanted to pull out my phone and call her and had to force myself not to. I didn't want to hover or make her feel like I was stalking her. But I did miss her presence as I went about my day.

"You'll never be Jarrod." The words went round and round in my mind.

Why couldn't I get that stupid conversation with Ava out of my head? She knew where to poke to get the best response, and she'd gone straight for the jugular. The thing about Ava was that she usually read people pretty well. She read me pretty well. Maybe it was part of her mother's legacy to her. The passing down of gifting. Or maybe she had just known me so well that my childhood resentment toward Jarrod was still obvious to her.

When Terry Machaelson, my friend and a chaplain in the army, showed up unexpectedly to help with the camp we had both founded, I welcomed the relief from the accusing thoughts. I showed him where I had stored the lumber for the new rock wall and where I wanted to put it up. Then I set aside what I had planned to make the best use of Terry's skills as a carpenter.

As we worked together, Terry shared about some of the new kids he'd signed up for the camp, and I started to look forward to the first session, which was coming up in just a couple of weeks.

"Looks like you could use more help than just this rock wall," Terry said as we began to measure two-by-fours and cut them to the right sizes. "Maybe I could get a team together to come out on a Saturday to help with the rest. I know you've been trying to deal with storm damage at your house."

I nodded. "A local woman came and helped get the cabins cleaned out yesterday, but she's not feeling well today."

"Every little bit helps," he said. He grinned.

"That was nice of her to give up her time for you. Is she someone special?"

I felt my face warm. "She's my cousin's widow. I showed her around the other day, and she wanted to help."

"Wish there were more people like that," he said.

I nodded and felt my heart lift as I talked about Corrie. Just the sound of her name on my lips brightened my day. "She mentioned maybe being a counselor." I marked a line on a board and set it aside to be cut. "I'm not sure she was serious."

Terry stopped what he was doing and straightened, stretching his back. He frowned. "Do you think her being here might be hard on the kids, though? With her husband dying over there, it might make them worry even more about their own deployed parents."

Honestly, that hadn't occurred to me, but I nodded. "She's still pretty broken up, so I'm sure it would come out, even if inadvertently."

Though he was easily fifteen years my senior, Terry was the only friend I had confided in about what had actually happened the day Jarrod became the town golden boy for saving my life and leg. "Can I ask your advice?" I said.

"You know you can." He leaned against my truck, so I followed suit.

I shared with him how my feelings for Corrie had hit hard and grown fast. "And the thing is, yesterday I thought she was feeling something for me too. I mean, something besides the friendship we've established over the past few weeks."

"What's changed since then to make you think otherwise?"

I shrugged. "I'm not positive anything has. But she didn't go to work at my mom's store today, and she didn't call. That's not like her. I can't help but think I did something that upset her or embarrassed her."

He offered a sympathetic smile. "Such as misread her feelings? Maybe she picked up on your expectations."

"And now I've scared her off and might never have a chance."

He folded his arms across his chest and stared at the ground for a second before turning his head to look at me. "Since you can't possibly know what she's thinking about yesterday, let's talk about what we know to be true. Your feelings for her. What is it about this woman that draws you to her?"

That was easy. Corrie was funny, witty, smart, sensitive, wise. Her blue eyes revealed every emotion, and I responded accordingly. If she smiled, I did too. If she cried, I wanted to hold her. I hadn't seen her angry—not with me—and I could imagine if she ever turned her anger in my direction, I'd want to die.

I didn't want to be a sap, though, so I took a minute to think about the right words. Finally, I gave a lift of my shoulders. "At the risk of sounding like a lovesick fool, pretty much everything about her draws me. Her looks, of course. She's got a perfect face and pretty eyes. She's pretty much the whole package, if you know what I mean."

"I can guess." He humored me with a wry smile. "Anything else?"

I nodded, and the words came pouring out. "I want to protect her and make her feel safe. I want to know every detail of her life, even what she's thinking, which I know doesn't make me sound very manly."

A chuckle came from deep in his chest. "It makes you sound like a lovesick fool." He grinned.

I didn't stop the return grin I felt stretching my lips.

"How are your feelings about her different than what you've felt before?" he asked.

The question struck me, and the first thing that came to my mind was Ava's face. We were only friends until she decided I would be her boyfriend. Wearing a tight cheerleading uniform and an encouraging smile, she didn't have to do any more than crook her finger and I came running. "I've had one serious relationship and almost got married. I think what's different is that then I felt like prey drawn into a web. With Corrie, I don't feel manipulated. She's not trying to seduce me. Does that make sense?"

"She sounds like a great catch."

"She is. Or would be if she were available."

His eyes narrowed. "She's dating someone else?"

"No." I felt a little foolish even bringing it up, but I'd already opened the door. "It's still Jarrod."

"So you're competing with a dead man."

In so many ways, I'd always competed with Jarrod, so I didn't deny the truth of his words. "You'd think the cousinly rivalry would have ended when he died, but I find myself feeling more resentment toward him now than I have in years."

Though I fought against revealing my discussion with Ava, I found myself opening up and telling Terry what she said to me that morning.

"I don't know why I let her get to me like that."

"Maybe because there's an element of truth to what she had to say?"

"That I want to be Jarrod?"

"Do you?"

I reflected on the question, though my first instinct was to dismiss the accusation. But I'd learned a long time ago to do an inward check of my motives. I wished I could say I didn't, but I wasn't sure. "Everything came easy to him. Accolades, hero worship, sports, girls. When he took credit for saving me instead of telling the truth about being responsible for the accident in the first place, something inside me started brewing against him. I could handle his accomplishments in the things he did for real. I accepted that to everyone except my grandpa, parents, and Ava, Jarrod was people's first choice. But that day something changed inside me."

"Then why didn't you tell anyone the truth?"

"I don't know. I suppose because I loved him like a brother. We grew up together, and it was natural for me to let him have the last say. He just always got what he wanted. I didn't want to drive a wedge between us. But things were never the same for us after that."

"But in essence, your silence still caused a wedge."

"I guess so. Pretty much."

"And now you've fallen for someone who loves him, even when he's not here to love her back. So it's pretty much a double whammy."

His words twisted like a steel knife inside me.

"Sometimes I get the feeling she's afraid that if she accepts her feelings for me, she's betraying his memory."

"That's pretty common."

I nodded. It had only been seven months since his death. I got that.

He turned toward me, leaning his hip against the truck. "So I guess the real question then is, are you willing to wait until she has healed from the loss?"

The scripture "love is patient" flashed into my mind. "I think I am."

"Settle that in your heart if you believe she's the one for you." He peered more closely, as though studying me. "The next important question has to do with you personally. It has less to do with her."

I frowned. "What's that?"

"Can you relinquish your bitterness toward Jarrod? Because until you do, not only will you always compare yourself to him and find yourself coming up short, but you'll also never be able to truly believe the woman you love—should you be so lucky as to win her heart—hasn't chosen you by default."

He was right. As we continued to work side by side, I reflected on the things he'd said. Somehow, the feelings of insecurity that had been festering all these years had come to a head in recent weeks. But Ava was wrong. I realized that now. I didn't want to be Jarrod. I wanted someone to think I was better than Jarrod.

Put simply, he hadn't seen that painting was important to Corrie. He'd allowed her to give it up to be his wife. My face burned as I realized my motives in going overboard for her birthday were for me. Not Corrie. So she would see that even though she gave that up for him, I was giving it back to her. I was the better man. Choose me.

I had only presumed that she'd sacrificed by not indulging in her art over the past seven years.

I'd just assumed that because everyone seemed to cater to Jarrod, she must have too.

The weight of my own arrogance pressed down on me until I felt ready to break.

Seventeen

Corrie

Even though I hadn't slept well the previous night, I awoke before the sun rose on the home Jarrod had given me. I shoved off the covers and sat up. I had to admit I was getting pretty tired of sleeping on the couch, but it was better than the thought of sleeping in the bed without Jarrod—flesh-and-blood Jarrod.

I stretched as I stood up. Drawn to my art room, I climbed the steps, treading lightly so as not to disturb Lola. I opened the door and went to the stool. I didn't come up here at all yesterday, but as I stared at my painting of Jarrod's violent death, I was once again overcome with the emotions of that night. Just sitting in the room with that painting, I was more convinced than ever that Aunt Trudy would be able to help me hear what he was trying to say. I shoved aside the tightness in my stomach. Shoved aside everything Sam had said to me. I wanted to believe it was Jarrod. I *needed* to believe.

My gaze fell on the painting I'd bought in town on my birthday, still covered in brown paper. I went to the corner, sat down, and peeled away the paper. I looked at my house, and my eyes shifted immediately to the attic window.

Something didn't feel quite right, and I couldn't put my finger on whether it was the artist's technique or the darkness of the entity that I was so sure was Jarrod. I'm not sure how long I sat there, staring at the painting, but as the light began to come in from the east window, I rose, gathered up the painting, and started downstairs.

I leaned the canvas against a wall in the living room and went to make coffee. I glanced at the clock and was surprised to see that I had been upstairs for two hours. It had seemed like no more than twenty minutes.

After starting a pot of coffee, I ran back upstairs and walked into my bedroom. Though I hadn't slept in my bed yet, I kept my clothes in there. I pulled out jeans and a short-sleeved top and tossed them on the bed, then gathered the rest of the things I'd need to get ready for what lay ahead in a couple of hours. In the midst of it all, Eli's face came to mind, and I was struck by the beauty of my new floor. He had taken the time to stain the wood and add a layer of sheen.

I wanted to call him and explain about yesterday, but I held back. What if Sam had told him about Jarrod showing up? He would most certainly believe it wasn't my husband, just as Sam did. I didn't want to give him the chance to scold me.

Lola had risen and padded down to the kitchen in her socks by the time I finished getting ready. She stood by the counter, pouring herself a cup of coffee. "Thanks for making this," she said. "Want some?"

I nodded and dropped to a chair.

"Are the guys going to be working on the porch today?"

I cringed inside. Why hadn't I thought to ask them not to come? "I guess I can't ask them to take off work and miss out on income for this. Hopefully it won't get too weird." And they'd never suspect anything.

"Want me to call Joe and tell him to wait a couple of hours?"

"What excuse will you give him?" I knew Lola's feelings for Joe were growing, and I hated for her to lie on my account.

"That you're going to have company."

She set a cup in front of me and shoved the sugar bowl and a spoon next to it.

"My phone's upstairs in my room," she said. "I'll go call him and be right back."

I stared out the window to where the porch was half-bricked. I missed my morning time in my swing, but I was the one who had thought a brick porch would look nice with the farmhouse, so I had to suck it up and be patient.

Lola was back in ten minutes. She grabbed another cup of coffee and sat, leveling her gaze at me. "Are you sure you want to do this?"

"Drink coffee?" I knew what she was asking and intentionally evaded the question.

A scowl twisted her face. "Funny."

I spooned an inordinate amount of sugar into my cup and stirred. "I'm sure, Lola. What did Joe say?"

She gave a little wave. "He said it's fine. He'll come after lunch. Whatever. Are you a little scared? I mean, considering how we were raised?"

I sipped my ultrasweet coffee and tried to pretend a confidence I was fast losing.

At eight fifteen, a knock at the back door interrupted a light breakfast of bagels and strawberries. "Are they forty-five minutes early?" Lola asked.

"Beats me." I glanced out the window. Sam's car was parked in my gravel drive. My stomach dropped. Guilt hit me as I hurried down the hallway to the back door, though I wasn't sure why it mattered to me what anyone thought about what I was about to do.

"I'm sorry to stop by so early," she said.

"Don't be. Come in. Is everything okay?" My voice sounded phony, and I cringed as I pushed open the door.

She shook her head. "I can't stay. They're bringing my new air conditioner today."

For the first time I realized she had something in her hand. "I don't know if you have one of these," she said, handing me a Bible. "But everything I said yesterday is written in here. I marked some scriptures for you."

I took the Bible. It felt heavy in my hands, and I was reminded of the unfamiliar feeling I had experienced when I picked up my first paintbrush in almost eight years the other night. "I had a Bible when I was a kid, but I haven't really been to church since I was a teenager."

"This one belonged to my husband," she said, her eyes suddenly soft and misty. "You'll find notes of his written on the edges of some of the pages." She smiled. "I consider them little nuggets of wisdom and truth."

I still couldn't bring myself to get rid of anything that had been Jarrod's, so I could only imagine what something as special as this had cost her.

"I don't know what to say," I said. I held it out to her. "But I can't take this from you. It must be special."

She shook her head. "It's only special when the words inside are read and taken to heart. I want you to have it, and he would have as well."

I could see she wasn't going to be deterred, so I held the book and smiled. I wanted to ask her if she would like coffee, but Aunt Trudy and her team would arrive in forty minutes, and I didn't want to chance her still being here.

"Well," she said. "I best go."

"Thank you for this," I said.

"You're welcome, Corrie. Just read it, and let Jesus reveal Himself to you. He wants you to know Him as well as He knows you."

"I will. I promise." And I found that I meant it.

She turned to go but hesitated and turned back, concern on her face. "I know Aunt Trudy is bringing Ava and Tonia Lancaster here for a reading today."

I hadn't known Ava had been invited, but it didn't surprise me as much as the fact that Sam knew I had asked them to come. I dropped my gaze, unable to meet hers. "Yes. I want to know what he has to say."

"I can't tell you how to live your life, hon, but remember that if you're afraid or if something doesn't feel right, you only have to say one name."

"I'll remember."

I walked with her to the back door and waited for her to get down the steep deck steps and disappear around the side of the house before I closed the door. I turned to go back in the kitchen and stopped short. The painting wasn't there. I went back to the kitchen, frowning.

Lola whistled. "That was intense."

"Yeah." I sat back down in my chair and took a

sip of my coffee. "Hey, why'd you move my painting? I was going to put it up today."

"What do you mean?"

"The one I bought in town? I unwrapped it when I was in the studio this morning. I left it in the living room."

"I haven't seen it. Are you sure you brought it down?"

"Yes, Lola."

"Well, sor-ry."

We were both on edge over what was coming, so I didn't hold her snarky response against her.

We had finished eating and cleaning up our mess by the time we heard a knock.

My stomach knotted, and Lola and I exchanged a glance. She stepped closer to me. "Last chance," she said. "We can tell them thanks but no thanks."

"I'm going through with it, Lola," I said, bolstered by renewed irritation at my nervous sister. I opened the back door. The three women stood on the deck. Aunt Trudy held a huge bag and smiled her toothless grin.

I opened the door wider. "Good morning," I said. "Come in." My voice sounded stronger than I felt. For that I was grateful.

They stepped into the mud room. Ava smiled tentatively. "Do you mind that I tagged along?"

"If it's okay with Aunt Trudy, it's okay with me."

"Well, I'm not much of a medium. I'm mostly here for moral support." She turned to the other woman, whom I assumed must be Mrs. Lancaster. "Mom, you haven't met Corrie yet, have you?"

The woman smiled at me and extended her hand. As I took it, I couldn't help but note the resemblance between her and Ava. Even with graying hair and a few wrinkles here and there, it would be hard to deny that she was beautiful. "Call me Tonia," she said in a warm tone. "I'm so glad to finally meet you."

"It's nice to meet you too. Thank you for coming."

"Of course."

I was a little surprised that Aunt Trudy had recruited Mrs. Lancaster. I knew they weren't exactly friends.

As if reading my mind, she inclined her head toward the other woman. "She has a gift for sensing the nature of a spirit."

Lola stepped out of the kitchen as we walked down the hall. "Nice to see you again, Miss Trudy."

"You can only stay if you don't bring negative energy," Aunt Trudy answered, her tone abrupt as she dispensed with niceties.

"I'm not leaving." Lola's tone was firm, and I knew better than to get in the middle of the power struggle.

"Then make sure you clear your mind of

negativity and open up to the spirits, or we may as well go home."

She shrugged. "I'm an open book."

I rolled my eyes and was this close to kicking her out to preempt any disruption to Aunt Trudy's juju, but I needed her there.

"She's staying, Aunt Trudy."

She shrugged. "Have it your way."

"Okay, then. How do we do this?" I asked.

"You stay here for now," she said. "Tonia and I will go into each room separately and try to see where the energy is the strongest. When we are finished, we'll discuss which room is the most active, and that's where we'll hold vigil."

"Vigil?"

"She means something like a séance," Ava said.

"Thank you, Ava," Aunt Trudy snapped. "I can speak for myself."

Ava averted her gaze. "Sorry."

"Should I lead you to the upstairs rooms?" I asked.

Aunt Trudy scowled at me. "Where do you think I grew up?"

My face warmed. "I forgot."

"I'm going to open myself to the spirits now and start my walk-through. Tonia?"

Tonia nodded.

They closed their eyes, and each breathed in deeply. A sense of unease swept through me.

What was I letting myself in for?

The walk-through took close to twenty minutes. Lola, Ava, and I remained in the living room while the two mediums did their thing. Lola seemed to have relaxed a bit. I thought maybe she hoped they wouldn't sense anything at all and we'd be off scot-free.

Instead, Mrs. Lancaster came down alone. "Trudy says you should come to the master bedroom. That's where the energy is the strongest."

We climbed the steps, wary. Lola held on to my hand tightly. The temperature seemed to drop by a good ten degrees when we stepped from the hallway into my bedroom. I might have made a *Ghostbusters* comment myself if not for the knot in my throat that choked off my ability to push out words.

"This is the room where we each sensed the strongest concentration of energy, and we believe it is where we should attempt our spirit communication."

Odd, I thought, since I never slept in here. Why would this be the room Jarrod chose to communicate with me?

But I kept my mouth shut and accepted their expertise. Tonia spoke. "I'm sensing a human spirit wanting to speak with you, Corrie."

Why was I suddenly so uneasy? This is what I had wanted all along. To hear Jarrod say something. Ignoring the twinge of fear, I nodded. "Okay."

"First, he wants you to know how much he loves you and that he's sorry he had to leave you."

Lola snorted. I knew she was thinking that anyone would say that about a husband who died. I squeezed her hand hard. Aunt Trudy glared at her, and she straightened up.

"He wants to say something to prove to you that he's here."

She cocked her head to one side, as though listening. Then she nodded. "He says to tell you he knows you were angry he died but that drinking is never the answer, and he's glad you haven't done it again since the first night you spent on the swing."

Suddenly, I couldn't breathe. The words she was saying were supposed to prove that the things I'd been feeling were Jarrod. But it was all too much. Too personal. He should have known I didn't want anyone to know about that night.

I glanced around the room, looking for something. My mind was beginning to play tricks on me. I saw shadows everywhere. Shadows that moved across the walls. I focused on an object leaning against the wall next to my closet. Something tapped my shoulder, and I jerked my head to the left, but no one was there. My gaze went back to the wall. The painting of my house stared back at me ominously.

"Corrie." Lola squeezed my hand. "Are you okay?"

"The painting I took downstairs this morning. It's up here."

"I didn't move it."

I knew that. I knew it instinctively, as I know that the moon is always in the sky, even during the brightness of a sunny day. I couldn't explain why, but I knew. As I stared at the image of the shadow in the attic, it seemed to come out of the painting and waft toward me as a gray cloud.

Maybe it was from my lack of sleep, but I suddenly felt lightheaded. My breathing came harder and harder, and my chest felt like something was pressing hard against me, trying to shove out my very life. "I . . . can't . . ." I reached for Lola.

"I'm getting you out of here," she said. "You're having a panic attack."

Ava followed us down the stairs and to the back deck. I dropped into a chair, and Lola shoved my head between my knees. "Deep breaths. You'll be okay."

"Should I tell those two you're not coming back?" Ava asked.

"What do you think?" Lola said. It was uncharacteristically harsh, especially considering Ava was a stranger.

To her credit, Ava seemed to understand. "Okay, I'll tell them."

"Think you could have been a little meaner?" I

said, sitting up. My breathing was returning to normal. "I think you owe her an apology."

She pursed her lips. "Probably." She turned to me. "Do you think it was him?"

I shrugged. "Maybe." I couldn't give voice to what I had experienced in that room. The overwhelming sense of dread as that shadow moved toward me.

I expected to feel love, joy at the confirmation of his presence. All I'd felt was fear.

Eli

Two days after my talk with Terry, I showed up to work at the camp with new perspective. I realized I had to surrender my jealousy of Jarrod and pretty much just get over it. As I went about the morning, actively choosing forgiveness, I felt there was hope that I might stop feeling I had to compete with him, even in death. My feelings for Corrie were just as strong as they had been, and I missed seeing her for the past two days, but I didn't want to impose, and I wanted to be able to go to her free of the weight I'd been carrying around for some time.

At noon Terry called to invite me to a men's retreat at a lodge in Branson for a day and a half, ending after a service Sunday morning. I started to refuse because I had a ton of work to do and a sermon to prepare for a ten o'clock Sunday service that I couldn't cancel with this little notice.

Terry interrupted me before I had the chance to offer my excuses. "I know there's still work to be done at the camp, but I've rounded up a few of my friends, and we're coming out next Saturday. I think the retreat would do you good. I also know you would have to leave early to preach your own service, and that'll be just fine." He continued on without giving me a chance to say no before he offered every reason to say yes. "Everyone needs to take time away for some R and R. We're going to do some fishing and praying and Bible study. What do you say?"

I was blown away by his generosity, and I didn't see how I could refuse the retreat. "First, I say thank you for getting the workday together. And second, I'll see you tonight."

"Great. I'll e-mail you the directions. Oh, and bring your bow. We're planning a manly target contest."

We hung up, and I decided to work for another hour before going home to shower and pack a bag. I was starting to look forward to the retreat.

Sweat poured from me as the sun beat down overhead. Mid nineties was a heat wave in southwest Missouri this early in the year. Just as I was locking the mower in the barn and knocking off for the day, I glanced up and saw a horse and rider coming toward me.

My gut clenched as I recognized Ava, but I

had to forgive her too. Friends quarreled and got over it. I was hoping we could too.

"Hey, there," she said.

She sat as regal as a queen high on her chestnut mare, Pinecone. Her cowboy hat shaded a pair of sunglasses. She wore blue jeans and a sleeveless shirt that revealed defined, deeply tanned arms.

"Hey, there," I said, hoping my tone didn't reflect the dread I was feeling.

"Catch," she said, and tossed down a round, basketball-sized watermelon. "From Daddy. He says thanks again for offering the firewood. They'll need it."

I caught the watermelon. "Tell him thanks."

Pinecone nudged me. Ava laughed. "Look who misses you."

Reaching up, I rubbed the horse's long face. "More likely she misses the sugar cubes I used to bring her. But I'm fresh out today."

"It's okay. She's gotten fat this spring. All that fresh grass in the field and no one to make her exercise." She smiled, flashing beautiful white teeth. One thing about Ava, she was beautiful. She'd grown from a cute child to a pretty teen to a beautiful woman. At thirty years old, she made Hollywood beauties look as though they were just trying too hard. Her straight dark hair blew around her face a little, and she definitely made a pretty picture. But pretty had never been our problem. And despite my appreciation of her beauty, I was wary of this impromptu visit.

She climbed off the horse, and I averted my gaze as her shirt slid up, revealing her midriff. Thankfully, she pulled the shirt down.

"What are you doing here, Ava?"

Her eyes clouded with what I thought might be hurt. "I'm here for two reasons. First, to say good-bye. I'm heading back to St. Louis tomorrow. Mom's all better, and the store is pretty much ready for the onslaught of customers."

I didn't know what to say. I wasn't exactly sorry to see her go. "When will we see you again?"

She shrugged. "Who knows? I thought I'd help out in the store over the summer solstice, but Mom hired a girl to help." She took a long breath. "So Thanksgiving, probably."

Ignoring my clear inability to respond, she continued. "The other reason I came is to apologize for what I said about Jarrod."

My heart went out to her, and I offered her a smile. "It's okay. Actually, your comment helped me work through some things. So I guess I should be thanking you."

I opened the door to the chow hall and stood back as she ducked under my arm and walked in. "Thank goodness it's cool in here," she breathed out.

"I just turned off the AC, so it shouldn't warm up too quickly."

She raised her eyebrows and turned to look at

me as we headed toward the kitchen. "Why'd you turn it off? It's melting out there."

"I'm knocking off early. I have a retreat to go to."

"Oh?"

"Yeah, it's last minute."

"Well, I should go, then," she said, but something about her demeanor seemed different. More subdued. It was clear something was troubling her and she'd come to talk.

"I have a few hours," I said, motioning her to the bar stool and moving around to the refrigerator. "I have water."

"That's perfect."

I lifted two bottles from the shelf, shut the door, slid hers across the counter, and leaned forward, resting on my elbows. "So what's bugging you?"

Her gaze jerked to mine, then she grinned as she opened the bottle. She lifted it to her lips and stared at me as she took a long drink. "Well, I sort of do have something to tell you."

Defenses rising, I eyed her, determined not to let anything she said make me mad.

But I could see her eyes beginning to mist. Ava wasn't a crier. She never really had been, so I knew this mattered and that it likely had nothing to do with me. I walked around to the other side of the counter and pulled her into my arms. She felt small. Thinner. "You okay?" I asked as she sniffled against my shirt.

She breathed out deeply. "I'm pregnant."

My heart sped up at the news and not in a good way. I pulled her away from me and stared at her. "Are you sure?"

She nodded. "Four months."

"I couldn't even tell."

"I have a tiny baby bump, but not much yet."

"Where's the baby's dad?"

"Back with his wife."

I stared into her eyes, a little shocked, I had to admit. "A married man?"

She gave my chest a light punch. "Hey, no judgment."

"Okay, sorry." My head was still wrapping around her news. "Just processing."

"Anyway, for your information, I didn't know I was dating a married man. He told me he was divorced. Turns out he was only separated, and two days after I got back from my last visit here, he realized he still loved his wife and didn't want to marry his pregnant girlfriend."

"Wow. I'm so sorry, Ava." I couldn't be sorry about a marriage reconciled, but the thought of anyone treating Ava like this got my back up. "What does the wife think about her husband fathering a child during their little break from marriage?"

"She doesn't know, and he asked me not to contact him." She gave a bitter laugh. "First he tried to buy me off. And when I told him to go to you know where, he changed his tactics and told me he is willing to give up all parental rights."

I couldn't believe how calm she was being about it all. "Well, too bad, right? You're going after him for child support, I hope."

She scowled at me as if she couldn't believe I'd had the audacity to say such a thing. "No way. I'd rather support the baby on my own and have him out of my life for good. It's his choice." Her eyes spilled over, and I pulled her back in.

"Well, I'm proud of you for keeping the baby. Do you know if it's a boy or a girl yet?"

"No. I don't want to know until the baby is born." She pulled back again. I grabbed a handful of napkins from the counter and handed them to her. "But Mom used a pendulum across my belly. She says it's a boy."

"Well, then."

"Don't start," she warned, giving me another little punch, and I knew she was doing better. "I've never known my mother's pendulum to miss in predicting the sex of a baby."

I let her comment slide. No sense giving my opinion about the old folk practice. "I guess now that you're going to be a mother I better be a little nicer to you."

"That's right, and if he truly is a boy, I might name him after you."

"I'd be honored." I reached forward and pressed a kiss to her forehead. Somehow, before I quite knew how, she was in my arms again, and her lips were on mine. She wrapped her arms around mine, snuggling herself closer to me. Corrie's face flashed to my mind. I grabbed Ava's wrists and gently pushed her away. "Ava . . ."

Tears filled her eyes. "You know, I'd hoped you might want to marry me out of pity and help me raise the baby."

I opened my mouth, but she held up a hand. "Don't. I would never have let you do it anyway. Besides, even if you haven't figured it out yet, I know you've fallen for Corrie."

Even though I wasn't inclined to share my feelings about Corrie with her, I didn't bother to deny it.

She nodded. "So you have figured it out."

"I'm still figuring it out." I smiled.

"She was pretty shaken up yesterday after Mom and your aunt Trudy did that reading."

A jolt hit me full in the gut, and I almost doubled over. "Why were they doing that?"

Narrowing her gaze, she looked me straight in the eye. "Well, they didn't shove their way into the house and tie her up. Why do you think they were there?"

"Corrie asked for a reading?" Didn't she know how dangerous that could be? "So what happened?"

"Mom and Miss Trudy found the highest concentration of energy in the master bedroom, so we all went up there."

"You too?"

"How else would I have known about it?"

I wanted to help Corrie avoid the slippery slope that someone could start down after opening herself up that way. "Anyway, tell me what happened. Did something . . . manifest?"

"You mean did some*one* manifest?"

I wasn't going to dignify her comment with a response. "I guess I mean, how is Corrie?"

The smug expression fell from Ava's face. "Jarrod, or whatever, spoke to my mom about an incident on the porch swing where Corrie was drunk." She finished off her water and stood, tossing the bottle into a large rubber garbage can at the end of the counter. Then she turned to me slowly, in her dramatic way. "She had a panic attack and ran out of the house. Her sister took care of her. Miss Trudy was pretty disgusted." She gave a short laugh. "I doubt she's ever going to speak to Corrie again."

I was pretty sure she would. Aunt Trudy never held a grudge.

"Well," Ava said, "I'm going to go so you can do what you need to do. Thanks for taking time to talk." She headed to the door. "Goodbye, Eli. I'll see you in a few months. Say hello to Corrie for me," she tossed over her shoulder. "You know you're hotfooting it over there as soon as I'm out of sight."

Eighteen

Corrie's Jeep sat in front of her house when I pulled up a few hours later. The retreat began at seven, and I had just enough time to tell her I would be leaving so there was no need for her to show up to help out at the camp, in case she had any intention of doing so after two days of silence. I couldn't leave for another day and a half without at least seeing her, hearing her voice, knowing she was okay.

Lola answered the back door. "Eli. How've you been?"

"I've been fine."

She stepped aside and welcomed me in. "It's good to see you."

"Thanks, it's good to see you too." I tried not to be too obvious about looking for Corrie as we walked down the hallway, past the kitchen. "I'm going to a retreat this weekend, but I was hoping to see Corrie before I go."

As if on cue, Corrie appeared at the living room door. "Hey, Eli," she said. Her smile seemed genuine enough, but there was a hesitance in her eyes that gave me pause.

"Is that for us?" Lola asked, pointing at the

watermelon. I nodded and handed it to her. "It's a re-gift." A sheepish grin tugged at my mouth, and I felt like a dope for bringing Corrie something so stupid.

"Great," Lola said. "We love watermelon, don't we, Corrie?"

Corrie nodded. "Thank you. We'll put it to good use."

Lola headed toward the kitchen. "Can I get you something to drink, Eli?" she asked in her soft southern tone. "I think we have tea and Coke."

I shook my head and found it hard to look away from Corrie, whose eyes had never left mine. "No thanks, I have to get on the road. I can't stay."

Corrie's eyebrows rose. "Going somewhere?"

"Branson, for a men's retreat."

"Oh. Sounds like fun."

"Should be." Being at a loss for words wasn't typical for me, and I found it extremely disconcerting. She stared at me, as though waiting for me to get on with it and get out.

"I just wanted to check on you before I go. It's been a couple of days, so . . ."

"I know. I'm sorry I haven't called."

The tension in the room was palpable. I wanted to go back outside and do this better—I'd leave the watermelon in the truck, for starters.

"I'll be gone until Sunday, so . . ."

"Everyone needs to get away every now and then."

The awkwardness was crazy considering how well we'd come to know each other. And as much as I tried to convince myself that I was only there to say good-bye, I had a much more important reason, and I couldn't leave without telling her.

"Listen, Corrie," I said. "I heard about—"

"I knew that's why you showed up." She glared at me and flounced to the couch. "Feel free to sit down, but I can't handle a lecture, Eli. Today's been hard enough already." She dropped onto the couch. She grabbed a couch pillow and clung to it. I knew enough about psychology from my seminary course work to recognize a defense mechanism. Stung, I sat in the rocking chair, trying not to be hurt that she needed to protect herself from me. "I have no intention of lecturing you. I just want to make sure you're fine."

"Well, I am, except for the fact that I freaked out and passed up a chance to hear from Jarrod."

Leaning forward in the chair, I rested my fore-arms against my thighs and met her gaze. The last thing I wanted to do was lecture her. But how could I express my concern over her unwilling-ness to hear the truth?

"You're not going to tell me that the things I've been experiencing haven't been Jarrod, are you?" Her tone was defensive, but she seemed small and vulnerable.

"Do you truly believe they are?"

"I honestly think they could be. He told me he

was glad to see I hadn't had anything else to drink since that night on the swing. How could that not be Jarrod? I haven't told anyone, and I don't think you have."

I shook my head. "Not even my mom."

"See?" Her eyes pleaded with me to say it was okay that she was welcoming a demon to stay and play house with her. But I knew better, and I didn't think she would be so conflicted unless she knew better too.

"At the risk of sounding like a nag, let me just help you put things in perspective. Don't you think any spirit, whether or not it was Jarrod, would have seen you on that swing? They're liars and deceivers, and this one is presenting itself in the form of your husband so you'll let it stay and interact with it. It's amusing itself at your expense."

She shook her head. "There were so many things we missed out on because he was gone so much, so maybe he came back to make it up to me. That's the kind of guy he was."

Frustration welled up inside me, and if this had been anyone but Corrie, I would have given her a good piece of my mind. "You don't have to tell me what kind of guy he was, Corrie."

"Yes, but you didn't know him the way a wife knows her husband."

"No, that's a given." But she didn't know him as I knew him either.

"Well, then?"

"It's not him. That's all I can say. We experienced that demon all through my growing-up years. After my grandfather's death, it would lie on the bed with Granny. She felt the impression on his side of the bed. She felt his hand on her hip. Why would Aunt Trudy feel so much energy from Jarrod in a room you barely go into?"

"I don't know!"

Her beautiful blue eyes filled, and my heart twisted inside my chest. "Corrie, I'm not trying to take something from you, but this can only end badly. I don't want you to end up getting hurt. And Corrie, neither would Jarrod."

"Jarrod wouldn't hurt me." Anger replaced the pleading in her eyes. "You're supposed to be my friend. Jarrod's so-called best friend. Why are you trying to keep us apart? Are you jealous or something? If that's it, you don't have to worry. I think we scared him off." Her voice broke. "He hasn't shown up since the reading yesterday."

"Well, I can't say I believe that's a bad thing, Corrie."

"Right. Because you don't want him in my life."

There was no getting through to her right now. Only God could show her the truth. The helplessness I felt ripped into me like the stab of a hundred knives as we sat in the living room, staring at one another on opposite sides of a battlefield.

Corrie

I watched out the window as Eli drove away. I felt like crying. I had hurt him with my outburst, and that was the last thing I'd ever wanted to do. When Lola came back into the room, I had slipped on my shoes and was headed for the door. "Hey," she said. "Where're you going?"

"For a walk."

"Want me to come with you?"

I shook my head. "I need to think." Mainly I needed to get out of that house. I hadn't been able to bring myself to climb those steps and take a chance on a repeat of my frightening experience since Aunt Trudy and the Lancasters had gone. Sam said if I felt fear or distress I should say "Jesus," but that thought didn't even occur to me at the time. As I headed toward the bridge, I wondered what might have happened if I had said His name. I approached my place of solitude, anticipating some calm. But then I recognized Ava's horse, and my stomach sank.

She had looped the reins around one of the posts and sat with her legs dangling, her arms resting on the bottom rail. She turned when she saw me coming. "I'm trespassing," she said.

I found it hard to be annoyed when she offered such a self-deprecating smile. "It's okay." I kicked off my flip-flops and dropped down next to her. "Everyone seems to like to come here."

"Does that bother you?"

309

I shook my head. It was true for the most part. Today, though, I would have preferred to be alone.

"You look down in the dumps," she said. "Most people tell me I'm too nosy, so feel free to suggest I mind my own business, but is this about the reading yesterday morning?"

I shrugged. "Partly. Eli stopped by on his way to his retreat just now. We had words."

"O-o-oh," she said. She released a breath. "That's my fault. I told him how freaked out you got yesterday morning. I guess I should have kept my mouth shut."

Yeah, probably. Irritation clutched at me, but I'd had enough confrontation today.

"So he really came down hard on you about the reading, I take it?"

"Not really. Sort of. I don't know." I rested my chin against my hands on the rail. "I was pretty hateful to him."

"Is he okay?"

I shrugged. "He drove off. He didn't seem mad, just hurt."

Gathering in a deep breath, she turned to me. "Corrie, I'm going to say something, and trust me, it's not easy."

Then don't say it. I thought the words but managed to refrain from speaking them aloud. "What?"

"Eli really cares about you."

My stomach fluttered. "I care about him too." I

deliberately misunderstood, because this wasn't a topic I wanted to discuss, particularly with his childhood sweetheart.

"I think you know we aren't talking about the same kind of caring."

"Look, Ava. I appreciate that you don't want to see him hurt."

"I don't think you do either."

I nodded. "That's where I was going with it. I don't want to see him hurt. I truly do care about him."

She paused, and I thought maybe she had taken the cue and dropped it. Rather, she seemed to regroup. "Listen, I know there was something in your house yesterday. And I know you want to believe it was Jarrod."

"You don't think it was?"

"Honestly? I have no idea. I'm not a medium like my mother. Not for her lack of trying, mind you." She gave a wry grin. "At any rate, let's say it is Jarrod."

"Okay . . ."

"He's not flesh and blood. He can't be a husband to you. The most he can do is let you know he's there." Her expression softened. "There's a real man standing right in front of you, practically begging you to notice him."

Her words hit their mark, and I had to look away.

"It's normal for you to feel guilty for wanting to

get on with your life. I don't think there's a widow or widower out there who wouldn't feel exactly the same way."

"Maybe I don't want to get on with my life. What if I just want to stay alone in that house with Jarrod forever?"

"If you did, why did you run away yesterday morning instead of letting Jarrod keep talking?"

"I don't know." I remembered the feeling of panic I'd experienced, the gray cloud coming toward me, and my heart picked up its rhythm. "It didn't feel right."

Ava maneuvered her legs out of the space between the deck and the bottom rung. She stood. "I think you already know in your heart that Eli could be the one for you. If you give him up, just know that you're making the biggest mistake of your life."

"Says the girl who already gave him up."

"Exactly. I have to be going. Mind if I take the road in front of your house so I don't have to go all the way around?"

"Go ahead, any time you want."

"I'm going back to St. Louis tomorrow, so this is my last ride for a while."

"So soon?"

"Yeah, I have to get back."

I took in the information.

"Well, then I guess whenever you're home again."

"Okay, sure. Thanks."

Her boots thumped across the wood as she walked the few steps to her horse. As I expected, she wasn't quite finished. "And just for the record, if I could go back and do things differently with Eli, we wouldn't even be having this conversation," she said as she climbed into the saddle. "I'd be married to him and would likely have a couple of his babies. So be glad I was an idiot. But try not to make the same mistake."

I watched the horse walk away, carrying Ava across the bridge. The sun had started to set, and the water below reflected its final rays of the day. I struggled with her words but even more with my feelings. How did I feel about Eli? True, he seemed to get me, maybe even more than Jarrod had, even after seven years of marriage. I laughed a lot with Eli. I had laughed with Jarrod too but not about conversation so much as TV shows and things like that. Outside sources.

I heaved a sigh. It wasn't fair to compare the two men. I loved Jarrod for who he was, and if I were ever to move on with Eli—if—the relationship would have to be separate from what I felt for Jarrod.

Suddenly I realized I was thinking of my feelings in the past tense. As though I didn't love him anymore. Everything in me rebelled. I did still love him. I still searched for him.

But he was gone. That thing in the house couldn't be Jarrod.

The thought came to me as though the very nature around me had spoken. Maybe Jarrod was there, as well as something else, something more sinister. That was possible, wasn't it? Had the other thing, the evil thing, scared me off so that I couldn't hear Jarrod?

I pondered the two sides of my confusion for a time, rationalizing on one hand, listening to my heart on the other.

As I walked back to the house a few minutes later, my mind replayed the entire conversation with Ava. She was meddlesome, but she seemed to truly care for Eli and want him to be happy. In a way, it made Jarrod's hold on me seem almost selfish. I pushed the thought away as fast as it had come. I was his wife. Of course he wouldn't want to see me with another man, even if that man was Eli.

An image flashed before me, unbidden, from someplace my imagination had never stretched to before. In my mind's eye, I saw a scene on the wall in Eli's chow hall. I gasped and stopped short to process it. As I stood there on my little path, surrounded by trees, the ground illuminated by beams of light, the image began to take shape.

I felt a presence, so unlike the things I'd been experiencing at my home. A feeling of hope filled me, maybe even just a twinge of joy, for the first time since Jarrod's death. I wanted to do something to show Eli how much I appreciated everything he had done for me over the past few weeks, giving up precious time to make sure my home was beautiful.

I grabbed my phone from my jeans pocket and dialed the first person who came to mind.

"Sam," I said, my feet picking up speed as I envisioned the task before me.

"Corrie, honey," she said, her tone rife with concern. "Is everything okay?"

"Yes ma'am," I said, breathless. "I have a surprise for Eli, but it's going to take the whole time he's gone to accomplish, and I need to get into his chow hall tonight. Can you help me?"

I could sense her hesitation on the other end of the line. "I have a key, but I've promised not to give it out. Can you tell me what you have in mind?"

By the time I explained what I wanted to do, I had reached my house.

"What do you think?" I asked, holding on to my next breath for fear she might turn me down.

Without missing a beat, she gave me her answer. "Come by and get the key." Her voice shook with emotion. "Honey, Eli does a lot of good for a lot of folks. What you have in mind will be nothing short of a kiss from heaven to him."

Nineteen

The wonderful aroma of paint began to fill the air in the chow hall, and I prayed as I worked, though I hadn't spoken to God much in years. Not one-on-one. The hope that infused me while I walked home stayed with me, dispelling any doubts that muddled my brain. I worried from time to time that Eli might not really want me to do this.

I had a brief moment of panic when I realized that even with my new paints, I had nowhere near enough to cover a wall. But Sam had me covered and called Jerry. Thrilled to be part of the surprise for Eli, he opened his art store, and neither he nor his wife would even consider payment for the supplies. So of course I bought another of Billy's paintings—this time it was a picture of kittens playing around my barn. Nothing spooky or dark. I joked I was going to have to charge him if he kept using all my props.

Sam called me three or four times before ten that night, asking how it was going. Finally, I had to laugh. "Sam, I'll never get it done in time if you don't let me work."

I had never been the sort of artist who painted

murals, so I had to rely on instinct to take over. This one challenged everything I had preferred in the past, and it began to take shape in an impressionistic style I hadn't used since art school. I found myself leaning toward a type of surrealism in certain areas of the wall. Those parts spoke peace to my soul as the image formed. I worked until the wee hours of the morning that first night and went home exhausted yet exhilarated at the same time. My heart soared with expectation of the next day's work, and I drifted into a peaceful sleep on the couch.

After only four hours of sleep, I rose, nearly panicked that this was my only day to finish before Eli returned early Sunday morning. But as the images began to emerge on the wall, I grew more and more optimistic that the painting would be finished in time.

Apparently, word of my project had spread around town, because several of the townsfolk, including Jerry and Verna, showed up to take a look. But Lola stayed on hand to answer the door and prevent anyone from coming in. I was determined that Eli would have the first look.

At lunchtime, Lola made a quick trip to the café. She returned with burgers and fries and a look of complete incredulity on her face.

"What?" I asked.

"The owner wouldn't let me pay for it."

"Did you forget to take money?" It wouldn't

have been the first time. I grabbed a fry and popped it into my mouth.

"No, I opened my purse, and the girl said it was on the house, so I asked to speak to the manager, just to be sure."

"And?" Lola had a way of dragging out a story.

"And he said, 'I heard what your sister's doing for Eli, and you can consider this our little contribution.' I was going to argue because I know how you are about paying your own way. But he said, 'Eli fixed my heater last winter and wouldn't take a dime. Been lookin' for a way to bless him back.'"

I grinned. "So we got free food because Eli is awesome?"

"Something like that. Man, this town loves that guy."

"You don't think anyone will spill the beans about this before he gets a chance to see it, do you?"

"No clue," she said around a fat bite of her cheeseburger. "I'm sure his mom has told everyone it's a surprise." She tilted her head. "Don't you think it would be cool to have a mom like Sam?"

"I guess so." Her words irked me a little. As much as my mother's control issues drove me crazy, I didn't want to completely disregard her. "Painting this mural had me thinking about what it must be like for the kids whose parents

318

are deployed. It's made me sort of miss Mother."

"Wow, you need sleep." She grinned. "Just kidding. Funny, I was looking at the outline you've done and thinking that at least their dads come back when their deployment is up. I haven't seen our dad in three years."

"And four years before that."

She nodded. "Yeah. I guess we just have to accept the fact that he isn't going to be superdad."

"It doesn't make it any easier, though." My appetite was gone, only halfway through my meal. I washed down my last bite with a swallow of diet soda and stood up. "I better get back to work." Lola followed, carrying the containers into the kitchen to toss in the trash can. I washed my hands at the kitchen sink.

I'd have preferred to drop the subject, but Lola seemed to need to talk about it. "I guess sometimes you have to let go of people who can't or won't be in your life, for whatever reason."

I pursed my lips, rolling my eyes. "So I guess you're not talking about Dad now. You're telling me to let go of Jarrod."

Her eyebrows went up. "Actually no, I wasn't thinking about you, really. I was just wondering if my commitment issues are because of him not being around. But if your mind went there, maybe someone's trying to tell you something."

I ignored her last comment and focused on what she'd said about commitment issues. "I thought

319

you were in therapy last year. Didn't you talk about him?"

"I only went six times," she said. "Six times equals six hours. I guess I never should have started the first session with Mother, because she's all I could get through in six hours. And it didn't work anyway, so I quit." She peered more closely. "What about you? Do you think it might help for you to talk to someone about your loss?"

But she and I both knew I wasn't ready to accept the loss as final. "I love you, Lola, but I have to work."

"I know, I know, and I need to be quiet." She grabbed the novel she'd been reading earlier and propped her feet on a chair. "Go get 'em, genius."

Someone knocked on the door awhile later.

"I'm on it," Lola said, and I didn't bother to turn around. She wouldn't have expected me to.

Ten minutes later, I reached a stopping point, and I stepped back and took in my painting with a critical eye. There was too much white in the sand. Frustrated, I turned, stretching my back. A baking dish sat next to a ceramic serving bowl, a bottle of salad dressing, and something else I couldn't make out from where I was standing. Lola had settled back in with her book and seemed engrossed. I set down my brush and grabbed a towel to wipe off my hands as I walked across the room. "What's this?"

Lola glanced up from her book and smiled. "More food from the natives."

"Did you get a name so we can send a thank-you card?" I lifted the foil from the baking dish, and tomato sauce tempted my senses, reminding me I'd skipped breakfast and eaten only half my lunch.

Lola hesitated. "It was Jarrod's mom."

"Liz brought this?"

"Yeah."

"Well, why didn't you let her in?" Wasn't there enough tension between me and Jarrod's family? Keeping her out just seemed like another push away.

"I invited her, but she didn't want to interrupt your work. And I'm pretty sure she's not holding her breath about the thank-you card, either, considering the birthday flowers and soup she made the other day."

Her words stung, but I knew she was right. Clearly, our encounter at the café on my birthday had tripped something and caused Jarrod's parents to reach out.

After grabbing the ceramic bowl, Lola removed the lid to reveal a leafy green salad.

"What's in the other thing?"

I lifted a linen towel and revealed still-warm slices of homemade bread. My mouth watered.

"She made all your favorites," Lola said, heading into the kitchen. She returned with place settings, and we sat to eat. "This is an olive branch if I've ever seen one. They're trying."

I knew they were, but I didn't have time to think about it. I would have started crying, and that would have delayed my work.

I took infrequent breaks the rest of the night and only stopped working when I could barely keep my eyes open. Finally, at three o'clock Sunday morning, I stood back and observed my finished work. I'd never painted anything like it. But somehow it felt right.

"Lola," I said, my throat hoarse from hours of not speaking, not to mention inhaling paint fumes. I hadn't had anything to eat or drink in a long time. "Lola!"

"Mmm." Lola stretched out on one of the tables and had been sleeping for the past three hours. I had suggested she go home to bed several times, but she refused. Moral support was the official reason, but I figured she didn't want to be alone in the house.

"I'm finished." And just in the nick of time. I knew from Sam that Eli was supposed to get home early Sunday morning.

I walked back to the door so I could get the full effect of what it would be like to walk inside and see the painting first thing.

But it was Lola who said what I didn't have words to verbalize. "Wow."

I turned to find her sitting up on the table, her

feet resting on the seat. "That's beautiful. Eli is going to freak when he sees it."

"I wish I could be a fly on the wall when he walks in."

"Corrie!" Lola said. "Are you kidding me?"

"What?" I walked forward to start cleaning up.

"You can't just let him walk in. Don't you want to do a big reveal so you can catch the full impact of his reaction?"

The truth was, the last thing I wanted was to be there when he saw the mural. What if he didn't like it? I was also afraid he might still be angry with me. He wouldn't show it, I'm sure, but I would see it in his eyes and know.

Lola scowled, clearly disgusted at my decision not to break out the band and fireworks. "Fine, then. Let's go home."

"Help me rinse my brushes and pick up the mess." I grinned at her. "You know the rules."

"I hate rules." I didn't begrudge her the weary moan. "Can't we come back and clean up tomorrow?"

I shook my head. "I want Eli to see the mural without all the clutter on the floor."

"Fine," she grumbled. "But since I gave up spending time with Joe for two evenings to help you, I think we could do something I want at least once."

"Stop trying to make me feel guilty. You've spent lots of time with Joe."

We cleaned up the mess, and within the hour we were home.

"Night," Lola said, yawning around the word. She trudged upstairs to the guest room, and I fell onto the couch and pulled up my quilt.

I closed my eyes, aware that for once I could sleep without that aching sense of longing for Jarrod.

My thoughts went to Eli. I imagined his reaction when he walked into the chow hall in the morning, and my lips curved into a smile and my heart fluttered. I gathered a deep breath and my body relaxed.

Eli

I unlocked the door to the chow hall. Normally I didn't go to the camp until after Sunday service, but after two nights away, I rose early and headed over to check things out. I recognized the strong smell of paint before I stepped inside the chow hall. Light from the rising sun blasted into the room. Something felt different. Frowning, I walked two steps, put my hands in my pockets, and tried to make sense of the unsettled feeling, the smell of paint. And then it hit me. Slowly, I lifted my eyes toward the back of the room. I drew a sharp breath, and my jaw dropped open.

For the instant it took for my brain to catch up, I actually felt dizzy. Then I refocused and walked to the middle of the room, where I stopped again to take in the sight before me. Only Corrie had heard me say I'd like a mural to help the kids remember that even though they were separated from their parents, God saw them both at the same time. My heart leaped in my chest as I stared at what she had done.

This incredible piece of art she had created exceeded my wishes. I stared at the beauty in front of me, and tears burned my eyes. I didn't even attempt to hold them back. I wouldn't have been able to anyway.

The scene in front of me showed a kid wearing jeans and a T-shirt standing in a kid's bedroom. The bed was made, but books were tossed across the twin-sized comforter, as though dumped there after a long school day. A few articles of clothing cluttered the floor. The kid stood looking into a full-length mirror, but the observer could only see the child from behind.

I don't know how Corrie accomplished it, but you couldn't tell the child's gender. The teen in the mural honestly could have been a boy or a girl. Any of my campers would be able to relate.

But the kid wasn't looking at himself or herself. Instead, the reflected image was of a soldier in full combat uniform. Again, the gender remained neutral. The soldier knelt in the desert sand, as though deep in prayer. I got the sense that the kid was so close he or she could step through the mirror and be instantly cradled in the soldier's arms.

A pair of long white wings surrounded them both, as though God had sent the guardian to hold child and soldier alike.

A soft gasp startled me, and I swung around to find my mother standing at the door, tears pouring down her face.

Smiling, I walked back to the door to stand next to her. "Well, that explains how she got in."

Without apology, she nodded. "When she told me she wanted to paint you a mural, I had no idea. Oh, Eli . . . What a precious gift."

I wasn't sure if she meant the mural was Corrie's gift to me or if she was referring to Corrie's God-given ability to paint a story.

My mom swiped at her tears. "You know what Dad would say?"

I shook my head.

"He'd say, 'The girl can swing a brush.' "

Joy welled up inside me as I looked back at the wall. I took it all in, as though seeing it for the first time.

I looked away only when Mom took my hand. "You know what I say?"

I frowned. "What?"

"Corrie is worth fighting for."

Twenty

Corrie

I wasn't sure if I slept. But when I opened my eyes, he was there . . . Jarrod. Sitting on the edge of the couch. I tried to sit up, longing to throw my arms around him. But he shook his head, holding up a staying hand, and my body refused to move. I shoved down the miniscule second of hesitation. He smiled but didn't speak. His fingers started at my eyebrows, then lightly trailed downward, closing my eyes as though I were dead. Only I felt completely alive. My body tingled. I sighed as his fingertips continued along my jaw line. My throat. Tears burned my eyes, and I tried to open them, but like my limbs, they refused to obey my brain.

"Relax," I heard him say, but not with my ears. It was as though he spoke directly to my mind, and I understood his presence there. I felt his fingers touch my collarbone. I tensed. As much as I missed his touch, making love in every room in the house, holding each other, this wasn't right, and I knew I had to stop it. But my body refused to move, no matter how much I wanted to sit up and push him away.

Fear clenched my stomach. In my mind's eye I saw myself thrashing about, fighting for release, but my body stayed immovable as fear multiplied.

Please, I thought. *Jarrod, I don't want this. It's not right.*

"*Shh,*" he spoke to my mind. "*Take it easy, baby.*"

I remembered Sam telling me if I felt it wasn't right, then it wasn't, and I could make it stop. But I couldn't remember what else she said because my head was so fuzzy, my stomach clenched with fear. I had never been afraid of Jarrod before.

I'm not sure if I prayed, to be honest. I do know I thought, *Oh, God, please.* I suppose that's a prayer.

In that instant, a knock sounded, loud and purposeful. I opened my eyes, trembling, and sat up. Disoriented, I looked around. Sunlight filtered in, so I knew I had been on the couch for at least a couple of hours.

The knock came again from the back door. Louder this time. I shoved back the quilt, stood on shaky legs, and stumbled down the hall.

I opened it to find Eli standing on the deck, staring at me and shaking his head wordlessly. I pushed open the screen, and at the sight of his kind smile, all my fear fell away. Stepping onto the deck, I went into his arms. "I'm so sorry for what I said, Eli. Please forgive me."

"I forgave you before I drove away that day,

honey." I felt the simple pressure of a kiss on my head and smiled as the disturbing dream faded from my mind. His arms felt strong and warm and good. But I knew I couldn't stay there forever. I stood back so he could come inside. "You saw the mural, I take it?"

He nodded. "I wish I had a way to express how it made me feel."

"You just did, Eli." My heart soared at his joy with the painting.

"Want some coffee? Plenty of sugar, since you can't drink my coffee any other way."

"You could just learn to make a decent pot." A wry grin slid across his lips.

"Ingrate." I rolled my eyes and walked down the hall to the kitchen, aware with each step that he was close behind. If I turned around suddenly, I'd be in his arms again. My face warmed at the direction of my thoughts. I started the coffee, using a few less grounds than I'd normally use.

He sat, stretched out his weak leg, and rubbed his thigh. "How late were you at the camp last night?"

"Till around four, I think."

He glanced at his watch. "It's only eight. I bet I woke you up, didn't I?"

Yes, but I was so glad he had. "It's okay. I don't want to sleep the day away anyway." I pulled two mugs from the cabinet while the coffee brewed.

I grabbed the sugar and cream and headed to

the table, where I sat across from him. "So you really like it?"

He grinned, spooning sugar in his coffee. "Corrie, *like* is so far from what I felt when I saw that painting. You have a rare talent." He sipped his coffee. "Did Jarrod ever see any of your work?"

Shoving out a sigh, I nodded. "Before we got engaged."

Jarrod had always told me he didn't get it. I laughed at him for being unable to see beyond the obvious, but he was military. He saw everything in black and white, and I respected his perspective. And he truly tried to encourage me, but I knew he had no real passion for my work. So when we married, I put it aside and found new interests. It was enough that he had passion for me.

Eli reached across the table and took my hand. I looked at him and felt my stomach flutter the way a girl's does when she likes a boy. The feeling took me by surprise, and I wondered if it showed on my face. "I hope this is only the beginning of your return to painting. It's a gift from God."

"Some other people had a hand in the process."

"Oh?" He sipped his coffee, then set it back on the table. I told him about Jerry donating the art supplies, the guy at the café whose name I'd never know sending lunch, and, of course, Jarrod's mother.

"There's still food in the fridge if you get hungry and don't feel like going to town to eat lunch. We put most of it in freezer bags so I could wash the dishes and give them back."

He laughed when I told him how people came and tried to get in to see the painting. "Lola ran interference, but it wasn't easy keeping them out. You're kind of a hero to these folks." He had definitely been a hero to me, but I couldn't bring myself to tell him that either.

As if on cue, Lola stumbled into the kitchen. "Can't someone make morning stop for a few more hours?"

" 'Fraid not," Eli said, softening his words with that easy laugh of his.

"Thank God. Caffeine—eight hours of sleep in a cup." She poured her coffee and walked over, bringing the pot with her. "I'll be drinking the first cup as if I'm in a chugging contest."

"You could have come home, you know."

"And leave you alone? No way." She closed her eyes and took in the aroma of her coffee.

"Sheesh," I said. "You look like a coffee commercial."

Ignoring my remark, she focused her gaze on Eli.

"So what do you think of Corrie's painting?" Lola asked, perking up a little.

"I think God gave her a piece of His heart, and she put it on the wall."

I sucked in a long, cool breath.

Lola lifted her mug. "Well said, Eli."

The words he'd spoken were beautiful but left me feeling confused. "What does it mean to put a piece of God's heart on a wall?"

He reached for the Bible that I had left on the table the day Sam gave it to me.

"Be my guest," I offered. "It was your dad's."

He didn't seem surprised as he opened it up and flipped through the well-worn pages. "Mom said she was planning to give it to you." He stopped ruffling pages and turned the Bible toward me. "Psalm 91 verse 4," he said. "Will you read it?"

I hadn't looked at an open Bible in so many years, I felt a little embarrassed. I wanted to ask him to read the verse but knew I was just being stupid about it. "He shall cover thee with his feathers, and under his wings shalt thou trust."

The words sounded strange, and the cadence felt unfamiliar on my ears. I flashed back to the image of my Gramps sitting in his corner wing chair, black book in hand, weeping from the beauty and comfort of the words he read in a Bible much like this one. But I had never understood. Give me *The Odyssey* or any of Shakespeare's plays, and I could read for days, but the Bible . . . I just didn't get it. Perhaps that was the reason for my spiritual apathy.

I tried on a smile. "That's nice."

I knew Eli wanted me to experience the same

feelings of awe he seemed to have taken away from studying the mural, but I wasn't feeling it, and he knew my face too well to be fooled.

"I like the Good News Translation," Eli said. He lifted his iPhone from his pocket and slid through the pages until he found what he wanted. "Here. 'He will cover you with his wings; you will be safe in his care; his faithfulness will protect and defend you.' "

"That's lovely, Eli," Lola said. "And exactly the feeling that painting gives." She shook her head and looked at me. "Your painting is going to help ease some of those kids' fear about their folks being in a war zone. How does that make you feel?"

I didn't know for sure what to say. The two of them seemed to believe my motives were so much purer than they'd been. I'd just had an apology to make, and this was my Hallmark card. I still needed to process exactly how I had been able to give creative expression to Eli's wishes for the wall. True, I was painting again, and, true, it filled a hole that had long been empty, even though I hadn't realized it. But I didn't want them to think I was going to preach through art. "I've never thought about painting religious pictures. I mean, I admit that this one was special to me because of the camp kids, and I sincerely hope they'll draw some comfort from it. But now that I'm starting to paint again, I don't know if I want to do a bunch of pictures of angels and demons and old Bible stories."

Eli closed his dad's Bible. "Corrie, art started in God's heart way before He painted His first sunset across His newly created sky. The gift He gave you is so that you can give expression to the thoughts and feelings inside you. If you're angry, paint that. If you're sad, paint that. If you feel like laughing, try to put it on canvas. Does it really matter what you paint as long as you're honest? Even though the mural shows God's ability to love and protect His own, it doesn't mean that as an artist you have to paint Bible stories."

"You should show him what you painted the other night when Joe took me to dinner," Lola said. "It worried me at first, but hearing you talk, Eli, I think maybe it was something she needed to get off her chest."

"I'm intrigued." Eli's eyes captured mine. "What do you say? Mind showing it to me?"

"I don't really think it's something you'd like. I was having a bit of a meltdown."

He smiled. "I've seen you have a meltdown."

"You saw the aftereffects of my meltdown."

Lola's eyebrows rose. "Hangover?"

My lips twisted. "Yeah, my early birthday present. The gift that made me miserable and thwarted any desire to ever sip another drop of brandy."

"Note to self," she said. "Only nonalcoholic gifts from now on."

"You had another meltdown?" Eli asked.

I gave a reckless wave of my hand. "It was after I got home from helping you clean the camp the other day."

"Did I do something to upset you?" Eli asked. His voice was soft, as though my careless words had just taken hold.

"Eli . . . what could you possibly have done? You fed me filet mignon medium rare."

"Wow," Lola said. "You had me at filet mignon."

Looking from one to the other, I felt like the Grinch whose heart had grown three sizes as mine swelled with love for the two people I trusted most in this world.

"Okay." I stood, even though I worried about what he might think. "Come on. I'll take you upstairs to the art room."

"That's what you're calling your studio?"

I nodded. "It just seems like more of an art room than studio."

"I'll stay down here and cook breakfast while you take Eli to see it," Lola said.

I led the way up the steps haltingly. I didn't want to share that picture at all, but especially not with Eli. Eli followed me slowly. His limp seemed more pronounced this morning.

"Does your leg hurt today?" I asked.

"Just aches a bit. Rain must be coming."

I opened the door to the art room, and Eli followed me to the easel.

I kept my gaze on the painting itself so I didn't have to watch his expression.

Eli didn't react badly. Most likely he had no idea what he was looking at anyway. When he finally spoke, his words surprised me. "So you prefer to create in the abstract instead of the realistic way you did the mural."

"It's the way I developed as an artist." I paused, looking for the right words. "But this was more anger poured out on canvas, like you talked about earlier."

He tilted his head and studied the painting, clearly trying to figure it out. His effort touched me more than I would have given voice to, but I was learning that Eli had even more layers than I'd imagined. "So we're looking at something that has to do with Jarrod's death?"

I nodded. "Most people wouldn't have gotten that in a hundred years."

"Well, if you weren't mad at me, I have to assume your anger was about your loss."

"I don't know about that," I said. "I can do some pretty frenzied painting every time Mother calls. I could have just gotten off the phone with her."

"Okay, I'll give you that." He chuckled. I had grown to welcome the pleasant sound. "Tell me about this story you've painted."

He focused hard on the painting, his hands stuffed into jeans pockets. Though I hated to tell him because I feared he might flip out, I had

336

allowed the door to be opened and had pretty much invited Eli to walk through. "It's a painting of Jarrod's death."

He didn't react, which I thought was to his credit. "It's honest."

"I know I shouldn't have painted it this way. It just kind of happened."

Eli turned to me and took my hands. He kissed one and then the other. With a feather touch, he turned each over and discovered my palms with his fingertips. He moved upward until his fingertips pressed against mine. "God isn't afraid of your honest emotions, nor is He afraid of how you express that anger in your art."

I couldn't hold back a laugh. I pulled my hands away and motioned toward the painting. "Even if it comes out looking like this?"

"Especially if it comes out like that. If we haven't got any pain, we aren't living. The need to express emotion is a sign of God's mercy for a very imperfect creation. He's not going to hold it against you."

"Thanks, Eli," I said, desperately aware that despite my gift for painting, words eluded me more often than not.

We left the room and walked toward the stairs. I shuddered when we walked past my bedroom. I'd been so busy the last few days I hadn't been in the house that much, and I still hadn't dealt with what had happened to me the day of the reading.

The door was wide open, though, and Eli stopped walking and stared at the far wall, which Billy's painting still leaned against.

"Is that a new picture?"

"Yes, but I'm getting rid of it."

"Why?" Clearly, he was too far away to see the figure in the attic window.

I hadn't even told Lola about my frightening experience with the thing coming out at me. Apparently no one else had seen what I had. I remembered Sam's words about how Jarrod would never want me to be afraid.

"Come in the room and I'll show you," I said. We walked to the wall, and I lifted it in both hands, holding it out for Eli to see.

"It's a good likeness of the house," he said. "Is it something the artist did that isn't up to your standard?"

"Look at the attic."

His eyes trailed to the image. "Who did you say painted this?"

I explained how Billy had come over the night Jarrod died and this is what he saw. "Aunt Trudy believes Jarrod's spirit returned here that day."

I had barely spoken the words when my hair-brush slid off the dresser and dropped to the floor.

Eli frowned. "Corrie," he said, "you know better by now, don't you?"

"I think so." With a heavy breath, I told him about the frightening day of the reading. Even now, as I relayed the story, I felt a chill, as though the temperature had dropped by a few degrees.

"Corrie," he said, "you know that's not holy. And you know it isn't Jarrod."

I swallowed hard as cold waves of fear moved over me. I grabbed his hand and held on tight. "I *do* know."

In a beat, the door slammed, a violent act of resistance by something that I now knew couldn't be Jarrod. Slowly, the door opened to its full width and slammed again, showing an angry response to my rejection.

"Can you make it stop?" I whispered.

"Jesus can," he said. He gathered in a breath and said a simple prayer: "Lord, You have the words that calm the storm. We're nothing in our strength, but Your name won't fail."

The door opened and slammed a third time. Eli opened his eyes and calmly spoke into the room. "Demon, you have no place here. You have to go because of the name of Jesus."

I held on to my breath, waiting, my heart pounding in my ears. "Is it gone?"

"Yes." His confidence was calming, and I loosened my grip on his hand but didn't let go completely. "It may try to come back," he warned. "It's been in this house for many years."

My fear returned with a vengeance, and I tightened my grip again. "I think I better move."

His hand tightened around mine. "You can do

that, but if things start happening again and you're alone, just call on the name of Jesus the way I did."

"I'm not a preacher, Eli. I don't really even know how to pray."

"A prayer is just communicating with God. The words don't matter. It's the heart that He sees clearly anyway. Even so, if you believe in Jesus, He's given you His name. It's not about the person speaking it. It's all Him."

I didn't want Eli to go, but when I saw him glance at the clock, I knew he wouldn't be in the house much longer. He confirmed what I had been thinking. "I wish I could stay," he said, "but I have a service to conduct in a little while, and my congregation is counting on me."

Finally, I released his hand. He flexed his fingers, and I could only imagine how tightly I'd been holding on. "Of course," I said, my voice stronger than I really felt. "Definitely get out of here." I picked up the painting that I'd dropped when the first slam startled me. "Will you take this out to the garbage bin? I don't want it in here." The memory of that thing floating toward me made me shudder.

He took it from me and slid it under his arm. We went downstairs, and the smell of bacon frying wafted through the house. My stomach growled. "You don't have time to stop for a quick break-fast?"

"I wish," he said. "I'm a bacon and eggs man, and that's making my mouth water."

Lola walked out of the kitchen. "I thought I heard you guys. What was all that banging around up there?"

"Long story," I said. "I'll explain later."

She noticed Eli was poised to leave. "You're not staying for breakfast? I fried a pound of bacon. It's Oscar Mayer, and you know that cost an arm and a leg." She gave a quirky grin. "Mine, not the pig's."

Eli laughed. "I wish I had time."

"He has a sermon to preach," I said.

Lola scowled. "Well, so much for my plan to persuade you to stay. At least wait so I can go get you a few slices of bacon."

"Okay," Eli said. "I can do that."

Lola returned in less than a minute and handed him a paper plate with six slices of perfectly crispy bacon. She motioned to the painting still tucked under his arm as he took the plate and thanked her. "What are you doing with that?"

"Corrie asked me to put it in the garbage on my way out." He bent and brushed a kiss on my cheek. "Thank you again for the incredible gift, Corrie. I feel like a kid at Christmas."

"You should see how well she paints Santa."

I rolled my eyes. "Don't listen to her," I said. "She thinks she's funny. I don't paint Santa."

Balancing the bacon in one hand and holding

the painting under his arm, he nodded toward the door. "Can you get that?"

"Sure."

"Thanks." He stepped onto the deck. "I'll call you after church—unless you want to come with?"

I shook my head. Two nights without sleep had caught up with me, and my body ached in ways I hadn't known were possible. "I'm dead on my feet."

"Okay, then back to the original plan. I'll call you as soon as I finish with the service." He peered closer at me. "Or maybe I should just let you call me when you wake up so I don't disturb you."

"No," I said. "I won't sleep for more than a couple of hours anyway."

He laughed. "Okay."

I could still feel the gentle pressure of his kiss on my cheek as I watched him limp down the steps. There was a long, low whistle, and I turned around. Lola stood there, smug and smiling.

"What was that little peck on the cheek?"

His kiss had definitely been less peckish and more of a caress. I felt my cheeks warm.

"I take it you might like Mr. Eli Murdock. Do I detect romance in the air?"

I brushed past her and headed to the kitchen. "Who knows what you detect?" I laughed. I dropped into the chair Eli had vacated when we went upstairs.

"Besides, maybe you should concentrate on your own love life. I haven't seen Joe around the last few days."

"Gee, Corrie," she shot back. "I wonder why. I've been kind of busy."

"Well, I appreciate the completely unnecessary sacrifice." I grinned. "Are you going to see him again?"

As I sat down in my chair, Lola opened the refrigerator and took out a dozen fresh country eggs that Sam had insisted I bring home one day last week. She went to the stove. "How do you want your eggs, scrambled or scrambled?"

"Um, how about scrambled?"

"Good, that's the only way I know how to make them." She grabbed a slice of bacon, broke off a piece, and popped it into her mouth. She brought me the other half of the slice. "Have an appetizer."

"Yum," I said as my taste buds enjoyed the perfect blend of crispy and chewy.

"So," Lola said, "now that you've accepted my bribe offering, I want to know honestly if you're having feelings for Eli."

"I should have known you wouldn't give me half your piece of bacon just because. Figures you had ulterior motives."

"And who did I learn that from?"

She glanced back at me and grinned.

"Mother," we said in unison.

Could I truly learn to love again? That seemed

to be the question of the hour. Could I love Eli? Could I love Jesus again?

They were two very different loves, but each required me to let go of Jarrod once and for all. I released a heavy breath. "We have time to figure it out," I said.

"So you're open to a relationship with Eli?"

"I think so." Thunder rumbled in the far distance. Eli's bum leg had told him right. It sounded like rain was on the way. "What about you? Are you going to see Joe?"

Shaking her head, she took out two plates.

"Lola! You like him. Why won't you see him again?"

Lola clammed up. She spooned scrambled eggs onto each plate, then grabbed the platter of bacon and headed over. I hopped up and took forks out of the drawer and a few napkins from the cabinet.

"Corrie, I've been thinking since yesterday that it's time for me to go home. I'm leaving today."

My heart sank. I realized how much I'd grown used to having her around. "Just like that?" That was Lola. Impulsive. She had shown up at my door out of nowhere, and now she was leaving as quickly as she'd come.

"Watching you paint just made me hungry to get back to using my own gift. I can't do that unless I go home and find another job."

I was glad Lola recognized her skills as a gift from God, but to go on the spur of the moment, without the chance to even have one more walk by the bridge, made me sad. "How'd you get a flight on such short notice?" I asked.

"I'm driving the rental and dropping it off at the Dallas airport when I get home. Mother's going to pick me up."

"You already spoke to Mother about this?"

"I had to make sure she could pick me up. I'm trying not to spend fifty dollars on cab fare."

"My, people come and go so quickly around here."

She rolled her eyes. "Dramatic much, Dorothy Gale?"

"Have you told Joe?"

She shook her head and pushed her eggs around her plate with her fork. "I thought I'd send him a text while he's at church."

"Lola! You can't do that."

Still she didn't make eye contact. "He probably turns off his phone when he's in church. It's not like it's going to disturb anyone."

"We both know that's not what I meant." I stood and brought the coffee decanter to the table, poured myself a cup, and pushed the decanter across the table for Lola. "If you're driving home today, you'd best pump more caffeine into your body."

"Thanks." She poured the coffee into her cup. "You know I'm not good at good-byes. And frankly, Corrie, I really like Joe. More than he likes me, as much as I hate to admit it. It's better just to send him a text, and we can both go back to what we were doing before we met."

I hadn't seen Lola this way about a man in a long time. It was pretty clear she wouldn't get over him very quickly.

"I understand," I said. The last thing I'd want to do was make her feel cornered. It wasn't my place to lecture her on protocol for breaking up. She had to do what was best for her own heart. Clearly, she'd made her choice.

"I'm glad you're ready to move on, Corrie," she said. "I was really starting to worry about you."

"I was starting to worry about myself, quite frankly." My admission today that the things I'd been experiencing weren't from Jarrod spooked me. I hoped like crazy the demon didn't come back.

The Bible still lay open to the verse Eli had asked me to read. Was I really ready to lay my heart back on the line? I had just come to the place where I could start turning Jarrod loose. It had been seven months since the funeral, and I'd been hurting for so long, I wasn't sure how to close my eyes and not see him in my mind.

PART THREE

You prepare a table before me
in the presence of my enemies;
You have anointed my head with oil;
My cup overflows.

Twenty-One

Corrie

Lola and I cleaned the kitchen after breakfast. Then I followed her upstairs to the guest room and sat on her bed while she packed. The faint rumblings of thunder continued in the distance, but so far there was no real threat of rain that would hinder Lola's drive home.

When she was all packed, she and I walked outside together. We got to the car and she hugged me tight. "I guess I can go back home and report to Mother that you're doing well so she should stop trying to get you to come back to Dallas."

"I'd appreciate if we could stick to that story."

I waved after her as she inched the rental down the hill. When she was gone from sight, I stood in the middle of my circular drive, hugged my body, and fought against overwhelming dread at going back inside. I glanced at the trash cart and saw the picture leaning against the container, waiting for the trash guys to pick it up in the morning.

I'd already missed my nap and was too keyed up to sleep anyway. My mind replayed Lola's question about my feelings for Eli. I had been in Saunders Creek only a month, and my friendship with him had grown fast. I couldn't help but wonder how Jarrod's folks would feel if I got involved with Eli. Clearly, they still considered me part of the family. Or at least they were making an effort to get in touch with me. I hadn't even tried to return the effort.

I searched around every corner as I walked inside, hoping, half praying that the demon Eli had made leave wouldn't be there. I didn't feel or see anything paranormal, and I was relieved. My phone rang, and I grabbed it and answered Eli's call. I told him about Lola leaving. "Did you get to nap?" he asked.

"No, but I've got a second wind, so I think I'll just go with that."

I walked into the kitchen as we talked. The coffeepot was empty, and so was the can of grounds.

"I have to meet with my camp counselors in a little while," Eli said, "but if you're up for dinner, I'd like to take you out later. We could go into Springfield. I know a nice Japanese restaurant."

"Sounds great."

"Pick you up around six?"

We hung up, and I set my phone on the counter. I desperately needed coffee if I was going to make it through the day and then have dinner out. I suppose it was our first date. A smile touched my lips. I hadn't been on a first date in nine years.

I knew I had another can of coffee somewhere in this kitchen. I opened the pantry and spied it on the shelf. Something else stared out at me from the closet too. The American flag I had so despised. Forgetting about the coffee, I pulled it out. I knew what I had to do. I headed upstairs, showered, and picked out a light blue summer dress. I started to walk out of the room but heard my mother's voice in my head. *"I can see straight through that dress, Corrine. Put on a slip."* With a sigh, I yanked off the dress, pulled on a silky slip, and then put the dress on again. Once I was presentable, I went back down the stairs, packed up Liz's dishes, grabbed the flag, and headed for my Jeep.

I gathered all the courage my body could muster and drove to the Saunders' farm. Mr. Saunders had all but stopped farming, but a few head of cattle still grazed in the field behind the house. The sky had clouded over, and we were about to get our first rain in a week. The temperature had dropped ten degrees since Lola left, and the thunder had gotten closer.

Jarrod's parents were sitting on the porch when I arrived. They stared at me wordlessly. My hands shook, and my legs barely held me up as I approached the porch. Liz stood up and went into the house, and my courage nearly failed. Tears welled up in my eyes. Clearly I'd hurt her so badly she didn't even want to be in my presence.

Swallowing down my fear, hurt, sorrow, and guilt, I stopped at the bottom of the porch. I didn't want to go any farther if Jarrod's folks didn't want me here.

"Well, it's about time you got yourself over here, gal," Fred said. He smoked a pipe, and talked around it.

"Yes sir," I said. "I'm so sorry it's taken this long to come by."

"We thought maybe you just been hurtin' too bad to see Jarrod's folks." His gaze narrowed. "That it?"

I wasn't going to lie to this man. "Partly."

He puffed on his pipe. Raindrops began to fall on me, but he still didn't invite me onto the covered porch, and I didn't impose. "Partly, eh? What was the other part?"

The screen door opened and Liz reappeared. "Good Lord, Fred! Why didn't you ask Corrie onto the porch?"

"Figured she'd come on up iffen she wanted."

"You know well and good our Corrie wasn't raised that way. You have to ask her. She's got manners." She turned to me. "Honey, get out of the rain before you get soaked. I brung you some tea. It's good and sweet just the way you always liked it."

I stared at her. Then him. And I saw Jarrod. I remembered how I loved listening to these two and their incessant, but oddly affectionate, bickering. Tears began to trail down my cheeks, and the sobs began. I dropped to my knees in the grass at the bottom of the steps. I clutched my gift to my chest and wept. Somehow, Mrs. Saunders had descended the steps and knelt beside me. I clung to her, and we held each other for I don't know how long. The rain was still falling when, finally, we climbed the steps, still in each other's arms. We sat on the swing, soaked, cried out, but reunited in our grief over Jarrod's death.

Even Fred teared up when I presented them with the flag that had covered Jarrod's coffin. "But that's for you, Corrie," he said.

I shook my head. "If I had a son, I'd keep it. But it should go to you."

He gathered me close and held me. "It's good to have you back, gal."

I stayed at the Saunders' home for hours. We looked through photos, and I listened to stories about Jarrod's childhood. We cried together and laughed together. I felt safe, wrapped in wings of love. We lost track of time until Fred announced he was going to starve to death if he didn't get some supper.

Gasping, I jumped up from my seat at the kitchen table. Eli would be at my house any minute. "I have to go," I said. "I'm late for dinner with Eli."

Fred and Liz gazed at each other. Silent words passed between them.

I hadn't told them that I wanted to start dating Eli, and even though I knew I had a perfect right, I hated the pain in their eyes. I sat back down. "You know I'll always love Jarrod."

Liz reached out and covered my hand with hers. "We know, Corrie, honey. We couldn't pick a better man for you to love again than Eli."

"Well, it's only dinner."

She nodded. "Jarrod wouldn't want you to be alone, and life is too short to spend it grieving."

"You said that really good, hon," Fred said, his faded brown eyes misty. Jarrod had been the image of this man in his youth, and as I looked at him now, I imagined what we might have been as an older couple.

"No one will ever take his place in my heart."

Liz's hand trembled on top of mine. "I know. Now you go and have a fine time with Eli. We've always said God must be saving him for the best girl out there. Looks like that might be you."

I didn't bother to say "It's only dinner" again. In my heart, I knew better. And as I said good-bye and drove home, I realized there was a new place in my heart with Eli's name on it.

Eli

Corrie's Jeep was gone when I arrived to pick her up for dinner. I walked around to the back of the house and sat on the deck, enjoying the cool air the rain had brought. I dialed her number, just to make sure she was okay, but when it went to voice mail, I smiled. She must have just run out for a quick errand if she forgot to grab her phone. I relaxed into the cushions and allowed the breeze to flow over me. The sky had grown darker again as clouds continued to roll in.

After a clap of thunder, I heard a little whine that sounded like one of the cats might be in trouble. Normally, I left the barn cats alone, and they left everyone else alone, but since Corrie had made an attempt at domesticating "Kitty," he showed up from time to time to cozy up long enough for her to give him something to eat. If she didn't love him so much, I'd have left him, but I knew she would go looking for him the second she heard that distressed meow.

Better me than her. I walked toward the old barn that hadn't been used for anything since Pop passed away. Without Pop to take care of the place, Granny had sold off all the cattle and horses. I would have stayed longer, but she hadn't wanted to keep me from my dream of going to seminary. At least, that's what she'd said.

I opened one side of the heavy double barn doors and went in. I called out "Here, Kitty, Kitty," feeling stupid for doing it. But I also felt a little heroic. The whining was coming from high above, and I realized with a slight groan that he must be in the loft. That explained why he was whining. He must have gotten up and now couldn't get down.

I went to the ladder, and it struck me just how hard I'd fallen for this girl. I wouldn't have climbed an old barn ladder to the loft to rescue a bawling cat for just anyone. "Kitty," I called. "Come here, you dumb animal." I climbed a few more steps, hoping without much conviction that he would just come to me.

I heard Corrie's Jeep coming up the road and turned for a second toward the sound. As I turned back to the ladder, my equilibrium left me, and I felt a weight slam against my chest. A face in the loft loomed over me. I tried desperately to regain my footing, but I knew in a sickening beat that this could be my time. I fell twelve feet. My body landed hard, and I lost my breath as my head connected with old, stale hay on a hard earth floor.

Twenty-Two

Corrie

More thundershowers were moving in, and as I crested the hill that rose to my drive, my heart sped up. Eli's truck sat in front of my house. Thankfully, he had waited—not that I'd really doubted he would. I glanced around, but I didn't see him. I remembered he had a key to the house. Still, I was a bit surprised that he would let himself in when there wasn't an emergency. I didn't mind. I was just surprised. I killed the motor and headed to the house but stopped short. My trash cart was tipped over, presumably from the storm. I righted it, glad none of the garbage had scattered. The container was still firmly shut.

I hurried around to the back and tried the doorknob, but found it unyielding. If Eli had gone inside, he'd locked the door behind him. I slid the house key into the lock and turned the knob.

"Eli?" I called out. "Hey, did you use your key? It's okay if you did."

I walked around a little, knowing he wouldn't go upstairs, even if he did come inside. He had too much respect for my privacy. Had he gone to the bridge?

I dismissed the thought as unlikely. The guy wasn't stupid. He wouldn't do that with a storm coming on.

As if to echo my thoughts, the sky let loose with a loud crack of thunder that shook my house. I walked into the kitchen and saw I had a missed call on my phone. I picked it up. Eli had called just a few minutes ago. I rested my hands on my hips and glanced around the room, truly perplexed.

"Eli!" I don't know why I called out again when

it was clear he wasn't in the house. Maybe it was because I suddenly had a sense of foreboding. And then I felt the presence that Eli had sent away only hours earlier.

Dread made its way through me as I realized my reprieve had been short lived and, as Eli had promised, the evil spirit had returned. My heartbeat quickened as my stomach roiled from the sudden foul odor wafting through the room. That was something new. I recognized its malevolence, and everything in me wanted to run away.

My brain muddled. I knew there was something I could do, something I could say, but fear paralyzed me. *Eli, where are you?*

For some reason, the image of my trash cart lying on the ground flashed to mind. Then it struck me: the painting hadn't been there, where Eli left it. My mind tried to rationalize. Eli must have decided to take it somewhere on the property and permanently destroy the thing. Maybe even burn it.

But no.

I knew where it was, and my body went weak with fear.

The water faucet turned on, and water poured in full force down the sink. I wanted to whimper, *Help me, God. I don't know what to do.*

My eyes found the Bible on the table, still open. In my mind's eye, I could see the wings surrounding the soldier and child in my painting. I walked to the table and lifted the open Bible. I heard a crash behind me and spun around. My coffeepot lay on the floor, the decanter broken into shards of glass.

Anger flooded me. I knew I would have to confront this spirit if I was going to live in my home. I could move away, as Eli said, but I didn't want to. I loved this house, and I had a right to live here. That thing didn't.

I didn't have the courage to close my eyes, but I lifted a prayer just the same. *Tell me what to do, God.*

I had seen the demon leave this morning when Eli spoke. I searched my memories for the right thing to say. Doubt assailed me as I felt my hair being tugged. Would it even listen to me? I wasn't Eli. I didn't have his faith or his goodness. A second later, I remembered Eli's admonishment: it's not about the person, but the name.

I clutched my Bible to my chest as if it were my shield and gasped as the kitchen cabinets began to rattle. This had to stop. I was tired of this evil thing playing with my life. I was so ready to live without soul-wrenching grief and fear.

I stood in the center of the kitchen, so afraid I honestly believed I might pass out from fear. The hair on my arms and the back of my neck stood up. It was now or never. "I know you aren't Jarrod." The cabinet doors banged so hard they seemed about to come off the hinges. My throat tightened, threatening to shut off my air. But somehow, I found the courage to whisper.

"You can't stay. I want you to leave this house in Jesus's name. And don't come back."

The cabinet doors stopped banging; the water stopped pouring from the faucet. The putrid smell dissolved, and I was left holding my breath, waiting.

I remained still, as peace flooded the room and washed over me. Standing there I came to realize that Sam and Eli had been so right. My breathing returned to normal, and I stood in wonder that so much power resides in one simple name. All these years I had lived without the Person behind the power, but He had come through for me despite my failure to so much as acknowledge Him in years.

I climbed the steps to my bedroom and was not at all surprised to see that the painting had been returned. I stepped in, bolstered by what had happened downstairs. I walked to the painting and grabbed it. Once outside, I marched to the trash cart. I slammed the painting onto the ground, knowing this time it would not be coming back into my house. For Billy's sake, I hated to trash it. No artist wants to have his work tossed out like that, but I had to make an exception this time.

As I turned around to head back to the house, I saw movement from the barn. From my vantage point, I saw the barn door swing open and bang shut.

Eli? I couldn't imagine why he'd want to go to the barn, especially when it was about to storm. Surely he'd be in any second. The wind caught the barn door again and blew it open.

I approached cautiously, knowing there were loose boards on the ground and scrap metal here and there. I'd planned to clean it up eventually, but the guys hadn't gotten to that yet since we'd focused on the house remodel. I caught the door midswing as the wind whipped at my skirt and blew my hair across my face.

I walked inside. "Eli?" The door slammed hard behind me, and I jumped as it opened again with a groan. And then I heard another groan. It sounded human. Just then my eyes caught movement in the darkened old building. "Oh my goodness! Eli!"

I rushed to the side of the room and knelt down next to him. Barely conscious, he mumbled as blood stained the hay beneath his head. My phone was inside, so I lifted his cell phone from his front shirt pocket.

"Pushed," he mumbled.

"Shh," I said. "Don't try to tell me what happened yet. I'm going to call for an ambulance."

His breathing was ragged, and I wondered if he had fluid filling his lungs. *That's it,* I told myself. *No more* Grey's Anatomy *for me.*

I dialed 911 and dispatch answered within a couple of rings. "I need an ambulance," I said. I gave the rural address and then told him point-by-point directions. I gave him Eli's phone number and insisted he call if they got lost. "Hurry," I said. "I don't know for sure what happened."

"Is he conscious, ma'am?" the dispatcher asked.

"Barely. Please, just hurry."

I knelt next to him as he drifted in and out of consciousness. Somehow, his hand was between my hands, and I kissed it over and over. "Eli, listen to me," I said as my heart nearly exploded with fear that he wouldn't recover from whatever had happened here. "You're going to have to fight. I'm not strong enough to lose the only two men I've ever loved in less than eight months."

His hand tightened around mine, barely, and only for a second, but I felt a sense of peace. Still, I prayed while I waited for the ambulance. The rain finally began to fall. It dropped onto us. "I guess the barn roof leaks, Eli," I whispered. I did my best to keep my hands over his face so he wouldn't get rained on, but it didn't do much good. While I waited and prayed, I looked him over. His head had a gash by his ear. That's where the blood was coming from. I wasn't about to leave him, not even to go inside for a towel. He had gotten hurt because I wasn't home, and I wasn't about to leave him to get hurt again. But I needed to find something to stop the bleeding.

There wasn't much to my dress. No jacket or anything. "Oh," I said aloud as I remembered I had put on a slip. It wouldn't be very absorbent, but maybe I could use it to apply pressure. I stood, reached under my dress, and yanked it down, then stepped out of the undergarment. It wasn't much, but I folded it and pressed it against the bleeding wound.

Eli mumbled something barely audible. My heart soared. If he was lucid, maybe he was okay.

I leaned down close to him. "What did you say, Eli?"

"I saw you take off your slip."

For a second my mind registered only confusion. He saw me? Then I rolled my eyes. He was trying to tease me. Battered and wounded, and he was being Eli.

"You behave yourself," I said, pressing harder against the wound as the blood began to soak into the worthless silky material. "Can you tell me what happened?"

"Kitty," he murmured.

"Kitty?"

"I thought he was in the loft, so I climbed up."

I turned to see the ladder. Close to the top, three rungs were broken. "You fell off the ladder." Now it made sense. "Oh, Eli. You were going after Kitty and fell. I'm so sorry."

"Shh," he said.

I could see there was effort involved, and I wanted him to just be still. "Don't try to talk," I said, trying to control my tears.

I heard the sirens outside, coming up the road. "The ambulance is here," I said. "I'm going over to the door to wave them in. Just be still."

"Wait, Corrie. Wait."

But I didn't want to chance the ambulance missing us.

"I'll be back."

I waved to the ambulance, and they drove past the house to the barn. By the time I got back to Eli's side, he was unconscious again.

Twenty-Three

Eli

I could tell as soon as I woke up that someone had filled me with painkillers. I was woozy and could barely stay awake.

"He's coming to again." My mom's voice.

"Mom," I said, keeping my eyes closed, not that I could open them through the drugs they'd given me. I heard her name come out, "Mum."

"I'm here," she said. She took my hand.

I nodded, wishing I had words or energy to ask for Corrie, but blackness overwhelmed me again.

The next time I remember waking, Corrie sat next to me in what looked like an extremely uncomfortable chair. Her legs were pulled to her side and covered up with a thin hospital blanket. Her eyes were closed, her head resting on her hand.

My heart swelled with love for her. Slowly, the memory of what had happened came back, from falling off the ladder—no, I was pushed by human hands—to seeing her take off her slip. I grinned. Her eyes opened, and she caught me staring.

"Eli," she said, my name almost a gasp in her throat. "Oh, you're smiling." She stood, and the blanket dropped to her feet. Without bothering to pick it up, she stepped over and came to me. She took my hand. "How do you feel?"

"Like I could wake up every day to watching you sleeping next to me." I'm sure it was the drugs talking, but hey, I wasn't lying.

Mom came to the end of the bed and touched my leg. "The doctor said you're one lucky guy. Especially after Corrie told us what happened. It's not often a man can fall from that high up on a ladder and walk away with a concussion and a sprained arm."

Relief moved over me. No wonder I couldn't stay awake.

"You have a gash on your head too, and sixteen stitches," Corrie said. She hadn't dropped my hand.

Mom seemed to anticipate my next question. "The doctor said you can go home tomorrow. The blow to the head was pretty bad, and he wants to watch you one more night. And only if you have someone to watch over you." I knew what that meant. Mom would insist I go to her house, and she'd likely win that argument, so there wasn't any sense in attempting to talk her out of it.

"I've been here a whole night already?"

Mom nodded. "It's Monday afternoon."

I groaned. I'd never get the camp ready in time. "I wonder if I will need to cancel the camp. Or at least the first couple of weeks."

Corrie shook her head. "Joe has that covered. He went after Lola before any of this happened, so he won't be back for a couple of days, but he's got some guys working out there. He told me to tell you not to worry about anything."

"That's a relief. I'll call him as soon as they'll let me use the phone. Wait, what do you mean he went after Lola?"

Mom cleared her throat. "I'll leave the two of you alone."

She patted Corrie's shoulder on the way out, and I noted the love in her eyes. I guess when a person saves your son's life, there would be nothing but love to reflect. I shifted my gaze back to Corrie. "So, Lola and Joe?"

"Oh, Eli, don't bother about that now. You need to rest."

"Sounds like something's going on. I'd rather know about it than wonder."

She pressed her lips together.

"You're denying a wounded man?"

She gave a little laugh. "Oh my goodness. Fine. Lola left to drive back to Dallas without saying good-bye to Joe. She figured they couldn't have a long-distance relationship, so she'd just high-tail it back without the drama of good-bye."

"And Joe went after her to change her mind?" I hadn't realized how much Joe cared for Corrie's sister.

She nodded. "Lola called earlier. They're going to try to figure something out." She shrugged. "I'm not sure what's going to happen, but best-case scenario—for me—is for them to fall madly in love, get married, and live right in Saunders Creek."

"I can't imagine Joe as a city slicker."

"I can't imagine Lola as a small-town girl, but you never know." She attempted a stern look but placed her hand in mine, and I felt anything but scolded. "Now enough about that. Okay? You need to worry about getting yourself all better."

I lay there, enjoying the feel of Corrie's hand in mine. I realized she was wearing the same dress she'd been wearing in the barn. "You've been here all night?" I asked.

"Yes." The simple answer spoke to me as— more than a word—a promise. I dared hope she might love me the way I loved her. I wanted to be careful, though. If I moved too fast, I might lose her.

"I'm so relieved you'll be okay." Her breath caught in her throat.

I laced my fingers with hers. "You saved my life."

She shook her head and tears filled her eyes. "You wouldn't be here if it weren't for me."

Shock bolted through me. She blamed herself? "Why do you say that, honey?"

"Do you remember why you went into the barn?"

Looking at Corrie, all I could remember was the way her sweet face filled with worry while I lay on the barn floor. I gathered in a deep breath and closed my eyes so I could think back.

"Let's see. I was sitting on the swing waiting for you to get home."

"Do you remember hearing Kitty?"

"Yes, that's what happened. The cat was whining, and I didn't want you to come home and have to go find him, so I followed the meowing."

"To the barn."

I nodded. "The sound was coming from the loft, so I climbed up."

"And you fell." She sighed. "Because of my cat, who by the way got down by himself. I saw him on the back porch when I went back in to get my keys."

"I remember falling." But there was something else I couldn't figure out. My head hurt just trying to remember.

Before I could put the foggy images together in my mind, two nurses came in. "Your mom told us you were awake." One turned to Corrie. "We're going to check vitals and look over the wound. You'll need to step out."

"Okay." She turned to me with a reassuring smile. "I'll be just outside the door, but I promise I'll be back."

Every part of me protested her absence. By the time the nurses left, the new pain medicine was taking effect, and I felt myself drifting to sleep.

Corrie

I walked toward the little waiting area, where there was coffee and a vending machine with snacks. My stomach dropped when I reached it. Aunt Trudy and Ray were in the waiting room with Sam, drinking coffee.

Ray spoke first. He stood up and offered me his seat. "How is he?"

"Lucid and feeling better. The nurses are with him now."

"Does he remember what happened?"

I nodded, and Ray's expression went white. "It was an accident," he said, his voice hoarse.

"We know. He fell off a ladder." Who would

have thought Ray would care so much? I still thought he was a bit of a creeper, but maybe I could overlook it, on occasion.

Aunt Trudy looked up at her grandson. Her eyes filled with compassion. "Tell them, Ray."

Samantha frowned and looked at me as though I should know what they were talking about. I shrugged. "I don't understand," she said. "What's wrong?"

He sat down in the seat across from me and looked at his grandmother and Sam, who sat side by side. He scrubbed his hand over his face and breathed out. His gaze met Sam's. "Aunt Sam," he began, "before she came"—he rolled his eyes quickly to me and then back to Sam—"I used to go to the home place. I visit a spirit there."

Sam's face went white.

He nodded. "Only it's my great-grandmother I commune with." He turned to me. "You know she's there. You can't pretend you haven't felt her presence."

I gathered a long, slow breath and leveled my gaze at him. "There was a demon in my house, Ray. It wasn't your great-grandmother. It was an evil demon, and Jesus helped me make it leave." I thought back to finding Eli on the floor, broken and battered. He'd said he was pushed. I stared at Ray as anger poured through me like acid rain.

Aunt Trudy's eyes narrowed. "That was no demon. I would know if it was an inhuman spirit.

What we felt that day was Jarrod. A wife should be able to tell the difference."

"Believe what you want, Aunt Trudy," I said. "I don't want to offend you. And I know you have tried to help me make sense of all the strange things I've experienced, but I was deceived. Things happened in that house that I know would never be Jarrod. A *wife* would know her husband."

She gave a *harrumph* and folded her arms across her chest. Clearly I wouldn't convince her, but as I turned back to Ray, his expression crumpled and tears filled his eyes. Instead of addressing me, he turned to Eli's mother. "Aunt Sam, she told me to push Eli."

Taking in a harsh gasp of air, Sam stared at her nephew, horror widening her eyes. "Wh-what?"

I turned quickly and looked at Aunt Trudy, who shook her head vehemently. "Not me. He means his great-grandmother." She frowned. "But that can't be."

Uttering a deep groan, Ray dropped to the floor, his head buried in his hands. The hands that had nearly killed the man I loved. "I'm sorry. I don't know why she'd tell me to hurt him, but I couldn't help it. I just did what she said." Tears dropped to the tiles as Sam stared down at him.

"We have to call the police," she said, her voice strangely calm, though her eyes flashed anger.

Aunt Trudy looked as though she might protest, but Sam had already pulled out her cell and was dialing 911. Compassion rose in me as Aunt Trudy sat back; her shoulders slumped as tears filled her eyes. She nodded simple acceptance.

Eli

Before I opened my eyes the following morning, I saw Ray's face in my mind's eye. The night before I had agreed to see him, even though I knew from my mother what he wanted to say. He confessed that he was the one who pushed me and begged forgiveness just before an officer escorted him from the room. A soft sigh forced me to open my eyes. Corrie was again in the chair next to me, legs curled up, covered by a blanket. Her cheeks were tear-stained, and I remembered.

"She won't leave," a voice said. I looked to my right at the nurse who was checking my vitals with her computer. "I didn't have the heart to send her away."

"I'm glad you didn't."

Corrie stirred then, and her eyes opened. "Hey, you're awake."

I smiled at her, and she burst into tears. I reached out with my good arm, and she came to me. Bending, she laid her head on my shoulder and wept and wept.

If my heart had been any larger in that moment, it would have burst through my chest. I smoothed her hair and held her close.

Even when the tears were spent, she didn't move, and I didn't want her to. Finally, she pulled back and pressed a kiss to my forehead. I was pretty sure those lips had been designed by God for me.

Her beautiful blue eyes glistened as she looked into mine. Words failed me.

"I could have lost you," she whispered.

"But you didn't," I said. "You found me."

I pulled her close and her lips touched mine, sweet and warm and filled with hope.

Epilogue

Corrie

I had thought spring in the Ozarks was beautiful, but fall took my breath away. I stood on my bridge, looking out at the gently flowing water dotted with red leaves and golden leaves traveling downstream. Joy washed over me as a cool breeze signaled the end of the long summer we'd just endured.

Eli's solid arm stretched across my back, his fingers curling around my waist, pulling me firmly against him. I slipped my arm around him and held him as close. My heart swelled with love for this man.

"How's the painting coming along?" he asked against my hair.

"It's going to make the perfect wedding gift for Lola and Joe," I answered. I had taken a photograph of the bridge and blown it up to eight by ten to look at while I painted. Lola loved this bridge almost as much as I did.

"Would you consider painting another one as a wedding gift for me?"

My stomach twisted for a second at the thought of Eli getting married, but then logic returned. He pulled back and knelt on his good leg. He reached into his jacket pocket and retrieved a velvet box.

He looked up at me with such tenderness in his brown eyes, I found myself kneeling to face him, tears springing to my eyes.

"Hey," he said softly, reaching out to brush my hair from my face. "You're supposed to stand there until I ask at least."

"I was too far away from you." I leaned my forehead against his and clasped my hand over the box. "Ask me."

With his forehead against mine and tears flowing down my face, he did. "Corrie Saunders, will you marry me?"

What had I ever done to deserve the forever-love this man was offering? I nodded, opening the box. He took the beautiful solitaire ring and slid it onto my finger. He held my face between his strong, capable hands.

Our eyes locked, and in the same calm way Eli had always approached me, he leaned close and pressed his lips to mine, sealing our promise that we would join our lives.

I prayed that the sins of the past were gone from this place and only God's Spirit would dwell here as we raised our family and left this land to new generations.

Surely goodness and lovingkindness
will follow me all the days of my life
And I will dwell in the house
of the LORD forever.

Readers Guide

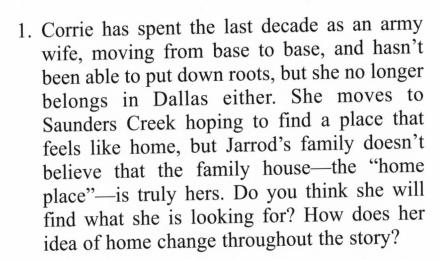

1. Corrie has spent the last decade as an army wife, moving from base to base, and hasn't been able to put down roots, but she no longer belongs in Dallas either. She moves to Saunders Creek hoping to find a place that feels like home, but Jarrod's family doesn't believe that the family house—the "home place"—is truly hers. Do you think she will find what she is looking for? How does her idea of home change throughout the story?

2. Eli loved his cousin, but they always had a rivalry. Which do you think he felt more strongly? How does this affect his choices in the book?

3. Most people in Saunders Creek see Jarrod as a hero, but Corrie wrestles with blaming Jarrod for his own death, which she sees as needlessly reckless. What do you think? How do you see the theme of sacrifice playing out in the story?

4. Corrie gave up painting when she married Jarrod. Do you think this was a good decision?

Have you ever made a big sacrifice for someone you loved? How did it affect your relationship?

5. Eli explains to Corrie that a lot of people in the area practice the "old magic," and Eli says his family has been filled with healers and naturalists for generations. This plays out in many different ways, from Sam's herbs and health food to Aunt Trudy's witchcraft to Tonia Lancaster's role as a medium. What do you think of the differences between these approaches? Where do you draw the line?

6. Strange occurrences happen at Corrie's house, some innocuous—like the spilled coffee and slamming doors—and some more menacing. Have you ever had an encounter you could not explain? What happened? What do you think it was?

7. At the beginning of the book, Corrie suspects Jarrod's ghost is haunting the home place. Rational Lola doesn't believe in supernatural events, at least at first. Aunt Trudy thinks it's Jarrod's spirit and it can be conjured, while Eli believes the presence is a demon. What do you think? What does the Bible say about ghosts? About spirits? Do you believe spirits are still active in the world today?

8. "Just be careful. It's seductive. It's also easy to justify it and make it much less dangerous in your mind and heart than it is," Eli says to warn Corrie away from Aunt Trudy's witchcraft. It is a warning that could apply to many situations. Have you ever been in a position where these words were relevant? What did you do?

9. "God's grace is all over situations like the one you are in," Eli tells Corrie. "But given the choice, He would much rather you turn to Him for comfort than anything else." What does Corrie rely on for comfort in this book? What do you tend to turn to for comfort in trying times? Is it necessarily a bad thing? How do you know when something good becomes a replacement for God?

10. What is the significance of the verses from the twenty-third Psalm that open each part of the book? Why do you think the author chose those verses? How do you see them relating to the story?

11. Eli tells Corrie, "Prayer might not change the immediate situation, but it changes the way I feel about it." Do you agree with his statement? Can you think of a time you've found this to be true?

Acknowledgments

My thanks to Kristine McGuire, who shared liberally from her experiences as a former medium and ghost hunter. Those two hours on the phone with you changed the direction of the book and deepened the authenticity. Thank you for not shying away from the hard places and for using your life to set the captives free. May God bless your efforts and use you mightily.

Kathy Helmers, for believing in the project and helping with initial development. *The Widow of Saunders Creek* would never have seen daylight without your confidence in me and your negotiating abilities. Thank you.

Shannon Marchese, editor extraordinaire. I definitely benefit from our partnership more than you do! Thank you for setting the bar high and challenging me to stretch myself.

To the WaterBrook team. From editors, to sales and marketing and publicity, cover design, copyediting and proofreading. I wish I had words to tell you how important you are. You handle each book with a loving touch and single-hearted commitment. I pray that God will bless each of you as you partner with authors like me to fulfill

His purposes. He gets all the glory, but please accept my sincere thanks.

Kathy Fuller, thank you for critiquing my work and reminding me that sometimes less is more.

To my family: Rusty, Cat, Michael, Stevan, and Will. You guys make me laugh and give me encouragement when I'm sure I can't write another word. Thank you for having my back and loving me in spite of my weaknesses. I love you more than any five people in this world.

About the Author

Tracey Bateman lives in the Missouri Ozarks with her husband and family. With more than thirty novels in print, including *Thirsty* and *Leave It to Claire*, Tracey spends all of her time telling tales, creating characters, and dreaming of other worlds.

Center Point Large Print
600 Brooks Road / PO Box 1
Thorndike ME 04986-0001 USA

(207) 568-3717

US & Canada:
1 800 929-9108
www.centerpointlargeprint.com